PROPHECY'S CHILD

An old prophecy, an ancient talisman, and a young girl with the fate of the world in her hands ...

After destroying the Harvester and suffering too many personal losses to count, Winnie Durham wants nothing more than a return to her normal life. But with Charmed permanently closed and the cost of her mother's medicine rising, Winnie's only choice is to continue running charms for crime lord, Artos Merrilyn.

But word of Winnie's magical abilities is spreading fast, and the head of the New Amsterdam Sable trade wants Winnie to work for him. And that boss won't take *No* for an answer.

Prophecy's Child

The Broken Throne Series
Book Two

JAMIE DAVIS

MERLIN WATCHED ARTOS VANISH INTO THE MAGICAL VORTEX.

He turned to face the tower room door, his home for so long. Crashes beyond the barred door grew louder, the attackers' axes slowly breaking through from the other side. The blows ceased as a voice rose above the din.

The old mage wove an invisible barrier before himself, sensing a gathering of magical energy in the hallway outside.

The door imploded in a blast of heat and force. Splinters of wood flew past Merlin, safely deflected by his magical barrier. Armed Saxon soldiers swarmed into the tower to surround him, blades aimed at his frozen body.

He remained still, indifferent to the menacing growls of the men around him. The circle of steel parted and a man in a black robe strode forward. "Where is the boy, Father? We were told that you took him up here with you."

A broad grin, then Merlin said, "Artos is far from here, Fenris, gone to a place that is mysterious even to me. I am afraid I cannot help you."

"Nonsense, old man. You are the most powerful mage of our time. How could you not know where you sent the boy?"

"I knew you would prevail, my son, and that you would use whatever means necessary to extract the lad's location. I could not take a chance that you might stop Artos on his quest. So I entrusted him to the Fae. They shepherded him somewhere of their choosing, based on their need."

"Bah!" Fenris groaned. "The Fae are weak, Father, and your loyalty to them over man is misplaced."

"The Fae offered their magic to us when we needed it most. And that was compassion, not weakness. The gift was a loan until we could set things in motion to return us from the dark after the fall of Rome. The magic was never ours to keep, my son. I taught you that long ago."

"They are weak because they surrendered such power, expecting us to return it without wanting to retain some for ourselves. They are stupid, foolish creatures, failing to see their foolish ways." Fenris pointed to his father. "Man was destined to have magic, and to use it to our benefit. We all see that. Why can't you?"

"Why can't you understand? Magic was a gift, offered to a select few in the most desperate of times. Man was never intended to hold it for more than a few hundred years, only until the once and future king was crowned. My mistake was in trusting you and the others to carry on my legacy should I fall before that time. Now the prophecy may never be fulfilled."

"It never will be if I have my say. You and your prophecy are mistaken. You can only count on what you can control. I have seen to the end of your prophecy."

"What have you done?" Merlin's fear showed through his facade. The prophecy was everything, ensuring that the gift of magic could be returned to the Fae, once the right person united the people in light.

"I have your precious sword in the stone, Father. I control the talisman of the Fae now. Only our chosen one will take up the sword and lead Britain to rule the known lands."

Fenris stopped and looked at his father, returning the old man's steady gaze, two mages standing toe to toe in silent battle.

"We could control everything together, Father. It is not too late to join me."

"You know I can't do that. If I don't release the charm on the sword, then only the prophecy's chosen child can remove it. Godspeed trying to circumvent my magic, Fenris, and I am sorry I won't be around to see your eventual defeat at the hands of those to whom you promised too much, those whose wishes you could never fulfill."

Merlin's face withered with pity for the son who had betrayed him and all he stood for — a sad smile for what he knew was goodbye.

Fenris bellowed in rage at his father's refusal, pulled a long dagger from his belt, and plunged it into his father's chest, pleased to see the smug smile wiped from his face as it twisted in shock and pain.

Merlin lay dead at Fenris's feet, blood pooling on the stone floor. The younger mage stepped backward as the spreading crimson pool worked to lick his boots.

He looked around the tower room, so familiar and yet so strange to him now. Fenris had grown up here, learning to work the Fae's magical gift beside his father. Now the room seemed somehow smaller as the man who gave it life lay, expired, on the floor. There were no clues as to where young Artos had been sent. Fenris would have to protect the talisman from the boy's eventual return.

Fenris had been the one to discover the boy's destiny. He remembered telling his father about it and how they could use him to control the kingdom once he claimed the throne. Of course, Father had refused, wrongly insisting that their task was to serve, advise, share, and counsel, so that the coming leader would know how to best unite the kingdom ... and, eventually, to return the talisman to the Fae.

Fenris couldn't abide by that choice. He had left his father's side and had taken the tale to the hated Saxons, helping them to unite their tribes and overcome the budding kingdom's meager resources.

It had been simple to draw the other mages to his side as well. All had secretly hated Merlin's plan to return magic to the Fae, and had joined him in overthrowing Uthur Pendragon's forces and taking the kingdom, one castle and fortress at a time, until all the old king's knights had either been killed or forced to swear allegiance to him.

Now, Fenris and the other mages would use their combined power to shepherd mankind into a new golden age, an age where magic could be used openly and men would learn to respect those who could wield its power. Fenris and his descendants would be kings among men for centuries to come, no matter what Merlin and his protégé, Artos, had planned for the future.

2

Nils Kane stared into the night sky, the moon's meager light dispersed amid the swirling clouds of orange dust that swallowed the capital and every city along the eastern coast of the United Americas.

Turning away from the window and the dust storm raging outside the Department of Magical Containment, the Director crossed his large office, past his desk, to the large stone sculpture. He told people it was a cherished piece of artwork belonging to his family. Only a few people in the world knew what it represented.

Nils stroked the large, hand-carved stone throne until he reached the sword embedded in its back. As he often did when alone, Nils gripped the blade and attempted to pull it free. But, like always, the sword wouldn't budge.

When he'd discovered that the sword in the stone still existed, Nils had personally financed the mercenaries who'd traveled to the ruins of old London, in what had once been the United Kingdom. The few surviving savages had made the

5

recovery difficult. Only half of the men returned with their prize.

Just as well. That made it easier to dispose of those who went on the quest, lest they discover the true meaning of the ancient talisman recovered from Europe's ruins. He could take no chances. That sword was his family's birthright. Mother had told him the legends of his family's origins, warned him to be patient and hide his abilities from jealous middlings who would use him for their own ends. She would be proud of him. He had followed her advice and now stood to reclaim all the world's remaining magic.

At least, that had been the plan, until Miss Guinevere Durham had spoiled it all. With that meddling Artos's assistance, she'd destroyed everything he'd had in place to capture the magic for himself. With the Harvester destroyed by the young chanter woman, Nils was forced to fall back on an alternative plan.

In the meantime, he needed to find a way to draw the girl to his side, or destroy her if she was unwilling. And he had a plan for that, too.

Nils turned on the large monitor mounted on the wall beside his desk. It was time for his interview with National News Channel's Rebecca Funk. He settled into his desk chair, leaning back as the program started.

"Today on NNC's Evening Report, we have an exclusive interview with Nilrem Kane. The Director of the Department of Magical Containment shares his thoughts on the causes of this strange weather phenomena affecting much of the East Coast."

The woman on-screen turned and the shot changed to a wide view of the Evening Report set, Nils seated across the news desk, his grin the perfect blend of disarming and friendly.

"Director Kane, thank you for coming. Let's start with a recent report from the National Weather Service, which is essentially throwing its hands in the air trying to explain these dust storms. But you have a theory. What, in your estimation, is causing these storms?"

"First of all, thank you for having me back. It's always a pleasure to stop by and share what is happening at the Department with your viewers, especially at a time like this." Nils watched as his TV-self took control of the interview, turning to the camera. "My colleagues and I, both at the Assembly and inside the DMC, are convinced the storms are magical in nature and relate back to some localized magical influence gone terribly wrong somewhere here on the East Coast. Our courageous Red Legs are investigating possible causes and specific individuals inside the chanter community."

"I see. So you think that chanters' misuse of magic is at fault?"

"I do. As you know, I have long been a voice of caution against the widespread use of magic by the public. As a result of several recent actions by the Assembly, we are addressing the reduction in use, creation of magic, and the registration of chanters so we may safely monitor their efforts."

"And the chanters' claims of Red Legs rounding up chanters last week and the list of missing chanters that some are calling the Baltimore Fifty? What about them?"

"We are cooperating with Baltimore law enforcement to locate the missing individuals. But we suspect that this is the result of a local Sable trade gang war, with abductions and deaths occurring on both sides of the conflict. I have it on good authority that my officers are close to cracking the case once and for all."

"So, none of these people were part of an official mass arrest and detention of chanters in the Enclave?"

"Correct. I think these erroneous claims are an attempt to shift blame for the strange and dangerous weather from the chanters at fault. The storms are clearly magical. Who else could be controlling or misusing the magical forces but the chanters themselves?"

"Well, thank you, Director Kane, for taking your valuable time to chat. I know our audience appreciates your efforts to solve—"

Nils killed the TV, then reached over and tapped the intercom to summon his assistant. The door opened and Miss Errand entered. He watched her approach his desk, admiring her dark skirt and tight, black blazer before giving her instructions.

He had two things to accomplish; provoking public unrest against the chanters was the perfect stone to fell both of his birds. Young Winnie Durham had evaded his efforts to eliminate her at the steel mill. Artos believed her to be the answer to an ancient magical prophecy. In the beginning, Nils had imagined that it was the old man's wishful thinking. But now he had second thoughts. If there were concerted attacks against the city's chanters, he might get lucky and she would succumb to one.

Nils wasn't one to leave things to luck. He had other plans that were much more likely to bring young Miss Durham down. Those plans were progressing nicely, but they were time-consuming and required finesse. Nils preferred more immediate solutions. He wanted to get his ultimate project back in place, but would be unable to while Miss Durham stood in his way.

The girl was dangerous, and not just because she had the power to stop him. Durham also had the ability to unify chanters against his efforts. He could not let her become that beacon for hope and unity among those who would stand in his way.

Nils had to stop Winnie at all costs.

3

WINNIE ROLLED OVER IN BED AND STARED AT THE CURTAINS OF her bedroom window. Streetlights outside offered a dim light, barely piercing her room's gray and black shadows. Like every other night in the last two weeks since her confrontation with Kane at the mill, sleep was elusive, short snippets broken by the hints of voices whispering at the edges of her darkest dreams.

Her hand rested on her stomach — another dream about her baby, and Joey. She remembered that much, before the whispers had forced her to wake. It was always the same: a little girl, about three years old, walking through a gorgeous forest, somewhere far away. "Why are you crying, Mommy?" she always asked.

But Winnie could never answer. When the voices came, Winnie always looked away, searching for their source. And when she turned back, the girl was always gone.

Winnie got out of bed, then made her way toward the kitchen, peeking into her mother's bedroom on the way. Elaine was sleeping, recovered from her recent hospitalization — the only bright light in her life's recent gloom. Mother's brush with death was now behind them, and she was recovering well. They no longer needed a nurse, and she was able to stand and move around on her own.

In the kitchen, Winnie set the battered old tea kettle on the stove and lit the burner so the blue flame heated the water for tea. She sat and waited while staring at nothing in particular. A buzzing fly circled the sugar bowl. Winnie reached out with her mind, directing thin threads of magic towards the insect. Winnie sharply inhaled, then exhaled with a satisfied sigh as the surge of Sable magic coursed through her.

The fly buzzed in complicated patterns above the table with Winnie directing the flight. She reveled in the euphoria that always came with working the forbidden magic on a living creature. It fed her addiction, and though Winnie knew it was wrong, she didn't stop, directing the insect as if it were a remote-controlled toy.

The teapot's thin whistle distracted Winnie from her casting and she released the fly. She immediately felt the hole, a bottomless emptiness deep inside her. She searched for the fly, wanting to reclaim the euphoria, but it had disappeared, leaving the room and the dangerous creature controlling it.

Winnie stood, picked up the teapot, poured it over a teabag in her mug, then sat at the table and spooned a few teaspoons of sugar into her hot tea. Sable magic was a problem, and had been before the night at the steel mill. Now she felt like she needed to touch it all the time. It was the only thing that made Winnie feel better since losing her baby, since all the captured chanters had died, since Danny had been taken away just hours after his return….

Winnie wondered where her boyfriend was. He'd been taken away during her battle with the machine. She'd been vaguely aware of him getting dragged off when Director Kane left her battling the Harvester. No one had heard from him since. She had even called his parents. The woman who answered must have been Danny's mother. She was frantic, asking who was calling, begging to know anything about his disappearance.

Winnie wondered if he was dead like all the others at the mill. The news had called the event "a terrible industrial accident," with a hundred workers' bodies discovered in the building's charred remains. Those bodies had been the discarded remains of chanters who'd had their magic harvested along with their life force. Middling news outlets knew nothing about that and accepted the official reports about an industrial accident.

That story was soon replaced by the dust storms descending like a hammer upon the city, starting in Baltimore and now a regular occurrence with people going about their days in scarves or surgical masks to protect their lungs from the swirling dust. After a few days, storms were raging up and down the East Coast of the United Americas, leaving experts scratching their heads.

That hadn't stopped pundits on the nightly news from positing a list of possible sources for the strange phenomena. A dangerous suggestion from one of the more conservative guests one night had led to a new populist movement from the more militant middling groups. The storms were proof of magic's danger, surely triggered by chanters from segregated enclaves.

No amount of denial had quelled the fear and anger surging from the middling population as they grasped for reason in the madness. They greatly outnumbered chanters, and there were now reports of gangs of middlings roaming the streets, randomly chasing and sometimes beating chanters as they went about their daily chores or work.

Winnie had heard of a few incidents directly from her friends Cait and Tris. They had witnessed a few ugly episodes in person. Cait had been forced to use her military self-defense training to fend off a group of toughs wanting to express their displeasure on a pair of chanter women they saw disembarking the bus. In the end, the girls had escaped the gang and had reached safety in the Enclave, where groups of chanter leaders patrolled in groups to discourage middlings from entering the area.

There was a noise down the hallway. Winnie looked up from her cup and saw her mom. Elaine was using her cane to support her weight as she walked with care down the hallway. Her arthritis had practically crippled her, but she was determined to make her own way around the apartment. A strong-willed woman, Elaine had insisted that she get back on her feet soon after regaining consciousness from her recent hospitalization. Winnie was proud of her mother's resilience, but worried about the unrelenting illness. She was getting worse, and the medicine needed to avoid further deterioration was getting more expensive by the month.

Elaine entered the kitchen and eased herself into a chair across from Winnie. "What are you doing up, dear? Still having those nightmares?"

"It's nothing to worry about, Mom. I'll be fine."

"No, you won't. At least not on your own. I wish you would tell me what happened. It's been weeks and you still won't give me a hint. I warned you that getting involved with Artos would lead to trouble. That man and his Sable trading are nothing to fool with."

"Mom, just let it go, alright?"

"I can't. It's not like we keep secrets from each other, Winnie. We've always been honest. But now it feels like you're hiding a lot more from me than your illegal little side-business."

"Just leave it be, okay?" Winnie stood and set her empty mug in the sink. She didn't like keeping things from her mother. But how could she tell her about the pregnancy, the loss, and her near death in some hare-brained rescue attempt against the Department of Magical Containment and the Red Legs?

No. Elaine was too frail to deal with that now.

A loud sigh from behind her. "I don't like this, Winnie. Have you watched the news lately? Dust storms are almost constant. Demonstrations against chanters and magic have made it even more dangerous to be outside the Enclave. And you still want to be out there running charms?"

Winnie turned and met her mother's eyes. "We have to make money somehow. The Red Legs closed our shop. I can't get it up and running again, even if I wanted to. Working for Artos is the only way for us to get by."

"It's dangerous, Winnie. And against the law. There are more than a hundred people from the Enclave missing — including Joey — and the authorities aren't even trying to search for them."

Winnie wanted to shout at her mother: It's because they're all dead.

Instead, she said, "Everything we chanters do is against the law now. We can't cross the street without people blaming us for something. You know we have nothing to do with these dust storms."

"We have to wait until decent people step up and do the right thing. There are good middlings out there — they'll stop these demonstrations and help us get justice."

"Justice might be whatever we can get for ourselves, Mom."

"So, what, you're some kind of freedom fighter now?"

"No." Winnie gave her mother a wry laugh. "I'll never be that kind of idiot. All I've ever wanted is to make sure that you and I can get by."

"I'm worried. You shouldn't have to support us both like this. I don't want to see you end up in jail, or worse."

Winnie returned to the table, sat beside her mother, took one of her gnarled hands, and looked her right in the eyes. "I promise to be careful, and I'll make sure we have what we need. You've always taken care of me. Now it's my turn to take care of you."

Elaine shook her head. This conversation was going nowhere.

"Let me walk you back to bed, then I'll lie down, too. We could both stand to get some more rest before morning comes."

"Promise you'll go back to sleep?"

"Yes, Mom," Winnie lied.

Once up from the nightmares, Winnie could never settle enough to fall back asleep. But she would lie down. And maybe tonight would be different.

Winnie helped her mother stand, then steadied her as she reached for her cane. They eased down the hallway towards their bedrooms and whatever else was waiting for them in the darkness.

4

THE NEXT MORNING, AFTER SHE GOT HER MOTHER SETTLED WITH breakfast, Winnie headed to the shop where Charmed had been located. The walk and short bus ride were uneventful, and Winnie was relieved to arrive early. She, Tris, and Cait were planning to plot their next moves going forward. They wanted to continue their charm running with Artos, despite their losses.

Winnie considered those losses as she unlocked the door and went inside. They weren't the happy-go-lucky crew they once were. Joey was dead. Winnie always saw his startled face in her nightmares, when the Red Leg strangled him to death.

Morgan was a traitor. That betrayal hurt more than when she'd believed that Danny had turned against her. Seeing her half-sister dressed in a Red Leg uniform, standing next to Constable Holmes with Director Kane nearby, had been devastating. Winnie and her sister had had their moments over the years, but she had never suspected the girl would become one of the Department of Magical Containment's most hated minions — the person informing on them all along. Now Winnie knew that it had never been Danny.

They hadn't recovered his body at the steel mill. If they had,

15

Danny's parents would have been in mourning rather than frantically looking for him. She hoped he would turn up like he always had before, his easy smile turning her insides to liquid and letting her know that everything would be fine. Winnie couldn't stop wondering what had happened to Danny after he was taken from the mill by Director Kane, Constable Holmes, and her sister.

A wild thought occurred to Winnie: Should she call Morgan?

She could try and use her to learn what had happened to Danny. They shared a father, and were surely still connected. Winnie pulled out her phone, punched Morgan's number, and contemplated making the call.

Her thumb hovered over the send button, but before she could press it, the front door opened. Tris and Cait entered together, deep in conversation. The sky behind them was orange — another dust storm coming.

Tris was mid-argument. "It's all connected, Cait. I know it. The storms, the declining city systems, the way magic's been waning for years."

Cait shook her head. "It doesn't matter if it's connected or not. It only matters that magic is involved. That gives the middling demonstrators a reason to vent their anger and fear on us and every chanter out there."

Winnie stowed her phone. She didn't want either of her friends to know who she was considering talking to. Morgan had betrayed them, too. They had all been strapped into that machine, having the souls sucked from their bodies. No … she'd wait and think on it before calling Morgan for help.

Winnie turned to her friends. "What are you two arguing about now?"

Cait hooked a thumb over her shoulder at Tris. "She's convinced the storms, the harvesting machine, and the explosion all have something to do with the recent changes in magic."

"It makes sense," Tris said. "The city systems were starting to fail before the explosion. So, the magic was already changing somehow. Then we destroyed … well, Winnie, you destroyed the Harvester, before all the storms started up and down the coast. It can't be a coincidence."

"What can't be a coincidence?" Winnie didn't want to hear any answer that might imply she had somehow broken magic when fighting that infernal machine. She remembered feeling something different after she opened herself to the storm of magic raging around the Harvester. She also remembered her strange vision of the lady by the lake. She'd said her name was Brigid and that Winnie must "heal the world as you know it."

Maybe she did have something to do with the changes wrought by the storms, if only to repair the damage magic use was inflicting on the world.

Tris approached Winnie, sitting on a tall stool by the old store counter. "We knew that magic wasn't working the way it should. I was way busier than I should've been, repairing old building systems. The magic kept changing even after its repair. I'd have to come back and fix the system again a few weeks later, as if the enchantments lacked permanence. The magic running the city's buildings is among the oldest and most stable magic we have, drawing far more power than our simple charms." Tris looked from Winnie to Cait, then back again.

Winnie gave her a blank look, not seeing where Tris was headed with her line of thought.

Tris sighed. "Come on, guys. Don't you see? It's like the magic is failing. Maybe the Harvester and the sudden release of magic stored in those tanks caused some sort of backlash and broke the magic somehow."

"What do you mean broke?" Winnie could still touch the magic, same as before. In some ways, it felt like she could hold even more. Still, Tris had a better idea of how the city's infrastructure was working — or, in this case, not.

"I'm still not sure. I need to do some research. I worked it out so I could spend some time working at the Archives Building during one of my upcoming shifts. I'll know more after I look into a few things."

Cait was doodling on a piece of scrap paper while Tris described her discovery. The girl was easily bored. Winnie looked over and saw her sketching a face, surprised by her friend's artistic ability. She'd always seen Cait as an athlete and soldier.

It took her a moment to recognize the face. She laid a hand on Cait's shoulder. "I miss Joey, too."

Cait stopped drawing and looked at Winnie. "I felt so helpless there. We went there to save those people, but we were too late for most of them. Then, all of the pain … I still wake up screaming."

"Believe me, I understand," Tris said. "I don't think any of us are sleeping well since the steel mill. That's why we have to do something. We can't just stand by, or return to business as usual."

"What did you have in mind, Tris?" Cait asked. "It's not like we have a lot of resources to draw on."

"And yet we managed to break the machine anyway." Tris was the group's scholar, and Winnie wasn't used to seeing her speak with such fire in her eyes.

"Winnie did that, though I don't know how. I could barely hold onto my sanity. And I'm not sure I succeeded." Cait gave a dry laugh, then turned to Winnie and asked her the same thing she'd already wondered out loud a hundred times before: "How did you manage to overload that thing like you did?"

Winnie shook her head. "I have no idea. I was angry and exhausted. In pain. I was desperate for it all to stop. Everything went kind of fuzzy until you guys woke me back up." Winnie said nothing about her vision, or the lady at the lake.

"Well, whatever you did," Tris continued, "you showed what

we're capable of. We need to do more to stop Kane and his thugs."

"We're not militants or revolutionaries, Tris," Winnie said. "Let's move slowly and with care here. I want to get some of our operation back up and running. The shop's lease is paid through the year. We can use it as a base of operations moving forward."

Cait looked back and forth between her friends. "You want to jump back into that frying pan? They know who we are and what we're doing. What makes you think the Red Legs won't shut us down the second we start running charms?"

"Let me worry about that," Winnie said. "I'm going to meet with Artos and see what he says. People still want what we can provide. This is supply and demand. We had something good going on. I don't want to give it up."

"But we don't have Joey or Danny, and Morgan is playing for the other side," Cait complained. "We're at half strength. In the military, we called that a depleted company. Nobody goes to war with less than their full strength."

Winnie winced at the mention of Danny, still worried about where he was and what might be happening to him. The sting of Morgan's betrayal and Joey's death were fresh wounds for them all. Still, both Tris and Cait had showed up here at the shop when she asked them to meet her. They wanted to do something. They might be resistant, like Cait, or have different motives, like Tris, but they were here. All Winnie had to do was conjure a plan to get them back in business.

She felt bad about manipulating them. But she needed them in her crew, and they had to run charms. In the end, Winnie needed enough to buy her mom's medicine. And she'd do whatever it took to get it.

Winnie was about to articulate her plans when the wind picked up outside the shop. She looked out the storefront's window. The sky had darkened to an angry tangerine as another furious dust storm settled in like a lid atop the city. This one was bad, swiftly turning afternoon to midnight outside the shop. Winnie was glad for the lights inside as she went to check that the door was secured against the wind.

A fine dust was forcing its way under the door despite the weather stripping seals, the incredible force of the storm buffeting the door. There was a muffled shout outside as a courageous, or perhaps foolish, pedestrian ventured by, hurrying on their way to whatever took them out in this abysmal storm — what looked to be the worst one she'd seen so far.

Winnie finished checking the locks and was turning back to face her friends when the electricity died and sent them into total darkness.

THE THREE FRIENDS WAITED OUT THE STORM FOR SEVERAL HOURS. The storms had caused blackouts in the city before, but only for ten or fifteen minutes at the most before power was restored. Winnie wasn't sure if it was the storm's fury that kept the power out longer, but even after it subsided, they had to wait another hour for the lights to return.

The friends plotted as they waited. Knowing they had been short-handed for their confrontation in the steel mill, they went back to basics. Tris had contacts in the downtown district. She would reach out to let them know they could start supplying charms again. Winnie would concentrate on securing their supply from Artos, or crafting the charms herself. Cait would take care of delivery and security.

They had everything worked out by the time the power returned, ready to start moving product again. Winnie was pleased with the progress, and secretly grateful for the storm and power outage that had provided a distraction from their differences of opinion. They would have to address them at some point, especially Tris's new militant streak, but that could wait for later.

For now, they would focus on recovering their momentum and serving their original customer base. They would expand as opportunity presented itself, but not until she was sure they could handle additional volume.

Winnie was crunching numbers as the three of them gathered their things. The front door opened and Winnie whirled around and saw three strange men standing there. They weren't cops or Red Legs, which was what Winnie feared the most; the men were dressed in overcoats hanging to their knees, surgical masks over their faces to protect them from residual dust. The one in front was short for a man, barely taller than Winnie. The other two were taller with broad shoulders and chests, masks obscuring their faces.

"I'm sorry, gentlemen, but the shop is closed indefinitely." Winnie walked forward, smiling. She sensed Cait and Tris coming up behind her.

The smallest one reached up and pulled his mask away from his mouth and nose. He had a pencil-thin mustache over his lip and a crooked smile. He looked back over his shoulder out the window. "I think the storms are worse down here than at home. I was a bit concerned at how fast that last one blew up on us. I didn't think we'd make it." The man looked up at the men behind him and nudged one with an elbow. "Garraldi, Dugan, take off your masks. Where are your manners? These ladies might think we're sticking up the joint."

"Sorry, gentlemen, but we've nothing to sell, and I'll have to ask you to leave." Winnie took another tentative step forward. "The storm has passed and I'm sure you can find your way."

"Oh, we found our way fine," said the little guy. "I've come looking for you, Winnie Durham. You're quite famous in certain circles."

"I don't know what you're talking about. Who are you?"

"I'm so sorry. Where are my manners? Name's Jimmy Constantini. Friends call me Cricket."

He stepped forward, extending a hand. Winnie shook it, then stepped back and waited for the man to continue.

Cricket stroked one side of his mustache with the back of a finger, still smiling. "My boys and I are here to meet you, and maybe, if the opportunity presents itself, to offer you a job with my boss. He's intrigued with you, Winnie." He paused and smiled again. "I'm sorry. May I call you Winnie?"

She nodded and he continued.

"Well, Winnie. Like I said, my friends and I came here to meet you and to see if you'd like to meet my boss, and maybe come to work for him. He can be … persuasive, and generous to those he takes under his wing."

"And who is your boss?" Winnie asked.

"Mr. Cleaver Yorke."

Cait and Tris both drew in a sharp breath.

They knew the name. So did she.

"What in the world does the head of the New Amsterdam Sable trade want with me?" Winnie looked around and gestured at the ransacked store. "In case you hadn't noticed, we're small potatoes here."

Cricket laughed. His two goons chuckled.

"Cleaver keeps his own counsel, and I don't make it a habit of asking the man why he wants what he does. The last guy who asked too many questions — well, let's say he was discouraged from asking anything else."

"You're saying he won't take it well if I say I'm not interested? Like I said, we're small time here, and that's just how we like it."

"We've heard things about you, Winnie. Impressive things." Cricket paced the store while Garraldi and Dugan stayed by the door. "This shop used to be bustling, so you can handle a larger scale. You might have had a setback or two, but that's never stopped you. Has it?"

Winnie stood still, not answering as she looked at him,

watching him circle the room. He walked slowly, taking his time as he considered the shop's empty shelves. When Winnie didn't answer, Cricket continued his circuit, finally returning to his spot in front of Winnie, Cait, and Tris.

"Cleaver Yorke wanted me to come down here and find out about you. You've checked out and seem to be in a bit of recovery. I get it. We all have setbacks. This is the ideal time for you to consider working under new management. Cleaver is making plans for expansion outside of New Amsterdam. He'll be moving in on Baltimore soon and wants to make sure the local talent —" Cricket pointed at Winnie "— understands that there are openings in the operations we'll be establishing along the way."

Winnie met Cricket's ice-cold eyes. "I'm not interested. We're not looking for new partners. Please express my regrets to Mr. Yorke, but our existing management is just fine."

"The existing management is stagnant, Winnie. Old fashioned." Cricket became more animated. "Artos Merrilyn is a small-time operator and will never be more. Baltimore deserves a better leader."

"What kind of things could you do for us that we don't already have?" Cait blurted, unable to wait.

Cricket laughed. "Ah, the blonde Amazon finally speaks. You're Caitlyn, right? Ex-army with an impressive set of skills. We could put them to more appropriate uses, and let you keep working with your friend." He turned to Tris. "You're Tristan, the fixer. Of course, we could use you, too. If Winnie wants to play along with Cleaver, you'll never have to worry about the Red Legs again. If Cleaver had been in charge, Winnie's cousin would still be alive and the city's chanters would all be safe. Cleaver protects his Enclaves."

"I'm impressed you've taken the time to learn about me and my friends, Cricket," Winnie said. "And I'm sure that all you've said is true. But we're happy with the way things are and will pass on this particular invitation. Please convey our regrets, and gratitude for the offer."

Cricket met Winnie's eyes and held them in silence. Finally, he said, "It isn't wise to land on Cleaver's bad side. He doesn't take no especially well. I urge you to be smart and reconsider."

Winnie shook her head. "No, Cricket. We're not interested in his offer. I don't wish to offend him in any way, but we don't want to work for someone we don't know, especially someone so far from Baltimore. It's like what you said about the storm. Things are different down here, and I believe it's best to stay with what we know."

"I'm warning you, Winnie. I'll pass along your refusal, but Cleaver won't be happy, and I can't promise that he'll offer a generous proposition again."

"Be that as it may, he has his answer. Now if you'll excuse me, we are leaving and I need to lock up." Winnie gestured to the door and waited for the men to comply, not knowing what she would do if they refused. She had faith in Cait to take on one of the two goons behind Cricket, but she wasn't sure that she and Tris could handle Cricket and the other man on their own.

Silence stretched for a few long and uncomfortable moments. Then Cricket nodded, shot Winnie a grin, and stroked his thin mustache.

"Very well, Winnie. I'll pass along your message. I'm sure this isn't our final encounter. As I said, Cleaver is looking to nurture his relationship with this city — I'd advise you to be careful and stay out of our way." Cricket motioned to Garraldi and Dugan, then the men turned and led the way outside.

Winnie watched them walk down the street and eventually out of sight. Once they were gone, she turned to her friends.

"Cleaver Yorke is bad news," Tris said. "He runs New Amsterdam with an iron fist. I heard he got his name because he chops off his enemies' hands with a meat cleaver ..."

"Well, I guess I better not double cross him, then," Winnie said.

Cait looked worried. "What are you going to do?"

"What I was planning to do already. I'm going to talk with Artos. He needs to hear about this, and we have to go through him to get our operation up and running again, anyway."

"And you're not worried about angering Cleaver?" Tris asked.

"No. I figure Artos already knows Cleaver's guys are in town. He's probably already made a few moves, and Artos seems to always know what's going on. I'm sure he'll know what to do."

Winnie walked over, grabbed her coat from the rack by the door, then turned to her friends.

"It'll be alright," she reassured them. "Artos will know what to do."

6

Winnie waited in the outer office watching Mr. Gunderson putter about his chores — or whatever it was he did for Artos Merrilyn. The small gray-haired man, dressed in a three-piece suit and tie like always, was fixing a tray with tea and coffee. He set a plate with scones on the tray beside a pair of cups and saucers, then turned to a French press and poured coffee into the silver pitcher.

Winnie was so engrossed in watching the assistant that she failed to notice Artos open his office door and invite her inside. She heard him on the second mention of her name and flushed, embarrassed at how scattered she was. This was how it had been since the fight at the steel mill. This wasn't like her — she always paid attention, and didn't like surprises.

Winnie stood and followed Artos into his office, and started toward his desk. Instead, he directed her to sit in the more comfortable lounge chairs next to the bookshelves lining the wall. As she sat, Mr. Gunderson entered and set the service tray on the table between her chair and the small sofa where Artos sat, smiling at Winnie as his assistant set up the tray. Mr.

Gunderson poured her tea and Artos's coffee before retiring to the outer office.

Winnie sat back and waited for the older man to leave before speaking. "I don't know what I've done to deserve this treatment, Artos. It makes me think you're up to something."

Artos laughed, picked up his coffee cup, then leaned back on the sofa. "Nonsense, my dear. You've been through a lot since I last saw you. This is my way of showing appreciation for all you've done, albeit in a small way. Nothing can truly compensate you for all you lost."

Winnie sipped her tea, wondering if Artos was referring to the loss of Joey in the raid or if he also knew about her pregnancy. Knowing what she did, it wouldn't surprise her that this man was somehow spying on her enough to know everything.

"It wasn't pleasant for any of us, Artos, but we got the job done."

"You're minimizing your role in the Harvester's destruction. I've felt things change in the magical field surrounding our city. That happened after the machine was destroyed. And your friends had nothing to do with it. My sources say you somehow resisted its power to draw on your magical life force and instead caused it to overload and explode. Is that true?"

Winnie shrugged. She didn't like to think about it, and couldn't remember much of what had happened when she was strapped to the machine, anyway.

Apparently sensing her discomfort, Artos changed the subject.

"So, my dear, what brings you to my offices today? Are you ready to return to work? There is much to be done, if so."

"Perhaps, but something else happened today that I want to talk about. I received a visit from a few gentlemen coming down from New Amsterdam. They came into my shop, told me they were taking over, and offered me a spot with Cleaver Yorke's crew."

Winnie left the statement dangling while she gauged the old man's expression. As usual, Artos seemed to know what was happening already.

"And you said … ?"

"I told them no, of course. What did you think I was going to say? You don't seem surprised. Why didn't you tell me about them coming if you knew that they would be? I could have been prepared instead of getting the crap scared out of me and my friends."

"I didn't know why they were in town. Things have been, shall we say, tense between Sable bosses since the dust storms started pummeling the coast. Director Kane has ratcheted up the pressure on chanters across the board. This has cut into profits. When the bosses lose money, they look for ways to make more, including expansion into new territory."

Winnie sat back. "So they're cutting in to Baltimore?"

"Are they moving in to try and claim a share of our business here? Yes." Artos met Winnie's gaze. "Are they taking over? No, far from it. I still control the Sable trade in this city, and fortunately, I have loyal people like you backing me up."

"Of course I backed you, Artos. I don't like being pushed around. You know that. But I want to know why they came to see me. I haven't been actively running for two weeks."

His eyes softened. "Winnie, they came to see you for the same reasons that I did. You're a remarkable young woman with substantial power. Word has spread since your confrontation with Kane. Yorke has friends in high places, and I assure you those friends have whispered about the girl who did the impossible, surviving where no one should have."

The chanter leader stood from the sofa, walked over to a map of the United Americas on the opposite wall, and pointed to New Amsterdam on the East Coast, just north of Baltimore. "It's no accident that Cleaver Yorke is the leader of the Sable trade in the country's biggest city. He's clawed his way to the top, fought and killed and claimed control through brute force. Someday, when the time is right, I'll tell you more about the man who rules New Amsterdam's charm runners with an iron grip."

"You're not helping ease my fears, Artos."

"I'm not trying to. You should deal with Cleaver Yorke carefully, especially if you meet him in person. Fortunately, you shouldn't ever have to do that. I'll take care of telling Yorke to stay the hell out of Baltimore. He should set his sights on Philadelphia or Boston. They're both closer and ripe for the picking."

Artos returned to his place behind the sofa and looked down at Winnie.

"The question for you right now is, are you ready to work? You and your friends must believe that it's time or you wouldn't have been meeting in the shop. I have a job that requires your abilities to mask a charmed object. So, Winnie, are you ready?"

Winnie looked down at her hands, holding a teacup and saucer while trying to keep it from shaking. She'd asked this question of herself every day since her deadly encounter at the steel mill. She still didn't know the answer for sure, but some things were certain: She still had to pay for her mother's medicine and medical bills. Plus, there was one other thing she longed to know.

Winnie looked back up at Artos. "I'm as ready as I'm going to be. But I do have one request."

Artos smiled and inclined his head for her to continue.

"I need you to find out what happened to Danny. I saw them dragging him out of the room while I fought the machine. I've searched for him, but no one seems to know what happened. I don't think that Danny is dead, so, where is he? Promise that you'll find out and I'll go back to work for you now."

"I'll do what I can to search for him, Winnie, but that is a promise I cannot make. Have you thought about what you will do if the news is bad? He was caught colluding against the Director himself. I will use my resources to search for him, and if it is within my power, I shall find Danny Barber, or discover what happened to him. But I can only promise to do my best."

Winnie felt herself relax. Artos was good to his word. That was one of the reasons she had told Cricket to pass along her NO to Cleaver. Winnie was loyal by nature. It was one of her strengths, helping her to command strong friendships with people like Tris and Cait. It also meant she was bound to those she chose to support. She'd cast her lot with Artos. That choice had been freely given and she would not turn her back on him.

Fierce loyalty was what had her so focused on locating Danny. She was ashamed that she'd believed the others who had said he betrayed her. She had to make that right, had to find Danny and tell him she was sorry for her doubt. She wanted him to forgive her and tell her they could become the friends and lovers they had been before the machinations of Nils Kane, Constable Holmes, and Morgan had torn them apart.

Winnie set her cup and saucer on an end table and stood, looking Artos in the eyes. "Find Danny and I'll be your charm runner forever."

He laughed. "Careful what you say, my dear. Forever is a long time. Why don't we agree that I'll do what I can to locate Mr. Barber for you and you'll take a few key assignments that have been awaiting your special talents?"

Winnie nodded, and that was it. She was back in the employ of Artos Merrilyn, running charms and defying the law.

Everything was fine, so long as she got Danny back.

7

THE DIRECTOR OF THE DEPARTMENT OF MAGICAL Containment marched down the corridor of the department's private detention facility, flanked by a quadrant of Red Leg guards. He stopped at a locked and barred door at the end of the corridor.

Kane waited for the lead guard to unlock the elaborate mechanism then open the door to a stark room with concrete walls, painted white to match the tiled floor. An examination table sat in the room's center.

Kane's subject was secured to the table by the broad leather straps attached to its frame. He nodded to the guard, waved a hand in dismissal, then stepped inside. The door was shut and secured behind him.

The guards would wait outside until he finished, as they'd done on each of his daily visits for the last two weeks.

It was a necessary distraction from his regular duties. He had so much to do, especially in the face of the citizens' unrest over these strange storms plaguing the coastal cities. The people wanted answers and were pressuring Congress, who were in turn nagging the Assembly. Everyone wanted to know where the dust storms were coming from, and how they might be able to stop them.

But, in truth, Kane didn't know. Only that they were tied to what had happened with Winnie Durham at the steel mill. She had survived the Harvester — a feat that no one had accomplished before — and had managed to somehow destroy it and trigger imbalance in the magical continuum that he'd not felt since he was a child.

Growing up in the United Kingdom, Nils had discovered his ability to sense the magic around him, just like his mother. She'd predicted Europe's coming destruction. It was the reason she had worked to get him on one of the final refugee boats when everything was collapsing. She had known what was coming but had been unable to stop it. In the end, she'd been killed by rioting middlings, venting their fear and rage on any chanter in sight. He had watched her get dragged to the ground and mauled as his transport to the coast drove off.

Nils had vowed to never be a victim again, to never again be helpless in the face of the middlings he hated so much. He would control the animosity that had ultimately killed his mother and use it to his own ends. He was more confident than ever: Winnie Durham was the answer. The challenge was in finding a way to manipulate her into doing what he wanted. If Nils could control her, he could steer the magic and restore the fragile ecosystem around the United Americas' most isolated cities.

Nils approached the exam table, discarding his suit jacket into a nearby chair. "Hello, Mr. Barber. Are we ready for our daily appointment?"

"I don't understand what you want from me. Ask me a question. Tell me what you want. I'll do anything. Please don't keep doing this to me."

The Director shook his head. "I want you, Daniel. That is all. The rest will come in time. Shall we begin?"

Danny wailed as Nils pushed up his sleeves and leaned over him. Practiced fingers found pressure points on the boy's skull, and with a surgeon's skill, Kane weaved a fine lattice of magical flow directly into his subject's brain.

Using the magic, Nils could see inside the boy's surface memories and his most basic desires. He manipulated the latter, as he did during each of these sessions, until he was satisfied. He was almost finished. Soon, it would be time to send young Mr. Barber back into the world, armed with his new destiny.

Kane stepped back several hours later, taking a handkerchief from his pocket and mopping his brow. He rolled his sleeves back down and buttoned them closed around his wrists.

He smiled at the unconscious subject sprawled on the table. He had enjoyed hearing the screams of pain during the most intense part of the session, but they had been distracting. So, Nils had knocked him out to focus on his task. He would return once or twice more to make sure his weaves stayed in place and that the magic worked in its intended manner. This time, Danny would serve the Director, same as his parents: effectively and without awareness of their actions on his behalf.

Nils straightened his tie and pulled on his blazer before rapping on the steel door to signal the guards outside. The door opened and he stepped back into the corridor. The guards came to attention.

"Take the boy back to his cell. Monitor him carefully and make sure he has something to eat and drink in the next few hours. He'll need his strength for what's to come. Understood?" Kane eyed the guards.

"Yes, sir!" the men barked in unison, then went inside for their prisoner.

The other two guards fell in behind Nils as he started back up the corridor toward the central hallway. He nodded to the Red Leg officer behind the desk on his way toward the elevators, then turned to the lead guard behind him.

"Make sure Mr. Barber is back in the treatment room at the same time tomorrow. I will be back to examine my work and to determine if there is anything else that must be done. If his condition changes in any way for the worse in the meantime, I want to know immediately. He is the key to my plans and I will not have him die because of lack of attention by you and your lackeys."

"Yes, sir, Director Kane. He will be watched and treated appropriately until you return."

The elevator door opened and Kane decided the man's answer was suitable. He nodded, then stepped inside the elevator. Nils had several meetings to placate concerned members of the Assembly. An annoyance. They were grown men and women — he failed to understand why they needed his reassurances that the strange weather events were under control. Perhaps he needed to raise the pressure on the chanter communities and shift blame on them more than he already had. But he couldn't be too obvious. This required a delicate touch from someone he trusted.

The special elevator arrived on the top floor, in an anteroom attached to his offices. Nils stepped out and saw his attractive assistant already waiting. She was excellent at her job, and he appreciated the way she anticipated his every need. He noted the slight signs of dark circles around her eyes, barely covered by her makeup. He would have to make sure he gave her something extra for enduring his rages these last few weeks. She had been quite the trooper.

"Director Kane, Assemblywoman Perez is here to see you. She is on your calendar for this afternoon, but came earlier because of the increased storm activity in and around her district in Florida. Should I tell her that you're out?"

Kane growled low in his throat. The girl blanched — an indication of their shared stress. She didn't usually show her emotions so easily.

"Five minutes. I'll be ready for her then. And Inspector Holmes. I have a task for him. It's time he earned his promotion. I'll see him tonight after the main department offices close for the evening."

"Yes, sir. I'll make sure he gets the message."

Kane watched her turn and head back to the reception area outside his chambers. Yes, he would have to reward her time and attention, and make sure she earned it over the next few evenings.

Nils went into his office and poured himself a Scotch. The smoky liquid was from his private reserve — one of the few caches of real Scotch left in the world. The same team that had recovered his throne and sword had procured several pallets of the liquor on their way out of the country.

He rested his hand on the hilt extending from the stone throne. Most people thought of his office centerpiece as a sculpture. But Nils knew its meaning and purpose. There was only one other person who might be able to recognize it for what it was, but there was no way that he was ever letting Artos Merrilyn anywhere near it.

Nils turned and saw the door to his outer reception area open. A stout, middle-aged woman entered his office. He downed the Scotch and returned the glass to its place beside the decanter.

Nils crossed the room. "Margret, it is so nice of you to come and see me. Please, sit, so I can ease your concerns."

He shook the woman's hand and directed her to the chair in front of his desk. This woman was one of the more persistent Assembly members, but her support of his position was important and he couldn't afford to lose her full backing. He put his thoughts about Merrilyn out of his mind and focused on his guest. Keeping Margret and her colleagues happy was the most important thing he could do to curb this volatile situation.

He would soothe her concerns, then return to his plans.

8

INSPECTOR VICTOR HOLMES STOOD IN THE RECEPTION AREA outside Director Kane's office. He had declined the opportunity to sit. There was too much on his mind to relax while awaiting his audience with the Director. He'd received his summons in the early afternoon and it had taken several hours to arrive by train. It had had to stop twice because the dust storms reduced visibility to nothing.

The storms had grown fiercer and were now impacting his officers' ability to get their jobs done. At least the charm runners were being affected, too.

The coincidence between the onset of the storms and the Harvester's destruction wasn't lost on Victor. He had a nagging suspicion that there was a connection between the odd phenomena in the sky and what had happened that dreadful night. He found himself absently rubbing his numb and tingling right hand as he thought about it, but forced himself to stop. Victor returned the hand to his side.

He'd been in shock when he and Morgan had escaped with Director Kane that night. He'd been gripping a railing of the collapsing catwalk as he pushed Morgan through the doorway behind the Director — the explosion had destroyed the machine, and a jolt of what he guessed was electricity had raced through the railing, into his arm. His right hand had been nothing but pins and needles ever since.

Victor shuddered. He had little fondness for chanters on any normal day. They were lying, cheating, conniving opportunists and criminals, for the most part. That didn't mean they deserved the terrible death conjured by Kane. Victor had been so shocked, he couldn't even react until much later. Now, the thought made him nauseous.

Morgan was even worse off. Because she'd feared for her sister's life and wanted her to stop engaging in illegal activities, she'd agreed to work with Victor. Morgan wanted her sister to get caught and quit her charm running. There was never any time when she'd wished her dead.

She'd been frantic about Winnie's fate in the aftermath of their escape, until Victor had checked his sources and discovered her survival. Now, Morgan had withdrawn from her usual enthusiasm as a future Red Leg. She used to attend Academy classes with an eager smile. Now she seemed beaten and listless when returning to their shared apartment.

Morgan was nearly finished with her training and would be assigned to Victor's unit in Baltimore. Director Kane had promised that it was the least he could do for such dedicated followers. Victor suspected the Director knew about their relationship and approved, despite its inappropriate nature. Still, as an inspector overseeing the Baltimore unit, he would have less interaction with the day-to-day street operations of a new officer like Morgan.

The intercom buzzed on the receptionist's desk. After a few words on the phone, she stood. "Inspector Holmes. If you'll come with me, the Director will see you now."

Victor nodded then turned to follow the woman into the lair of a man he had once idolized. Worship had changed to fear, even disgust, since the steel mill. But he dared not let those emotions show. This man still had the nation's interests in mind and Victor mustn't allow his personal feelings to get in the way of keeping the country safe.

Maybe if I keep telling myself that, I'll believe it.

Victor approached the Director's desk and stood at attention, waiting until the man had finished perusing a file before announcing himself.

"Inspector Holmes, reporting as requested, Director."

Kane looked up and smiled. "At ease, Inspector. Please, take a seat."

Victor forced himself to relax enough to sit, but his back remained ramrod straight, refusing to recline against the soft leather.

"I'm sorry I was unable to see you before now, Inspector. There has been a great deal happening since the events a few weeks ago, as you know. I wanted to thank you and your protege for such attention to my safety after the unfortunate equipment failure at the facility. But have no fear. This is but a minor setback in our final plans."

"It was my sworn duty to protect you and all citizens from danger, sir."

"Indeed," Kane said. "Still, I won't forget what you did. It proved your loyalty, to me and to the plans I have to secure magic in this country and support the greatest good."

"Yes, sir."

"This understanding is why you earned your inspector's rank so quickly. Your loyalty will be rewarded. I also personally requested that your companion, Morgan Bennett, is rushed through the Academy. I cited her excellent field work as the reason to push her past classmates to early graduation. She should be finding out about that today."

"Thank you, sir. I'm sure she'll be grateful for the reward."

"Yes, well, as I said, it is the least I can do."

Kane stood and stepped over to the window behind his desk, looking out at the sunset and the orange, glowing dust sweeping through the capital.

"I didn't just call you here to tell you about your rewards. I wanted to give you an important assignment, one I'll be rolling out to each of the city inspectors over the next few days. I thought it was appropriate to involve you first, since you were the inspiration for the plan."

"Sir?"

"The storms are not a natural occurrence, as I'm sure you have figured out. People want to know how we're planning to deal with the weather, and both the Assembly and the Department of Magical Containment need time to formulate a plan. In the meantime, your vigorous prosecution of chanters in Baltimore gave me an idea for a way to gain some breathing room."

Kane turned from the view back to Victor.

"The populace wants to blame someone or something for the storms. Some are protesting our inaction. Others are taking their frustration out on the chanter community. I'd like to encourage the latter actions over the former."

Victor shouldn't speak up, but couldn't resist. "Sir, are the chanters even responsible for the dust storms? It's only affecting the East Coast. Doesn't that point to another localized cause?"

He wanted to say more, but Victor had said too much already.

Kane's eyes narrowed, staring at Victor until the inspector dropped his gaze. "You are partly correct. The failure of our ecosystem is a direct result of the inappropriate use of magic in and around our cities. Chanters have brought this plague of storms upon us, even if it took them years. It's time people knew the cause."

Kane took a step toward him, and Victor's heart sped.

"I want you to start working with your street informants to spread 'official' reports that the storms can be tied directly to chanters in the Baltimore Enclave. Spread the word in dribs and drabs so that no one gets the whole picture at once. You don't want the rumors traced back to you, or me."

"Yes, sir. And this will be done by the other city inspectors as well?"

"Yes. I will be meeting with each of the East Coast inspectors over the next few days. Storms are at their worst in this part of the coastline, so let's start the rumors in Baltimore."

This was an … uncomfortable request. It would cause rioting in and around the Enclave. Victor was a proponent of law and order. This would encourage gangs of middlings to vent their fear and frustration on random chanters throughout the city, and could have widespread repercussions to Baltimore's infrastructure.

But Victor didn't dare express his concerns. The Director was clearly looking for any version of, Yes, sir.

He nodded despite his concerns. "Yes, sir. I will see to it immediately."

"Remember, Inspector, this requires a delicate touch. These rumors must take on a life of their own. Only you, myself, and the other inspectors can know what is truly going on."

"I understand, sir. Is that all? I should start back if I expect to catch the late train and start this task first thing tomorrow."

"Your enthusiasm is inspiring, Inspector. Keep this up and you may need another promotion sooner rather than later."

"Yes, sir. Thank you, sir." Victor stood. "By your leave, sir?"

"Yes, yes, by all means, catch your late train. I'll expect daily updates concerning your progress with this little initiative."

"Yes, sir." Victor turned and passed the odd stone sculpture on his way to the door, his mind a chaotic fog as he left.

Outside the Director's office, Victor pulled a surgical mask from his pocket, and covered his nose and mouth in the elevator back to the lobby. The storm was still hurling dust, turning the glow of streetlights overhead to an amber haze as Victor stepped onto the sidewalk and made his way to the train station on foot.

He could have hailed a taxi. There were a few cars out, even in this weather. But he didn't, preferring to be alone with his many conflicted thoughts. He had much to consider on his way home.

It was late by the time Victor reached his apartment. He quietly entered. Morgan was already asleep and he didn't wish to wake her. She needed her rest. She hadn't been getting much since seeing the horrors at the steel mill. He also didn't want to discuss what the Director had wanted. Morgan would have questions and he would have to be honest, or else suffer strain between them.

Victor set his keys down on the counter, pausing when he thought he saw something from the corner of his eye; a strange, flowing ribbon of azure light drifted past his vision … and then was gone.

He blinked to clear his eyes. He barely noticed that he was rubbing his right hand, the pins and needles now back to haunt him. He needed to see a doctor, but didn't want to field questions that he couldn't answer. Any doctor would surely want to know when the problem had started and what he'd been doing when it had.

"You're rubbing your hand again." Morgan appeared in the kitchen doorway. "Is the numbness getting worse?"

Victor started, then smiled to reassure Morgan that every-thing was fine. "I'm fine, honey. It's nothing."

"You should see a doctor."

"You know I can't."

Morgan looked at him sternly, but said nothing. They'd had this discussion too many times already. "What did Director Kane want?"

"He wanted to discuss our current investigations," Victor lied.

Morgan crossed her arms. "Bullshit. He doesn't summon someone to the Assembly Building unless he has something more important than daily reports to review. What did he want?"

Victor sighed. Morgan was persistent and obstinate — excel-lent characteristics for a law enforcement officer and investiga-tor, but a burden in a partner and mate.

"Let's not get into this now. I'm tired and need to sleep. We have a long week ahead of us."

"Something is upsetting you, Victor. I can see it in your eyes. You didn't tell the Director your concerns about what happened at the steel mill, did you?"

"Of course not. We can never talk about that with anyone."

"Then what, Victor? What has you so upset?"

Victor crossed to the fridge for something to drink. Morgan waited, her expression concerned as she stood watching and waiting. He opened the bottle, then took a sip, stealing seconds to consider his best path to confession.

"The Director had good news for us. He is promoting you from the Academy early. You should be hearing from the commandant soon, transferred to active duty."

Morgan met his eyes. "He's paying us off with favors."

"He's rewarding our loyalty."

"After what he's done in the name of 'law and order,' how can you even consider being loyal to him? He killed those people. He tried to murder my sister and did kill her baby. I saw your face in that horrible place — you were as disgusted with what was happening as I was. I know you better than this, Victor."

"You assume too much. I know more about Director Kane than you ever will; he has the nation's greater good in mind with everything he does. I'll not have you speaking treason."

"I don't know how you can keep believing in him like you do."

Morgan moved closer and Victor opened his arms to pull her close to him. He didn't like arguing with her, nor lying to her. He did have his doubts about the Director and his motives. But they had to move carefully. Morgan was impulsive and wouldn't keep her thoughts to herself if he didn't dim her vigorous opposition to Director Kane.

Victor let Morgan go, then held her at arm's length. He looked into her eyes. "I know you still believe in the greater good and in the law."

She nodded.

"Then trust my judgement. There is much at stake here. I'll watch and see what's going on. Make sure things don't go too far again. But I do believe that magic is at the heart of our present problems, and that we must do something to limit its use, or else everything will fall apart and we'll end up in a wasteland like Europe."

"I can trust you, Victor. But I can't trust him. Not ever again."

"That will have to do. I have early work tomorrow, and so do you. We need to sleep."

"Agreed. I'll be waiting. Don't be too long. I've missed you."

Morgan padded off to the bedroom. Victor watched her leave, his pins and needles returning with a flash of color from the corner of his eye. Another ribbon of color — now yellow and orange — flitted into sight to follow Morgan down the hallway, fading from sight as he started down the hall to see where it went. As the light faded, so did the odd sensation in his hand.

Victor wondered what he was seeing, turning the brewing ideas in the back of his mind, leading him down a path he was hesitant to contemplate. He rubbed at his hand, considering the complications at home and work.

Morgan's voice called out from the bedroom. "Victor, I'm sorry I jumped all over you about Director Kane's plans. Don't stay up worrying about it. Come to bed."

Victor killed the kitchen light and headed toward the bedroom. He could do nothing tonight, and what Morgan didn't know surely wouldn't hurt her.

10

Winnie grabbed her jacket and looked around for anything she might be forgetting. You had to have a jacket everywhere now, even in the heat. Dust storms and wind were a sand blaster on bare skin.

"You're going out again, I see."

Winnie looked up. Elaine was standing in the kitchen doorway, leaning on her cane. She didn't need this argument now. That was why she had tried to steal out without waking her mother.

"I was going to leave you a note. I have work to do and didn't want to wake you."

"Work for Artos, I assume." She pointed to Winnie's shoulder bag, stuffed with charmed items for uptown delivery.

"Does it matter? Look, Mom, I know you don't agree with what I'm doing, but we need the money."

"I know something happened to you on one of your little missions for Artos. You won't tell me, but I know you well enough that it's still bothering you. I don't like the way this is changing you. I worry … that you'll come home injured, or worse, not come home at all."

"That won't happen. I promise."

"Don't make promises you can't keep, Winnie. You could disappear like all those other chanters, snatched off the street and never been seen or heard from again."

And they won't be. Because they're all dead.

"I'll be back in time for breakfast. I'll grab some nice pastries at the Bun Shoppe. We can eat together." Winnie looked at her mother, hoping she'd take the hint.

A long pause. Winnie fiddled with the buttons on her shoulder bag, pretending that her mother's eyes weren't burning her skin, until Elaine finally spoke.

"Breakfast would be nice. A cinnamon roll for me, and please get cream for the tea. We're out."

Winnie sighed, exhaling her tension. "Great. I'll be back for sure by seven or eight in the morning."

"Be safe, dear." Elaine turned and started back down the hallway towards her bedroom.

Winnie watched her mother go, then picked up her bag and slid the strap over her shoulders. A final glance around the room, then she stepped out of the apartment door and into her next illegal run.

* * *

The dark was a blanket around her.

Artos had told Winnie that she'd meet her final drop of the night at this corner. Winnie decided to stay in the shadows of a nearby alley, check out the scene before her contact was supposed to show. She was glad for her jacket. The night was cooler than expected.

She stared at a nearby street lamp, weaving strands of magic to make the light shine brighter towards the intersection and sidewalk corner and less so in her direction. Shadows deepened around her. Winnie smiled.

Magic was more thrilling than ever. It wasn't like the deep kiss that came from using Sable on a living creature, but regular charms felt great all the same. Everything was different since the steel mill. Like the way she was now tuned to local weather patterns. She could sense the onset of storms well before they reached her and was thus always first to find shelter.

She looked east, sensing the location of the destroyed Harvester. Something tugged at her senses, a tickle on one side of her body, depending on which way she was facing. Probably some sort of residual magic field left behind after all the captured magic was released. She laughed to herself, imagining what Tris would say. Her friend would try and find out what had happened to her, try and explain the science of the magic Winnie could feel like blood in her veins.

She didn't care why it was happening. It didn't cause her to start crying, like thinking about her lost child, or Joey, or Danny did. And really, it was like having a compass. Winnie could sort of localize herself to the sensation wherever she was in the city, and always find her way.

A figure stepped onto the sidewalk from a nearby building. Winnie peered through the darkness. The shadow started walking towards the corner and when it passed beneath an overhead light across the street, Winnie spied the flicker of a man in his forties or so, wearing a black or blue windbreaker and a baseball cap. She couldn't make out the logo, but if it was from the Jaybirds, a rival team up north, then it was her guy.

He reached the corner and stood beneath another streetlight, looking around with hands in his pockets. He'd stopped at the right place and was wearing a cap. This was probably the guy.

Winnie's gut clenched like it always did before an exchange. She wondered if deliveries made Cait feel the same way. The ex-soldier always seemed composed, on or off a run. Winnie lived in anxiety's skin.

She stepped out of her hiding place, releasing her streetlight spell so that light spilled in every direction. The man turned toward the movement and Winnie saw the bluebird on his cap. This was her guy. One more delivery, then breakfast with Mom.

The cap cast a shadow across his face, so the man's face was a mystery until she was standing in front of him. He watched her approach, waiting for her to speak.

"A friend told me to pick Jays for the win."

"That's a professional bet."

They both relaxed as each said the expected phrase arranged by Artos. Winnie looked both ways up and down the street, then back over her shoulder before she continued. "I'm ready, if your payment is."

The man reached into his windbreaker and took out a fat white envelope. He handed it to Winnie, then she slipped the bag over her head and made a trade. He opened the bag, glanced inside, then nodded.

Winnie opened her envelope's flap and looked inside.

No cash. Just rectangular strips of newspaper.

Someone stepped up behind her and grabbed Winnie by the arms.

She stomped hard on her adversary's foot, was rewarded by a grunt of pain, then twisted to free herself. She pulled one arm free, turned, and found herself looking at Dugan, one of Cleaver's men, his face contorted in pain and anger. He raised a balled fist to strike at her. She pulled hard on her other arm, steeling herself to dodge his coming punch when someone shouted, "Stop."

Dugan's fist hovered in the air. Winnie turned to see Cricket and Garraldi standing a few feet away. The little man was shaking his head and clucking.

"I'm disappointed in you, Winnie. Based on the rumors, I expected some sort of magical attack or defense."

"I don't do Sable magic, Cricket. Not even against goons like you."

Cricket planted a hand on his chest. "Goons? Really? I'm hurt."

The little mobster looked at the man in the cap, took a wad of cash from his pocket, peeled off a few hundred-dollar bills, and handed them to the man. The man gave Cricket the shoulder bag, then shrugged at Winnie and hurried back the way he had come.

"Artos will be furious. Baltimore is his territory, not Cleaver's."

Winnie hoped her bravado was a bullet. Her gun was empty otherwise.

"I told you before, Cleaver is moving in on Baltimore's charm and Sable trade. And Mr. Yorke wasn't happy with the way you turned him down. He never takes rejection well." Cricket chuckled.

"Fine, you've taken my bag. What else do you want? I won't ever work for your boss, and this here is the worst way to convince me."

"This isn't about you. It's about the job. Cleaver wants something from this run."

"And what might that be?" Winnie had looked over the contents of her bag before the night's runs and saw nothing remarkable. Certainly nothing Cleaver Yorke couldn't find in New Amsterdam.

"I've learned to keep hush, not ask too many questions of my boss. Remember that, for when you have the pleasure of meeting him."

Winnie looked up at Dugan, still gripping her by the arm with his fist half-raised. "So, is this the part where you give me a beating to teach me a lesson?"

"Ordinarily, yes," Cricket admitted. "It's interesting that Cleaver told me to make sure you didn't get hurt if we happened to run into you. We weren't sure Artos would send you out. We're glad he did. Like I said, the boss has an interest."

"So, now what? I'm not going anywhere with you. If that's what you want, we may as well start fighting." Winnie tried to sound defiant despite her terror.

"Cleaver wants Baltimore for his own. You can join the winning side and support him, or stay with Artos and watch everything crumble around you. You need money to support your mom and pay for her care." Cricket paused, looked around the empty streets, then continued. "You can fight if you want, but we both know you'll come along in the end. No one is going to risk sticking their neck out in this neighborhood. Do yourself a favor and meet a man who wants to meet you, and won't waste your time."

Despite a few tricks up her sleeve, Cricket was right. Unless everything she tried went perfectly, Winnie would end up going along with them in the end, and could get hurt beforehand.

She looked at Cricket and nodded in defeat.

"Smart girl." He waved. A dark sedan pulled forward from the shadows. Cricket opened the door.

Winnie climbed inside and settled into the center back, between Dugan and Garraldi. Cricket got into the front passenger seat and motioned to the driver.

The car drifted up the street, then accelerated onto the interstate.

Winnie tried to appear calm, but inside, she was a tangled mess of emotions. She was leaving Baltimore for the first time in her life and heading into unknown territory at the hands of Cleaver Yorke.

11

THE PAIN IN DANNY'S HEAD REMINDED HIM OF SOMEONE dropping a cantaloupe from a ten-story window, and he was the cantaloupe.

His session with Kane had been longer this time. Danny never figured out what the man was doing. At first, he thought it was straightforward torture for information. He tried to resist saying anything, but after a few days under the Director's procedures, he was spouting off anything and everything that could possibly be of use. Anything to finally make him stop. But still, he kept going.

Danny opened his eyes then shut them against the harsh white light, stabbing at his eyes and sending slivers of pain into the heart of his brain.

It was weird. Usually when he woke up after one of Kane's visits, Danny woke in his dark cell. This was the first time he'd opened his eyes in the white room. It scared him at first. Maybe Kane wanted to double his session. He stayed still and listened, but heard no one else in the room.

Danny peered out at the room from under his lashes,

keeping his eyes mostly closed. The room was empty. No guards or Director Kane.

Danny was still secured to the table with wide leather straps. He yanked at them and noticed that his left wrist was looser than usual. He pulled at the restraint and was rewarded when his hand slid a bit through the straps. He pulled harder, wincing as the metal buckle dug into his skin. Then it was wet, the buckle kissed with blood.

Danny considered, then got an idea. He twisted his arm in the restraint and smeared the blood around his hand at the wrist. Maybe it would lubricate his hand and help him slip free of the strap.

He pulled and twisted, harder and harder, until he was finally rewarded. A grunt of pain puffed from his lips, then his hand pulled free.

He flexed his fingers, looking at his blood-smeared appendage. The cut was superficial and would heal if he could wrap it with something. But that could wait. Danny reached over with his free hand and pulled at the buckle and straps holding his other wrist. A few moments later, both hands were free. Danny sat up to undo the straps at his ankles.

Danny started toward the only exit but stopped at the sight of a large, cardboard file box sitting on a corner table, the name Barber stenciled on the side.

He looked in the box and saw his confiscated clothes. Great; he wouldn't get far in his jumpsuit. Dressed like a civilian, he might be able to blend in to escape this prison, or whatever it was.

Danny unzipped his prison garb and stepped out of it, then pulled on his blue jeans and tee from the box. His wallet was still in the jeans. Unfortunately, his cell phone wasn't — they were probably hacking into it for info on their operation.

He slipped on his sneakers, crossed the room, and pressed his ear to the steel door. The other side was completely silent.

He put his hand on the knob. This was going to be either an epic prison break or history's shortest escape attempt.

His nausea was almost crippling. Vomit burned the bottom of his throat. Something pulled at him, a tugging at the corner of his mind telling him to go through the door.

He pulled it open. No one there.

The long corridor was empty, though Danny spied lights at the far end, revealing the cell block doors and a steel door that was surely the exit.

He hurried down the hallway, pausing at the cellblock door to peer over the lip of its window. A guard watched a series of monitors on the other side, not looking Danny's way.

He ducked past the window, continuing down the hallway until he was greeted by an antechamber with an elevator door set in the far wall, opposite the corridor entrance. There was also a desk and chair, both unoccupied.

Danny rushed to the elevator doors, then pressed the button to summon it.

Something chimed then the UP arrow turned red.

Someone was coming. Danny looked around, but there was nowhere to hide.

The doors started to open. Danny flattened himself against the wall.

" … You'll take the shift change, then? That's great. The wife wants a long weekend away from the city — that'll give me a chance to get out past the barrens to the countryside for a few days."

A pair of armed Red Legs stepped off the elevator and approached the corridor's entrance, never looking his way.

"Yeah, I'll take the shift. Lord knows we could all use a break. Just remember, you owe me one … "

Their voices receded. Danny stepped into the elevator and let the doors close. He looked at the control panel, numbers going from S4 - S1, then Lobby, then numbers from 1-12. He was on Sub-level 4, according to the readout. He punched L and stepped back, watching the number count rise as the elevator ascended to the lobby.

It chimed again, then the doors slid open to a broad, marble-paved lobby that Danny recognized, both from memory and ample news reports cast, as the Assembly and Department of Magical Containment Building.

Everyone seemed to be minding their own business, with no one paying attention to the young man stepping off the elevator. Danny looked for an exit and was rewarded with a bank of double glass doors lining one wall.

He walked toward them, trying to look as though he knew where he was going. That was the trick: You could go almost anywhere if you looked like you belonged and you knew where you were headed. Danny was going outside. He'd figure something out once there. He had to. Winnie needed him and he needed her. That was a beacon in his mind amid the constant, throbbing ache.

No one stopped him or looked his way as Danny strolled past the guards and citizens coming and going from the building. The guards were intent watching for trouble on its way inside, and the workers were working, with no time for him. Danny soon found himself walking through the parking lot, towards a nearby commuter train.

He took out his wallet and checked inside. Some cash, his credit cards, and his student rail pass — it had been purchased with cash and Danny didn't think using it would identify him as an escapee to the systems running the trains.

A train pulled into the station as Danny approached the terminal. The guards waved him through at a flash of his student pass. He slid the card into the magnetic reader and the light turned green. He pushed his way through the turnstile, placed the card back in his pocket, and boarded the train to Baltimore.

He was certain that that's where she was.

Danny could feel her like the beat of his heart.

Nils Kane stood in the operations center of the Red Legs security wing, watching Danny Barber make his way out of the prison, amused by his precautions and careful attempts to avoid guards that had been instructed to allow his escape. The boy was resourceful and made the escape look easy, if it had been an actual escape. The security commander standing beside Nils spoke up as they watched their subject board the train.

"I don't see how letting this criminal escape will help you shut down the terrorist cells, sir."

"I know you don't. That is why I'm the Director and you're a security officer. We are done here. This boy will lead me to my quarry and end our problem once and for all."

Kane turned to the officer. The man was tedious, but the son of a prominent senator, so Nils had had to put him somewhere. This was a reasonably prominent position, with little real authority, to serve Kane's objectives: reaping a favor from a senator and keeping this idiot far away from important field operations. Still, the man was useful for simple tasks like this.

"Tell your men to stand down. They may return to their usual duties and security protocols."

"Should we prepare a cell for Mr. Barber's return?"

"No, he'll not be returning here. You may clean it and prepare for the next subject."

The commander nodded, stood at attention, and saluted the Director.

Nils nodded, then the commander turned and left the room.

The Director shook his head. Perhaps, after they rid the country of those chanters not allied with him and the Assembly, he could look into basic intelligence testing for children and cull the idiots from the rest.

He waved off the other salutes from the operations center staff, then left for his offices. Danny would serve his purpose and help him bring Winnie Durham — a girl he now knew to be a child of prophecy — to justice.

12

WINNIE RODE IN SILENCE WHILE THE FOUR MEN AROUND HER engaged in lively conversation about everything from the women they'd bedded to speculation about the dust storms. She was frightened, even with Cricket's assurance that she wouldn't be harmed. Getting kidnapped then coerced into conversation with a man named Cleaver sent the opposite message.

She was tired of getting pushed around and tricked into doing things she didn't want to do by people who wanted something from her. Cleaver was just another boss, same as Artos. She already had one of those, and didn't need to meet with him to see that.

The ride to New Amsterdam took about five hours up a broad stretch of barrens between the cities. Many activists blamed these arid and desolate areas surrounding the cities on the continued and high-level use of magic. Others said it was nature's reaction to the pollution created by large clusters of people living in close proximity. Winnie had never left Baltimore, nor seen the barrens, so she couldn't help staring at the great swaths of brown and blackened ground passing outside her window.

She'd always envisioned a desert, with endless sand and arid ground, void of all life. But it was worse than that. There were plants of some sort, but they were wrong. Winnie couldn't explain it any other way — the plants were just wrong. They weren't green or in any way lush. The plants, grass, bushes, and stunted trees were all sickly shades of mottled browns, peppered in a sickly black. She didn't know how they could possibly grow, but their disease seemed to reach out with bent twigs like crooked claws to poison the ugly sky.

"Look ahead," Cricket said. "You're about to see a real city. New Amsterdam makes Baltimore look like a park by comparison. A talented young lady like you could do well in a place like this."

"Do they treat chanters any differently here?"

"We chanters get treated like crap everywhere, but here, among all the richest and wealthiest people, there are plenty of opportunities for those willing to help those middlings at the top. They're always trying to one-up one another. With your special abilities, Cleaver thinks we could crack a new market."

"I told you, Cricket. I'm not interested in a new boss. Artos is enough for me. Same for Baltimore. I'm not looking for a bigger and better place."

"I urge you to reserve judgment until you've talked to Cleaver. He has a way of convincing people to see things his way."

That's what I'm afraid of.

Winnie stared into the city's skyline ahead, packed with the tallest buildings she'd ever seen, stretching from one horizon to another. She had always heard that New Amsterdam was the largest city standing, and of course she'd seen it on film and TV. But still, Winnie could never have imagined what that might look like in person.

Plant life changed as they got closer to the city, shedding the withered browns and blacks for the lush green of something growing. They crossed a massive suspension bridge of steel and concrete. Winnie muttered a viewing spell under her breath — something so massive must be supported in some way by magic. As the spell left her lips, she saw the countless strands of woven magic in and around all the steel supports and thin cables holding up the road span. She wished Tris was seeing this with her.

They crossed the bridge and entered canyon-like avenues, walled on either side by buildings screaming into the sky. Winnie ignored her captors' amused grins and tried to take it all in at once. Streets swarmed with the masses on their way into work.

They drove through the city's beating heart until they reached a residential area that bordered on the industrial, with apartment buildings and warehouses lining either side with old-world construction. This felt familiar — it must be New Amsterdam's Enclave.

The car slowed at an industrial park. The driver pulled between a group of warehouses, then stopped at a building with no special markings that Winnie could see. The driver slid the car into park and killed the engine.

"We're here," Cricket said.

Dugan and Garraldi opened their doors. Cricket got out and waited for Winnie to exit the vehicle.

"It's not impressive for a headquarters," Winnie said. "Have you seen the Mender's Hall in Downtown Baltimore?"

Cricket gave her a wry smile. "You shouldn't judge a book by its cover. This is where Cleaver has chosen to lead his empire because this is where he's most comfortable. Don't be fooled by the surroundings. Come on. Let's see if the boss is here."

Cricket walked towards a door in the unmarked warehouse to their right. One of the others nudged her from behind, and she followed the diminutive mobster into the warehouse. The other three followed.

There were a few cars parked inside the warehouse, all in various stages of disassembly. Cricket led Winnie to an area of offices walled off from the rest of the warehouse, in the far corner of the cavernous space. It was like a small two-story building, built inside another and set against the wall.

Cricket opened the door and gestured for her to enter.

Winnie did, then found herself in some sort of clubroom. A pool table occupied the middle of the room, while the far corner was situated with a seating area, a massive TV, and a trio of sofas and several chairs. There was another door set in a wall with a large multi-paned window of frosted glass across the room.

"Come over here, Winnie." Cricket walked toward the windowed room. "The boss is in and he'll want to see you right away."

Winnie followed Cricket into the other room. Inside, there was a giant metal desk strewn with papers and folders, a few chairs in front of the desk and one larger one behind it, and a large, flat-screen TV. Nothing else.

A tall man with a shaved head stood in front of the TV, his back to them. He was broad-shouldered and muscular. Massive arms bulged from his short-sleeved bowling shirt. He was engrossed in something on the TV and didn't turn when they entered. He waved to shush them.

" … There are few reports coming in so far, but it appears that some sort of massive natural disaster has occurred in Boston. We are unable to reach our affiliate station or any local authorities by phone or video conference. National response agencies are rushing resources there to try and get to the bottom of whatever is happening. We'll have more details as they come. Again, some sort of natural disaster has struck Boston and severed all communication with the city. Stay tuned for details."

The big man picked up a remote control, muted the audio,

then turned around. Blue eyes pierced Winnie. He looked her up and down, then turned to Cricket. "This her?"

"Yeah, boss. She's the one you wanted. Cleaver Yorke, meet Winnie Durham."

Winnie didn't like Cleaver Yorke's smile as he eyed her again.

"Good. It's about time." He gestured to one of the chairs in front of his desk. "Please, sit. We've much to discuss. Boston's been destroyed, and I think you might be the only one who can keep that from happening here."

13

THIS WASN'T WHAT WINNIE HAD EXPECTED FROM HER FORCED
meeting with this man. She stared at the New Amsterdam Sable
trade kingpin, her mouth open for what seemed like a full
minute before she could make any words. Cleaver didn't wait.

"You are the key. Everything I've heard suggests that you're
the one who tipped the scales and set this all off." He circled
around, sat on the front edge of the desk, and leaned over
Winnie until she could smell the stale stench of tobacco. "I want
to know how you did it. How did you beat the Harvester when
so many others died?"

Winnie's thoughts tumbled. How could Cleaver know about
that, or about Project X at all? Few people had been there, and
fewer had lived. She knew most of them personally and
couldn't believe that a single one had said a word. She'd told
Artos most of what had happened. He'd also spoken with Tris
and Cait, so he probably had a reasonably full picture of what
had occurred. But it seemed unlikely that he would have
passed that information to Cleaver Yorke, especially given
what she knew about his attempt to claim the Sable trade in
Baltimore.

"You tell me, if you know so much about it. I was unconscious. My friends had to all but carry me out of that place."

She held Cleaver's gaze for a long moment, until he slapped his hand on the metal desktop. The loud smacking made Winnie jump.

Cleaver grinned, then stood and crossed behind the desk, talking as if to himself, or with himself. "That's true, it matches what I've heard. How could she remember? The girl could be lying, trying to hide her ability … have you considered that? Yeah, but people who do that don't last in my organization."

The big man stopped and looked Winnie's way again.

"Don't mess with me, girl. I don't like being lied to. I take it personally." He wagged a finger at her. "You might not remember the end, but you were there for the beginning. I understand the machine's basics; it should've stripped your magic. But it seems to have released what it had collected back into your body instead." Cleaver eyed her, his head cocked to one side, an eyebrow raised in question. He wanted an answer, and her racing heart said he'd know if she lied.

"I woke up strapped to the machine. It was agony. I couldn't stand it. Then it did something that made me snap." Winnie stopped and looked up at him, feeling like an ant in her seat.

Cleaver nodded and gestured for her to continue.

"I don't know how it happened. I was trying to resist but then I felt it. The machine was … killing my baby, taking its magic and life, then turning both to dust. It was like one minute a candle flame was lit, and then it was gone with a puff. I didn't want to live, and I was done with all the pain, so I tried to speed things up. If it wanted all of my magic, then I was prepared to give it. So I opened up and let it have everything."

She remembered the moment, pushing and pushing to send more of her personal flow into the machine.

"Then it stopped pulling and started pushing back, I guess. Next thing I knew, all the magic was coming back at me, faster than I could handle it." Winnie looked at the floor, shaking her head. "That's it, Mr. Yorke. That's all I can remember, I swear."

She kept her eyes on the floor. Cleaver's feet turned and Winnie heard him circle back around his desk. There was a creak as he settled his bulky frame into the chair and leaned back. This was the first time she'd confessed everything that had happened inside the machine. Artos had only inquired about the Harvester's destruction.

A deep, rumbling chuckle came from across the desk, and then, "She's the one, Cricket, the girl from the prophecy, just like I said. That's why Artos has been keeping her to himself."

"You said it, boss. Seems strange from this wisp of a girl, though."

"Nonsense. You're the one always saying that big things come in small packages."

Winnie listened to the men, trying to piece things together.

Artos had plans in which he thought she had a part. That was why he'd sent her after the Harvester. A prophecy would have sounded like a stretch a few weeks ago, but she'd seen that forest glade after the machine's explosion; she'd met the lady by the lake. It wasn't a dream or her imagination. Something had happened when all that magic snapped back through her, and Cleaver wanted what Winnie now had, even if she didn't know what it was.

"I want you to come and work for me." Cleaver pointed to the silenced news reports about Boston on the TV. "Now that I've seen what's happening to this side of the world, I need you to fight for me against what's coming, here in New Amsterdam."

Something finally clicked. She looked up at Cleaver as it hit her. "You have the sight. You can see into the future. That's how you hold on to all this power. That's how you beat the Red Legs in New Amsterdam."

Leaning against the door, Cricket said, "I told you she was smart, boss."

Cleaver nodded, smiling at Winnie. "Yeah, I have the sight. I can see some things that are going to happen and sometimes make adjustments to smaller events before they do. But I've seen things coming that I have no control over. And that makes you the only way to survive what's coming."

"What's coming?"

Something changed in his eyes. Cleaver went from imposing to almost … apprehensive. He looked at Cricket, then back at Winnie. "It's the end of the world."

Winnie puffed nervous laughter at the gangster's ridiculous claim, then saw his stone-cold face and looked over her shoulder at Cricket and his matching expression.

Even if Yorke had the gift of foresight, it was a rare quality, unreliable and limited to events directly related to the individual seer. He would hardly be able to see the apocalypse.

"Don't laugh at me, little girl," Cleaver growled from somewhere low in his throat. "I've done my research. I couldn't make sense of what I saw in my visions, so I looked back to accounts of the European destruction. I found former chanter refugees here in New Amsterdam, talked to them about what they saw and remembered from their youth overseas. It was already happening here, and it started spiraling out of control after you destroyed the Harvester two weeks ago."

"I didn't do that." Winnie pointed to the TV. "I had nothing to do with what happened in Boston."

"I know. It was the machine. But you're still the key. Somehow, you are the answer that keeps that —" he jabbed his own finger at the TV "— from happening everywhere."

"I don't want to insult you, Mr. Yorke, but I don't know how to stop what happened to Boston. I only found out about it after I got here."

Cleaver sighed and grumbled under his breath. He cocked his head to one side again and looked at her, examining her face and expression. She met his gaze, as hard as that was to do. After a moment, he nodded.

"I believe you. But that will change, and I want you here when it does, because you're going to keep this city and the people in it from falling into a giant sinkhole."

"I'm not the one you want." Winnie didn't believe it, knowing there was something she was supposed to do, somewhere down the road. But if she was going to save any city from destruction, it had to be Baltimore first.

"Look, kid. I'm offering you a great gig. Work for me. You'll stretch your skills. Together, we can figure out how to stop these dust storms and keep the cities from falling apart. Then you can write your own ticket."

"But I don't want to work for you, Mr. Yorke. I mean no offense, but I have a mother to care for and friends I'm committed to helping in Baltimore. I can't drop everything to move here. Not now."

"I don't think you realize how desperate this situation is. Boston is gone. There were more than a million people in that city, and according to early reports, less than one in ten survived the night. That will happen to every city on the East Coast before working its way inland all the way to the west."

"I'm not working for you, Mr. Yorke. I'm not the girl you're looking for."

His eyes narrowed and Winnie was certain he caught the lie at the end. He might be right about her, but she didn't know how to help and longed to go home. She held her stare. If she was right, Cleaver wouldn't hurt her because he might need her help in the future.

He scowled, then spoke to Cricket. "Drop her somewhere downtown. She can find her own way to the station."

"What about her gear?"

"Keep it. Leave her a few dollars to catch a train. Keep the rest to pay for my trouble trying to be nice." Cleaver turned to

Winnie. "And I was nice. Much nicer than you'll find me next time we meet. Remember that. I'm not known as a gentleman and won't befoul my image on your behalf."

Cleaver turned his back on Winnie, picked up the remote, and cranked the TV's volume.

Cricket tugged on Winnie's arm until she stood and followed him out of the office, then outside.

"Downtown is that way." Cricket pointed. "Start walking now and you might make it to the station in time to catch the last train south."

"Cleaver said to drop me downtown. Doesn't that mean to drive me?"

"It might. Feel free to go back in and ask Cleaver for clarification. I'll wait here."

Winnie turned, stalked past Cricket, and started down the alley between the warehouses, trying to remember the route they'd taken to get here. She couldn't even remember if it was left or right, but wouldn't give Cricket the satisfaction of begging for directions. She knew he was watching.

Winnie squared her shoulders, walked the rest of the way to the main street in front of the warehouses, then turned right and walked out of sight, alone in New Amsterdam.

14

EVEN WITH THE SKYSCRAPERS IN PLAIN SIGHT, WINNIE WAS NO closer than she had been when she'd started walking downtown an hour before. She hadn't even reached the edge of the New Amsterdam Enclave. This city was a lot larger than Baltimore and laid out on a flat island, so distances were difficult to judge. She thought of hailing a cab, but she barely had enough for a ticket home. For what had to be the hundredth time this morning, Winnie cursed Cleaver Yorke.

She'd been afraid of what would happen when his men picked her up. The ride into New Amsterdam had been full of random, scary thoughts about what could happen. She'd never imagined that he'd let her go and force her to find her own way home. Winnie walked, eyeing the downtown skyline and trying to gauge the distance again.

Someone grabbed her and yanked her into the alley.

She tried to scream, but a hand was clamped over Winnie's mouth. She struggled against the iron grip, trying to bite the hand on her mouth and digging her fingernails into the bare arm across her chest. Neither stopped the attack.

Winnie was let go. She spun around to face her assailant.

She was about to scream and throw a wild punch at the person's head when recognition swept her.

"Danny?" Winnie embraced her assailant, tears streaming down her cheeks. "What are you … ? How did you … ? Where … ?"

Winnie had too many questions and didn't know which to ask first. She was thrilled to see him. At first, she had thought he was probably dead, killed in retribution for her destruction of the Harvester. Then, when nobody turned up, she had desperately tried to find him. Now here he was, without any announcement, holding her close, in New Amsterdam of all places.

Winnie buried her face against his chest, surrendering to her sobs.

"Shhh … " Danny soothed her, his hand stroking her hair, tracing her cheek and jawline.

She leaned her head back and the two of them shared a deep, desperate kiss. It was a homecoming, something she'd dreamed of doing again. After a long moment, the wonder passed and she broke the embrace.

"Why did you pull me in here like that? Are you insane?"

"You were being followed. I waited until you turned that last corner to pull you off the street. Look." Danny pointed past the shadows. Garraldi hurried past, his head swiveling around, looking for Winnie, missing her in the alley's open mouth.

"Come on. Follow me. We'll lose him first, then we can talk."

She fell in behind Danny and eyed him from behind. His clothes hung loose on his much lighter frame, the same ones he'd been wearing that night. They were filthy, as if he'd not changed since.

He led her down the alley until it crossed through the city block to emerge on another main thoroughfare. He turned right and headed back up the street until he reached a sketchy-looking hotel. He checked his pockets, counting out a few bills, then led her up the steps, into the lobby.

Danny approached the clerk, standing behind a panel of bullet-proof glass. Winnie tried not to lean against the walls. The place was grimy. The clerk leered at her before turning his attention to Danny.

"Twenty for an hour, thirty for two. You want the room for a whole day, it's eighty. In advance."

Danny looked back at Winnie with a half-smile. She thought he was trying to reassure her. "I'll take two hours, please."

He counted out two tens and two fives then handed them to the clerk. The man was eating a greasy sandwich. He set it down, wiping his hands on his formerly white tank-top before reaching into the window slot and taking the cash. Turning on his stool, he reached back, pulled down a key tied to a plastic tag, and slid it through the slot to Danny.

"Room 314. Up the stairs over there. Elevator's broke. Don't make me come up and fetch you two when time's up or I'll charge you double to leave without a beating."

Danny took the key, then grabbed Winnie's hand, leading her up the stairs and into their two-hour room. Winnie found herself following along on autopilot. Danny unlocked the door and led her inside.

The room was about as disgusting as one would expect from a two-hour rental. The naked mattress was riddled with stains that Winnie would never want to identify. The space was barren except for a single wooden chair and an old dresser with most of its knobs missing. A peeling door led into a tiny bathroom with a badly stained toilet and a sink that was more rust than anything. The floor had a cluster of small holes that looked like they may have been put there on purpose, perhaps by a prisoner of circumstance paying to tweak by the hour.

She tried not to cry as Danny locked the door behind them. He slid the key into his pocket, and Winnie wondered what exactly he thought they were going to do in this place. He pulled her into another embrace.

"I've been so worried about you," he said. "I didn't know if you were dead or alive and they refused to tell me. All I could remember was you strapped to that machine before they dragged me away, unable to help you. When I finally escaped, I only wanted to find you, and make sure you were safe. Now that I have, I never want to let you go."

"Where have you been? I've been looking for you, too."

"Director Kane had me in some sort of private prison. He kept questioning me about you, wanting to know what you were up to. I didn't tell him anything he could use against you. Promise."

"I believe you."

So he'd been a prisoner of the Red Legs. That made sense. Winnie figured his parents couldn't get him out of this one, despite their connections.

"How did you find me, Danny? What are you doing here?"

"I followed you. I had to tell you that I was alive and let you know how much I've missed you."

Danny reached out for Winnie again, but this time, she pushed him away. She didn't want to get physical, especially in this dump. Besides, he looked like he might break. His eyes were sunken and his face was pained. Sure, she cared for him, but she wasn't ready to make love. Not so soon after losing the baby.

Danny fell a step back and winced, putting a hand to his head, sitting on the bed with a loud creak of rusty springs.

"Danny, what's wrong?"

"It's these headaches. They keep getting worse. I've had them since Kane started his experiments."

"Experiments?"

"He tortured me for information. But I didn't tell him anything." He gasped in a sudden spasm, obvious agony pulsing through.

"I wish I could do something for you."

Danny gritted his teeth. "You might be able to. Once, when the pain was too much, Kane worked some sort of magic on me that made it disappear for a while. Think you could do something like that?"

"I'm not a mender like Artos, Danny. Sorry."

Danny groaned and rolled on his side, curling into a ball on the mattress, head touching his knees.

She put a hand on his hip as he writhed on the bed. "Maybe we can get on the road and head to Baltimore. We can go straight to Artos. He's been looking for you. I know he'll help if he can."

"I … don't think … I'll … make it … that long."

Winnie had only just found him, and now this.

If it was a magical attack of some sort, it wasn't something she understood. She had no idea what was wrong, or how Kane had hurt him. She didn't even know if there was a magical solution. But as Winnie watched Danny deal with his pain, she knew she had to try something, anything to make it right.

She cast a viewing spell and observed Danny's head in the magical spectrum. She could see a flicker of something, but couldn't identify it. Winnie probed toward the flickering pinpoint with a gossamer thread of energy. She touched the thread to the point and Danny sighed, visibly relaxing.

She pulled back and broke contact. Again, he groaned in pain.

God, what was she doing? She doubted her ability to do any good. Winnie didn't know the first thing about healing, but she'd obviously had a positive effect.

Again, she reached forward, thickening the thread. And again, Danny seemed to relax. She pushed forward, trying to tie the thread around the flickering pinpoint of magical light.

A surge of euphoria cascaded through her body; the spell embedded in Danny's mind was Sable for sure.

She inhaled the addictive rush. Her skin bristled with the weave of magic she reflexively sent into Danny. He visibly relaxed as her pleasure centers exploded. She hadn't crafted any Sable magic for so long … Winnie had forgotten how much she missed it, how much she needed it. It was easy to continue; she was feeding her need. She tied one thread into another, until she'd woven a complex net of orange-yellow strands around the flickering speck in Danny's brain.

He was smiling, staring up at Winnie with pure affection. She'd done it — healed his pain and probably whatever Kane had done. She released the threads, feeling the sorrow come as energy and pleasure faded. Sagging back until she sat at the foot of the filthy bed, Winnie looked at Danny reclining at the other end. Beads of sweat still showed on his forehead but his expression promised that the pain was gone.

"How do you feel?"

"That's the first time I've been without pain since Kane started working on me. Thanks. I don't know what I'd do without you." Danny took Winnie's hand and pulled her towards him. She leaned over him and kissed him, but when his hands roamed up her torso and made their way under her shirt, she pulled back and gripped him by the wrists.

"No. I'm not ready for that. It's too soon after … "

Danny looked at her, puzzled. Then he said, "After the baby."

Winnie nodded, then stood and crossed the room to look out the grimy window. She turned back to Danny. "Did you bring me here to get me into bed?"

"We had to get off the street, and I figured we could use some rest. That's all. I swear."

Winnie looked at Danny, trying to judge his intentions. She wanted to believe him, but this was a strange place to hide. "How's your headache?"

Danny put a hand to his head and smiled. "Like it was never

hurting at all. I didn't know you could do that, but I'm glad that you tried."

"I didn't know what I was doing. There's the edge of a spell I can barely see in your head. Kane did something, but I don't know what. I couldn't even tell what it does. Still, I was able to contain it with a sort of magical bandage. I bound the threads like I do with charms to make them last. I think it will last awhile, at least as long as it takes to get you some professional help."

"No." Danny's face grew stern. "You're the only one I want messing around in my mind. Promise me that if it comes back, you'll fix it again."

"I didn't fix anything. It's still there. I only managed to cover it up. You need someone to take whatever it is out of there."

"I don't care. After I had Kane in there, I can't have anyone I don't trust poking around inside my head. I only trust you. Promise that you'll help me if it happens again."

Winnie considered the strange surge and her connection to Sable magic. She already wanted to reach out and touch it again. "Yes, I'll do it."

Danny's smile returned. But Winnie didn't go back and sit by him on the bed, not wanting him to get the wrong message.

"So, we wait here for a while, then we'll head back to the city and catch a train to Baltimore. Is that the plan? I don't have much money. The men who grabbed me took my purse."

Danny nodded. "I have some cash. Definitely enough to get us both to Baltimore safely. I want to make sure we leave here and go straight to the train station without anyone following you."

"Great. I wasn't even sure I had enough for the train ride."

"So, what did those guys want you for, anyway?"

"To poach me for their charm running operations in New Amsterdam. They're taking over Artos's Baltimore operations and wanted to cherry-pick his best people. I need to tell Artos what's going on, and figure out why they think I can stop the storms and other disasters."

"You heard about Boston?"

"A little. What did you hear?"

Danny filled her in. He'd watched a news report while looking for her and knew about the massive sinkholes that had opened to swallow entire neighborhoods of the city. Winnie listened as he described what the rescue crews had discovered when they responded from nearby cities, and she wondered why Cleaver thought she could stop anything on that scale.

Winnie didn't know of any chanter strong enough to channel that much magic at one time, no matter who they were.

It surely wouldn't be her.

15

AFTER TWO TENSE HOURS IN THE RENTED ROOM, DANNY WENT outside to make sure that none of Cleaver's goons were hanging around. She wondered why Cleaver had let her go and then had Garraldi follow her anyway. Danny thought it might have been to make sure she made it safely back to the train station. She asked why he thought that as they started downtown.

"Makes sense if what you said about his foresight is true," he said. "You pissed him off when you refused his offer, but his vision is his proof that you're supposed to work together. He wants to make sure you survive long enough to see it happen."

"'Prophecy's daughter' should get a ride to the station."

"Sounds like he wants to teach you a lesson. Besides, you wouldn't have run into me. I was on foot. If you'd driven back to the train station, I wouldn't have found you."

Their fingers almost brushed each other. She wished that they had. A part of her craved him, like all of her craved the way she felt when tapping into Sable. She wanted them to connect, in every way. But she needed space.

Danny's route took them by a park. A family played with a baby, who was laughing in her swing. Could that have been them, if not for their loss? She hadn't even had the chance to tell him. He'd only found out when she was connected to the Harvester and it was ripping the life force from her. That was no proper way to find out that your girlfriend was pregnant. Or that she no longer was, in their case.

They walked forever with little conversation. She thought plenty. They were together and yet they weren't, standing with a ten-thousand-pound weight between them. It ached to be near him. It was agony not to be closer.

She thought about Cleaver and what he had said, how similar it was to what Artos had hinted at. Something had happened when she took on the Harvester. Artos knew it. So did Yorke. Winnie wasn't sure.

Mostly, she felt the same. There were slight changes in how she saw the flows when casting. Her control of fine detail had clearly improved. Danny's missing headache was proof. It was like she had once woven burlap and now crafted lace.

That ability didn't give her the power to affect the weather, though, no matter what Cleaver Yorke had imagined. The problem was proving that to him, and Artos, who also had ulterior motives. The men were vying for her obvious skills, and powers that she didn't have. Soon, they would realize that they'd overestimated her value. Then Winnie would be just another charm runner again.

They reached the station's east entrance. The building was giant and felt larger inside, sprawling as they descended into the transportation hub's bowels. Danny told her to wait away from the ticketing area, in case Garraldi or another of Cleaver's men was around. He took her spare cash, added it to his, and bought a pair of tickets on the last train to Baltimore. It left in a half hour — enough time to trade their few remaining bills for something to eat.

They sat on a bench in the corner, eating hot dogs and sharing a bag of chips. The food settled her stomach, despite the grease. She grew queasy when Danny left to buy the tickets, but the feeling faded once he was back by her side. Hopefully, her nausea was just hunger, because damned if it was the flu, or something worse.

The train arrived in the station. Danny searched the platform for signs of Cleaver's guys before he signaled Winnie to follow him onto one of the passenger cars. He boarded first. The second he was out of her sight, Winnie felt queasy again. She was one wrong move from vomiting.

But then it passed and she boarded the train. Danny was waiting.

He held a seat and they sat by the window.

Winnie smiled at him, then turned to the view. They were talked out. Nothing left to say. Winnie was afraid that their next conversation might not be as friendly as their earlier ones. Tension between them was fine porcelain about to be dropped.

<hr>

They arrived in Baltimore's Central Station a few hours later. It was almost midnight. They stood on the sidewalk outside the station in silence.

Winnie didn't know what to say. She was thankful for Danny's help getting her back to Baltimore, but now that she was home, she wanted to check on her mother. She was still recuperating and Winnie hated leaving her unattended so long.

Then she had to tell Artos what had happened with Cleaver, explain how she'd been unable to finish her run. Those errands left little room for Danny. She had to let him know that.

"I need to check on Mom. What about you?"

"Guess I'll find some place to hole up for a while until the Red Legs stop looking for me. I can't go home."

"I'm sure they'd look for you at my place."

"True." Danny shifted his weight, kicked a pebble on the

sidewalk. It skittered across the lot into the darkness. He muttered something else that she couldn't hear, then reached for her hand. "Look, I'll be fine. I've got a few friends who will put me up for a while. Dad has a work apartment downtown for when he has to work late. I know where he hides the key. I'll get a place to hide out for now and let you know when I'm around to catch up."

"Sounds good," Winnie lied.

She needed him closer.

He nodded. Her hand slipped from his. She wanted to ask him to come back, but she wouldn't cave in. She drew a deep breath and smiled. Then she let him walk away, turn the corner, and disappear.

The dizzying, curious joy she'd felt since healing him circled the drain; in its place, the bubbling nausea stained her insides.

The nausea refused to leave.

So, with something dying inside her, Winnie walked to the nearest bus stop and waited for her ride home.

16

TRIS CHECKED HER WATCH, HURRYING TO REACH THE intersection so she could cross with the light. The dust storm threw orange grit everywhere, making her way to work difficult if not impossible. It was worrying how bad it was getting.

The dust storms seemed to coincide with failures in the city's infrastructure. Tris had a nagging feeling that she was missing something. She'd barely managed to get her job back, even though it was painfully obvious that she was desperately needed, and had shifted her schedule to work in several different downtown buildings, monitoring the powerful magic that worked with the building's tech and electrical systems to keep everything running.

In the past, it had often been a matter of observing energy in the magical spectrum to make sure the flows were unbroken and headed where they were supposed to go. She'd been spending a lot of time in the past few weeks working in the same building on a major repair project when the internal systems started going haywire.

Garbage disposals were backing up and elevators were moving too fast, or too slow, or not at all. At first, Tris figured it was isolated to her building. Things sometimes required adjustment and magical realignment. But with the storms, Tris considered the other buildings in the city's center, and the other downtown structures, all reliant on magic to make them work.

That was why she'd changed her schedule, giving herself the chance to see about three different structures each day. But her discoveries weren't good. The issues she'd noticed in each location were an indication that the magical energies feeding the city's infrastructure were failing at an ever-increasing rate.

The building ahead was the control center for the primary pumps that sent drinking water throughout the city. This was her second stop today. She'd already visited the sewage treatment station. Trouble there had led Tris here. Her concerns were validated at every new location. She dreaded what might happen if the city's water supply became affected by changes in the magic.

The spells running these pumps were supposedly permanent, but Tris had found fluctuations in the flows driving the sewage station pumps and magnified the electrical energy needed to power them. Something seemed to be interrupting the thick, cable-like threads comprising these powerful magical feeds, breaking them up into stuttering sections instead of long, unbroken flows, straining the electrical systems.

If they failed, so did the pumps.

Tris made it to the corner as the light turned green, then crossed with the other pedestrians before turning toward the pumping station entrance. She heard shouting as she crossed the threshold.

"We can't stop it! The whole system is going to overload."

"We have to leave, or we'll die when this pump explodes!"

Tris rushed down the hall to the open door at the far end, and found herself looking over the pump room from a raised catwalk running above.

The shouting was from the other two techs already there,

Jim Something or Other and someone else, arguing about whether to stay or run. She muttered a viewing spell and saw the problem. The normal flow of magic into the pumps was interrupted so completely that it looked like some sort of Morse code of dashes and dots. Without the continuous, uninterrupted flow, the pumps would back up and overload. An explosion was possible, and maybe imminent.

"You can't leave the pumps like this," Tris shouted over the whining machinery.

The two techs below looked up, seeming to consider for a moment. Tris swung her legs over the catwalk railing, then hurried down the ladder to join them on the deck grating below. A pool of water rushed beneath them, pumps drawing in the liquid and forcing it into the pipes that fed the city.

"When did this start?" Tris asked Maybe Jim.

"Around midnight. I managed to pull the flows back together, repair the breaks so everything kept working. I heard the pumps change pitch again when you arrived. It's much worse this time."

Jill, the other day-shift tech, squinted at the magic entering the station. "I've never seen flows with interruptions like this before. I don't know if we can repair it. We might have to rebuild the spell from the ground up."

"We can't!" Tris shouted. "It will cut off the city's water if this system goes down for more than a few hours. We need a patch."

"A patch? For something this bad?"

"We have to try," Tris insisted. "I have an idea, but I need you both to help me."

"What is it?" Jill asked, moving to stand beside Tris.

Jim looked at the women, then joined them. "What did you have in mind?"

"We surround the point where the flows enter the pumps. Then each of us pours fresh flows into the stream. If we fill the system with enough energy, the spell should shift and repair itself."

Jill cocked her head. Both she and Jim were older than Tris by about a decade; she was sure they were skeptical about taking orders from someone so young.

"Trust me, guys. We can do this if we hurry." Tris pointed to a spot on the far side of the pump housing. "Jim, you go over there. Jill, position yourself between the two of us around the housing."

Tris waited until they assumed their positions, then drew in the magical energy around her.

"Watch what I do and try to match me."

Tris opened her senses, trying to draw as much as possible. She didn't have the power of someone like Winnie, with her raw ability to gather and manipulate the magic around her. Tris's skill lay in her ability to plan and see what each flow would do in the grand scheme of a large municipal project like a water pumping station. She set large sections of magical flows into gaps in the support stream powering the pumps. Soon, Jim and Jill were doing the same thing on their sides around the massive flow pouring into the station.

The machinery still whined, but seemed to be settling. Tris spared a glance at the pressure gauges and winced. They were touching the red zone on the readouts. If she couldn't stabilize the interruptions, the system would overload and the station would experience a catastrophic failure. She and her colleagues would be killed in the explosion, or drowned when the water flooded the full city block, including their building.

Tris shouted to her co-workers, "Keep it up; it's starting to work."

"What do the readouts say?" Jill asked. "The pumps are making a terrible sound."

"They're still in the green," Tris lied. "We're fine. Just keep pulling in the flows and weaving them into the station stream. We can fix this."

"I'll try," Jim yelled from across the platform. "But I don't know how much longer I can keep this up. I'm starting to lose control."

"Stay focused, both of you. If this fails, everyone in the city could be without water for days. Maybe weeks. After Boston, this could be devastating."

Tris was exhausted. This type of brute-force work was only done when launching a new public works project. Chanter techs lined up to step in and take over so each person could periodically rest throughout the construction and activation. They didn't have that luxury here. There were only the three of them, with limited resources. When one of them lost the strength to continue, it would all be over. They had no one else to help them.

She refused to think about that, focusing instead on laying each new section in place to fill the gaps in her side.

Tris felt rather than saw her colleagues falter. Jim collapsed first. She caught his movement from the corner of her eye after sensing a cessation of magical flows from his side of their casting circle. She spared a glance and saw him lying on the floor, his back to the metal grate, chest heaving as he battled exhaustion.

Sweat beaded on her forehead, some running down into her eyes. She wiped at them, doubling her efforts to account for Jim's loss. The repairs seemed to be holding, and there were fewer gaps in the massive flow powering the pumps. They might pull this off, even without Jim, if they could keep going.

Tris shouted encouragement to Jill — she'd shifted to a position directly opposite her to help fill the hole opened by Jim.

"We've almost got it, Jill. Keep going. The repairs are holding."

"I don't know how much longer I can keep this up. I've never channeled energy like this before."

"I know, but if we fail, the entire city could be affected."

Jill simply nodded and kept working the flows. Tris did the same.

It seemed like it took forever, but then, all of a sudden, there were no gaps to fill and the flow of energy powering the station was steady.

Tris stumbled backwards to rest against a railing. Jill crumpled to the grating, hands to her head. Tris knew how she felt. Her headache was the worst of her life.

The three techs rested for several minutes before moving to the control room where they all sat in chairs scattered around the small room, staring at the readouts. Everything looked normal again, the pumps operating within their normal, safe ranges.

Tris leaned forward, picked up a phone on the panel, and dialed a number on the printed list beside it. After a moment, it began to ring.

"Who are you calling?" Jim asked.

"We need to report the system's near-failure. If this is happening here, what about the other main tech program centers around the city? We need to warn central control and tell them to schedule extra techs at every station in case they need to run repairs like we did."

The phone rang for what felt like an hour before Tris hung up, puzzled by the lack of response. That primary line was supposed to be manned twenty-four hours a day. "There's no one there. I'll send an email, but one of us should stop in the central office to make an in-person report. Any volunteers?"

Tris didn't want to do it. She thought it was more important to tell Winnie and Cait about what was going on. They might want to report this up to Artos as well. She looked at her co-workers, hoping one would raise a hand. But they looked at each other, then back at her, both of them shaking their heads.

"You should tell them, Tris," Jill said. "You were the one who rallied us to make the repairs."

"Then you should both stay here until I get back. Jim, you've been here all night. Are you good for a few more hours?"

Jim's sunken eyes belied his fatigue, but he nodded with a half-smile.

"Alright, I'll go right now and come back as soon as I'm done with my report. I'll call in when I arrive to see if anything's changed here. Have any updates ready, including any recent readings from the pump control panel."

Jill nodded and picked up a clipboard to record a set of panel readings for Tris to take with her. Tris stood. The sooner she reported to headquarters, the sooner she could finish her shift and find Winnie and Cait.

She took Jill's paper and left the station, her brain occupied with potential disaster.

17

ARTOS MERRILYN WELCOMED WINNIE INTO HIS OFFICE, OFFERED her a chair in front of his desk, and then sat himself. She had much to tell him and didn't know where to start, so she chose the previous night's initial encounter with Cricket and the other three members of Cleaver's gang.

"I didn't finish last night's run. It was interrupted by Cleaver's men, just like they warned me."

"I assumed as much when you didn't return with the cash."

"You don't seem surprised. Did you know they were going to kidnap me and take me to meet Cleaver?"

"I suspected he might want to meet the girl who took on Nils Kane and lived to tell about it."

"How does he know about what happened? You didn't tell him."

Artos shook his head with a smile. "I'm sure Cleaver has his own sources inside the Assembly, or among the Red Legs. They'd have fed him information on the Harvester and Kane's plans. I'm sure there was a shakeup at the upper levels of the Assembly and the DMC. Cleaver's operatives would've given him a report. Of course he'd want to meet you."

"Why didn't you warn me, then? It would have been nice to be prepared. I could have brought Cait, or you could have lent me some of your security team."

Again, he shook his head. "If I had intervened or warned you, the odds of someone getting hurt would have risen dramatically. That kind of direct confrontation always ends badly in our line of work. I didn't want you or anyone on your team getting injured while trying to prevent the inevitable."

"So, you've no intention of resisting Cleaver's push into claiming Baltimore's Sable trade and charm running operations?"

"I'll resist, but not through direct confrontation. That kind of fight is precisely what Cleaver wants. It plays to his strengths, and that's never good. People I care about will get hurt. People you care about, too."

Winnie was getting annoyed, wanting more from Artos than what he seemed willing to share. "You seem to know a lot about Cleaver Yorke."

"I do. He's not a person to cross lightly. I'm sure that was your impression, too."

"He's scary. We met when the Boston disaster was being reported, so he was a bit distracted. But when it came down to business, he was direct. And forceful in his arguments around why I should work for him rather than you."

"Cleaver is the way he is because of his upbringing, and how he came to power. The man hasn't had an easy life. I prefer finesse; he chooses brute force."

"I guess that makes sense for someone with the nickname of Cleaver."

"Cleaver's not a nickname, entirely, although he does appreciate the additional connotations his name brings to mind. 'Cleaver' is his mother's maiden name. He took it when he was twelve in her honor. A sad story, but it tells us why he became the man he is today — one of this country's most feared Sable bosses."

"Did she die in some tragedy? Cleaver vowed vengeance on the people who killed her?"

Artos's eyes grew serious, to match the lines around his mouth. "You shouldn't discount such an event in someone's life so easily. The death of a loved one at a young age can have a significant impact on a child's life. Such has shaped many of our most powerful leaders. Director Kane's own origins stem from the death of his mother at the hands of those who sought to harm him. Cleaver's mother was the mistress of the former Sable boss in New Amsterdam, Grim DelTorio — a brutal man, known for his terrible treatment of women. He took Cleaver's mother when he was only a boy."

Artos leaned back in his chair and continued.

"Being such a hard and brutal man, Grim beat Cleaver's mother, and the boy himself whenever he tried to rescue her. Eventually, Grim apparently beat her to a pulp, raped her, then cut her throat while the boy watched. Ever since, Cleaver's been known by that name. He's made vows and threats that forever change a person's path through life."

"Who took care of him? He must have been traumatized."

"Cleaver freed himself eventually, started working his way up as one of DelTorio's runners, working small-time charms for a local captain until he'd learned the ropes. Then he claimed that man's area by murdering every lieutenant in his way, one by one, drawing others to follow him until the captain saw the writing on the wall and sought early retirement in Florida. Cleaver took over.

"Grim thought it was amusing and applauded the boy's initiative. But that was a foolish mistake. Cleaver continued to gather influence and power through brutal displays of blackmail or violence. Soon, he controlled all of the captains. He was only a couple years older than you when he finally took over the entire operation. The story goes that Cleaver just strolled into Grim DelTorio's office and beat the man to a pulp in front of the other captains. No one lifted a finger to stop him. He destroyed his former boss in body, mind, and soul before leaving him for dead on his own office floor."

Winnie shuddered at the brutality of it all. She'd stood in front of this man and faced him down. It might've been the most foolish thing she'd ever done, given what she knew now. "Aren't you scared he'll do the same to you? Kill you in front of your crew here in Baltimore?"

"No. I've never wronged him, and have always treated Cleaver with the respect due to someone in his position. If he moves in here, I will counter him in my way, but violence would be a foolish way to cross Cleaver Yorke."

Artos leaned forward, picked up a folder, and flipped it open.

"I did find some information for you about your friend, Daniel Barber. Seems he was held under a special warrant from Kane himself. I don't know where they were holding him, but it appears he was recently released from confinement."

"He was released? He said he escaped."

"So you've seen him?" Artos looked down at his folder and flipped through the pages. "Says he was released from custody the day before yesterday. No mention of any escape. Where did you see him?"

"New Amsterdam. He told me — well, it doesn't matter what he told me. It's good to know he's out. Thanks for looking that up." Winnie was grateful, though it was a little too late. She wondered why Danny had told her about an elaborate escape. She hoped it wasn't a lie.

Artos cleared his throat. "I'd like to get you and your team back out on the street. You need to recover your losses from that last unfortunate run."

Winnie nodded. "I'm ready, though I need to check in with Cait and Tris."

"Cleaver will try to take our nightclubs in the Fells Point district. That's his preference, taking over the smaller operations one at a time, setting things up so the owners will think they can only get their magical charms from him. We need to spend a day reaching out to each of the local business owners, invite them to a central meeting, let them know we have their backs. I'd like you to do that. There are rumors in the community about the girl who stood up to Kane. Now we shall add a shout to those whispers."

"I don't want that kind of attention on me." Winnie shook her head. "I don't want people thinking I'm anything special."

"It's too late for that, my dear. You are special. Cleaver knows it. I know it, and so do you. People need a figurehead to believe in. You're our best option. Business owners will take our side and resist Cleaver's intrusion."

"That might work in the short-term, but a confrontation is coming. You can't hide behind me."

"I assure you, Winnie, I hide from nothing. There are specific things I need from you. Don't mistake the splinter of information I'm sharing for my final plan. There are things happening that you do not understand."

"Then tell me what I don't know. I don't like being put in the middle. You're playing me and I'm the one with her neck on the line!"

"My dear, all of our necks are very much on the line. You know what Director Kane is capable of, and how far he's willing to go. A turf war between two Sable bosses is nothing compared to finding a way to foil the Director's end game. That is where my focus shall remain. Cleaver Yorke is the least of my worries."

Winnie didn't like the way Artos downplayed the influence of New Amsterdam's Sable boss. Kane might be their ultimate problem, but Cleaver's plans for incursion into Baltimore was a significant short-term challenge. She would hear out his plans for the upcoming meeting with the owners of the Fells Point clubs, but Winnie's mind was on her encounter with Yorke. She couldn't stop thinking about Artos's description of his mother's death and his subsequent takeover.

It didn't bode well for anyone allied with Artos.

18

"I don't give a damn about Baltimore, Cricket. I need Durham on my side or New Amsterdam is going the way of Boston. The world will follow."

Cleaver punctuated each sentence with a jab at the heavy bag dangling from a chain in one corner of his office. Cricket winced with every punch. He was on the other side of the bag, steadying it for his boss, feeling the power with every hurl of his fist.

"You sure she's the one in your vision?"

A hard punch sent dust raining from the overhead beam. Cleaver turned just as Cricket sneezed.

"She's the one. I wasn't sure 'til we met, but looking at that girl leaves no doubt. She's the one. Artos must know she's important, too, or else he would've traded her when I asked. It's not like him to risk a turf war over a runner."

Cleaver looked up at the flatscreen mounted in the corner, watching coverage of the refugee camps out of Boston. He knew what was coming. Unless someone stopped whatever was happening to the world, it would be Europe all over again. And nothing would stop the devastation this time. The entire human race would be reduced to ribbons of survivors, scrambling for scraps in a wasteland.

Winnie Durham represented hope. Something she was going to do, or some power she possessed, would turn the tide, but she had to be allied with Cleaver. That was why he had treated her with kid gloves. He had been sure he could charm her into compliance. But it hadn't worked, and now she was pissed at him because he'd lost his temper.

Cleaver turned to Cricket. The idiot was blowing his nose in a handkerchief, his hair chalked in white dust.

"So, Cricket, question is, have I fucked it all up after that first meeting?"

Cricket thought before he answered. Cleaver liked that about him. The diminutive man was a prized counselor, because his insights came regardless of their potential popularity.

"I don't know, boss. Might be she needs some persuading, like she has to be shown the way, you know, for her own good, so to speak."

Cricket paused. Cleaver waited, forcing himself not to tap his foot.

"On the other hand, she didn't seem the sort who appreci-ated getting pushed around. I tracked one of the guards from when she blew up the Harvester. He was still shaken by the whole thing weeks later. I asked him what happened and he swore the girl got more pissed as the machine drained her, said she wasn't like none of the other chanters they strapped into it." Cricket shrugged. "I say more force is a big mistake. We need to hit this from another direction."

Cleaver sat in his desk chair. "Where is she now?"

"She went back. We checked on the guy she was with — an occasional boyfriend. He'd been detained after the incident with the Harvester, but seems to have been released since. She met with Artos, as expected. I'm sure he's warning her against you, and probably leaving her with a healthy respect."

"What about his operations?" Cleaver asked. "We need to take him down so she has nowhere to turn but me."

"It hasn't been cheap, but we've bought off most of his upper-level customers. I'm sure he has other places to move inventory, but he won't have the cash flow to keep his operation running without the whales."

"Perfect. I want to see him squirm. Artos has been a sanctimonious pain in my ass ever since I took over here."

"I know you've always refused, but why not just fix the problem? Garraldi is looking for a way to move up."

Cleaver shook his head. "No killing chanters. The Red Legs are doing enough of that and we'll need all of us for what's coming. Besides, Artos knows more about what's happening than he's letting on. I may be able to see what will help me out in the future, but he knows the why behind it all. I'm missing something in the big picture. I bet Artos knows what it is. We take over, but keep him alive, for now."

"Suit yourself. Either way, Winnie will have no choice but to work for you if she wants to keep her mommy in medicine."

"That's exactly what we're going to do. Artos should be working to consolidate his power base. Find out exactly what that means and let me know immediately. It's time to take the boys for another visit to Baltimore."

19

The shop felt like home and helped to settle Winnie's nerves.

She'd been on edge ever since being accosted by Cleaver's men. Old wounds from the Harvester incident had opened and she had a nagging itch at the back of her neck. The more she scratched, the worse it got — raging when she thought of Danny.

She had confronted him about some of his story's more bothersome details when they'd met at the shop yesterday, but Danny insisted that he had indeed escaped. His headaches had returned with a vengeance and he begged Winnie for help. She was pissed about his lies, but that didn't stop her from wanting to heal him, to feel the tender kiss of forbidden magic as it filled her with adrenaline and opened her eyes to a new shade of magical light.

Even now, while waiting for Tris and Cait, Winnie opened herself to draw in the magic, able to take in more than she ever could before.

Winnie was tapping into something elemental. Something impossible. Something she shouldn't be able to touch.

The thrill was beyond anything she'd ever felt.

Her senses threatened to overwhelm her. This was euphoria. But she couldn't succumb. Not entirely.

If Winnie surrendered that last little bit of herself to the flow, then she might as well die. She'd be a slave for the rest of her life.

Cait was first to arrive. The tall blonde came through the back entrance, pulling the surgical mask from her face and slamming the door behind her. She unwrapped a linen scarf from her head and shook the orange dust onto the floor. "Hey, Winnie, have you heard from Tris? She hasn't answered my texts for days."

"I heard from her earlier. She did say that something was up, but that she'd tell us about it later tonight."

"Something's going on. She's never gone AWOL before. And my old sergeant wants us to form Response Units from our old squads and be ready to respond if we're needed. She wouldn't say what she had in mind, just that we might be needed."

"Sounds ominous. You going to do it?"

"I feel like I have to. There's too much going on. And it's not like we have options if everything starts falling apart." Cait shrugged. "We'll see. Maybe she won't call for us."

"I don't see her broadcasting a message like that if she didn't think it was necessary. Do me a favor. If you get that call, let me know right away. It might have something to do with some of the other things that are happening."

"Like what?"

The front door swung open to a swirling cloud of dust. Tris entered, then shoved it closed behind her. She stomped on the floor and orange dust showered the ground. When she removed her mask, Winnie practically jumped.

"Tris, you look like hell. What happened to you?"

"I look like hell because it's all going to Hell. I've been working non-stop, only stopping to sleep a few hours at a time."

"Doing what?" Cait said. "What's happening, Tris?"

"I think I know what happened to Boston, if what I've seen here in the city is any indication. Techs in Baltimore have been put on round-the-clock duty. I could only get away here after I said I was going to check on a node nearby."

"So, what did happen to Boston? What does it have to do with what's going down here?"

Tris hung her coat and scarf before coming over to her friends. "I think Boston's magical infrastructure suffered a catastrophic breakdown that caused all of the public works and large structures to fail at the same time. It would have caused buildings to collapse, holes to open in the earth as the magic failed…. It started to happen here at a pump station two days ago. We barely patched the flows in time."

Tris told them all about her discovery at the pumping station, how she and her colleagues had had to wrestle the failing system until they could repair it. Winnie and Cait listened to her tale. Tris wasn't one to exaggerate, and if things were as bad as she claimed, then everything really was going to Hell.

"We've notified all the other cities on the coast. So far, all have reported back with similar findings, though not as severe as what we found in Baltimore." Tris looked at each of her friends. "I don't think we can patch the flows indefinitely. It's only a matter of time before we miss something and the failures cascade across the systems."

"So the systems will fail this week?" Cait asked.

Tris shook her head. "Not that soon. But eventually, maybe within a year, we'll be unable to keep up with the failures. Then this will go the way of Boston, and so will all the others."

"Then someone needs to find the cause," Winnie said. "If the magic is failing, and all of this started with the Harvester, then Kane has something to do with it. He might know how to stop it."

"Makes sense," Tris agreed. "But how will we make him tell us what's happening? We're not exactly on his list of good little girls and boys."

"Artos will know," Winnie said. "I'll talk to him after our next job and tell him what you told me."

Cait turned to Winnie. "You said we have another job? I could use the cash."

"We're going to make some deliveries in Fells Point tomorrow and talk with all the club owners while we're there. Artos wants to gather them for a central meeting and prepare them for what Cleaver Yorke will be trying to do."

"So you met him in person," Cait said. "What's he like?"

"Big. Scary. Everything you'd expect from a Sable boss named Cleaver."

"We sure we're on the right side to win?" Tris asked. "Sounds like Artos doesn't have Yorke's muscle. If he wants Baltimore, he'll take it, whether Artos lets him or not."

Winnie nodded. "I agree for the most part. But Artos says he's got it. And I know one thing: Cleaver Yorke won't scare me off just because he nabs me off the street and leaves me stranded in New Amsterdam. I'm with Artos." She looked at each of her friends. "You guys in, or what?"

Tris glanced at Cait, then to Winnie. She nodded and Cait followed suit.

"Good, because this run is a haul. Artos wants to impress the club owners with our volume. We push these charms through their club, and we prove ourselves invaluable. Then we can have whatever we want."

Her friends nodded, then she continued.

"Tris, we could use your help. Can you get away again tomorrow afternoon?"

"Maybe. I've gotta check an electrical transfer node down in that area, so I might be able to slip away. Two birds, one stone.

I'll try and meet you there. Just tell me where to pick up whatever you want me to grab."

Winnie smiled. This was what she wanted to do. She could help her mother and her friends without getting caught in the politics and drama.

Too bad it couldn't stay like this.

They wrapped themselves in their coats, scarves, and surgical masks, then stepped out into the storm. Winnie looked up at the dark orange sky behind the setting sun, barely visible through the haze.

At least the escalating storms kept the roving bands of middling thugs indoors. A small blessing in the face of a terrible problem. They'd taken every opportunity to accost wandering chanters, blaming the storms on them, along with anything else in their miserable lives.

Heading toward the bus stop, Winnie thought about the challenges of tomorrow's job. She was so deep in thought, in fact, that she didn't see the two figures emerge from the shadows to follow her down the street.

20

Cait met Winnie outside her apartment. Both of them wore backpacks over one shoulder; they looked like students heading to their classes, but the bags weren't full of books.

Winnie had been up all night and most of the day using her unique ability to invert the magical weaves so they could remain undetected by the Red Legs. Though the law enforcement arm of the DMC hadn't been as active over the last few weeks, they would surely still love to stop Winnie and Cait if they caught them on the street.

They kept their eyes out for trouble, either from Red Legs or the middling gangs plaguing the Enclave's edges. The gangs looked for lone chanters coming or going. They often hurled curses; other times, they chased their quarry. Sometimes they beat them. Winnie figured she and Cait could hold their own in most situations, but it didn't make sense to draw attention to themselves, especially while running charms.

They passed the bus stop, walking until they reached a nearby alley. Waiting at the bus stop drew attention and left them out in the open. After a few minutes, the bus approached. Cait wasn't paying attention. Winnie followed her gaze to a group of men in their twenties walking down the opposite side of the street. A few carried bats. She judged the speed of the oncoming bus versus the distance she and Cait had to cover. The charm runners traded a glance, then took off running.

Winnie didn't turn her head when she heard a shout from behind. The middlings had seen them.

The bus driver saw Winnie and Cait rushing toward the bus. It slowed then stopped. Cait bounded onboard a beat before Winnie. The bus lurched forward and left the chasing men behind, waving their bats at the curb.

"That was close," said a woman seated across the aisle. "Those thugs are getting more brazen. I'm afraid to go to work."

The bus driver looked at them in her mirror. "There's been talk of limiting routes to the Enclave. A few of our buses have been boarded and the drivers assaulted. Make sure you check route updates with the transit authority before you leave home."

"Thanks for the advice," Winnie said. "I wish there were some way to show them that we're not a threat, and have nothing to do with the dust storms."

"From your lips to God's ears, my dear," said the woman. Mumbles of agreement rang through the bus.

The girls sat, Cait with her mouth closed and her fists clenched, irked at having run from a fight. She wanted to teach those men a lesson. Winnie did too. But she also knew it was important to finish what they had started before adopting personal vendettas. Artos was depending on them.

Winnie looked forward as the bus rolled through its route. Tris was supposed to meet them two stops down the line. It was closer to one of the substations she'd been monitoring for the city. Tris had troubled Winnie, talking about such an unfortunate and perhaps even inevitable fate. There had to be a magical solution, even though magic was part of the problem.

Tris was waiting for the bus as the driver pulled to a stop.

She climbed on and startled Winnie with her corpselike fatigue, her eyes sunken and her skin the color of a melted candle.

Winnie glanced at Cait. Too late.

"Jeeze, Tris, you look like crap," Cait said. "You need to get some rest."

Tris shook her head and sat beside Winnie. "No time. If I wasn't going with you, I'd be staying with the duty crew here. We're all dragging. I couldn't just go home and rest."

"Nonsense," Winnie said. "You're going to get sick if you keep going like this. Don't they have more people they can call on to help?"

"Everyone is scared of the middling gangs. Refusing to go out if they don't have to."

"That's only going to make things worse," Cait said. "If public utilities fail, middling troublemakers will be out in greater numbers than ever."

"It may not matter," Tris said with a wry laugh. "The deterioration is getting worse faster than we anticipated. The other cities aren't seeing it, but breakdowns are coming closer together in Baltimore, and are more severe."

"And no one can find a central cause?" Winnie asked. "There has to be a reason this all started."

Tris leaned forward and lowered her voice so that only Winnie could hear. "It all started after the Harvester blew up. I think it broke something."

"What do you mean, 'broke something?'"

"I mean magic used to work a certain way. And now, at least for the larger spells that control the city's infrastructure, that magic is failing. There has to be a connection."

"If you could figure it out, how would you prove it?" Winnie asked.

"At some point, we need to visit the blast site. Then we could try and see if there's something in the magical spectrum."

"No," Winnie said. "I'm not going back there. Not ever."

Cait leaned across the center aisle. "What are you two whispering about? People are starting to pay attention."

"Just Tris suggesting that we go back to the site of a certain machine," Winnie said.

"That's crazy, Tris. Winnie has plenty of good reasons not to go back. I'm sure you can think of plenty."

Winnie flinched. Instinctively, her hand found her belly.

Tris squeezed her hand. "Sorry, Winnie. I wasn't thinking. It's not something you have to do. I just need to follow up on any potential source of the failures before it's too late for us all."

"I don't get how Boston happened if the machine is down here," Cait whispered. "They didn't have a magical explosion up there. It should've been like all the other cities."

Tris nodded. "My boss said there was a labor dispute. A bunch of the regular techs had a sick-out that day. Usually, it wouldn't have been a big deal. If a key system broke down during a surge, there wouldn't have been enough techs to stop the failure. We don't know for sure because none of the working techs survived, only those on the sick-out."

"I bet they feel like crap," Cait said.

"They do now that we've started putting the pieces together. Still, there was no way to predict it. We only know that kind of thing can happen because it did."

"I don't know about that," Winnie said. "Mom talks about Europe at the end. She remembers news reports from when she was younger. She's told me stuff that doesn't sound much different from all those horrible stories we heard from the refugees fleeing to the United Americas before ... "

It was maybe a minute before the bus pulled to a stop.

Winnie looked up. "Hey, this is our stop. Come on."

They got off, then stood on the curb. The bus pulled away.

Winnie swung her backpack onto one shoulder. "I think we should revisit this conversation, ladies. For now, there's work to do. You each have a list of clubs to visit along with the owners' names. Once you have them alone, make the delivery then ask them to attend the gathering at the Fells Point Meeting Hall. Tell them it's a chance to chat with us in a group setting so they can let us know how to improve what we're doing."

"So it's a focus group?" Cait said. "That's a first. A focus group to see how we can better serve our illegal endeavors."

Winnie shrugged. "It has to be done. Artos is dealing with a loss of business based on the New Amsterdam incursions. This is a chance to solidify some of what he's already doing. Artos has done the heavy lifting here; we just need to gather some discussion points."

They quickly divided, and each went for their marks. It was mid-afternoon, so the owners should all be in, prepping for their evening. They were all supposed to be expecting the deliveries, after all.

Winnie picked the first club on her list and opened the doors, oblivious to the two black sedans pulling up to a nearby alley, unloading Cleaver, Cricket, and six of Cleaver's crew onto the streets of Fells Point.

21

WINNIE STEPPED INSIDE THE BRASS SEAHORSE SALOON AND looked around. Dark wood paneling and antiqued brass hardware made the bar seem ancient. It made Winnie imagine a world in sepia, with seedy villains and the detectives seeking justice. She smirked. She could use someone to bring a few villains to justice right now.

"Can I help you with something, young lady?"

A bearded bartender in his early thirties stood behind the bar. He wore a pressed white shirt with a black apron tied about his waist. He held a damp rag and appeared to have paused midswipe.

"I'm Winnie Durham. I'm here to see the owner." She glanced at her list. "Mr. Nick Wells. He's expecting me."

"I'm Nick. And I wasn't expecting you. Artos said he was sending over a rep with a few new items I might be interested in. He said nothing about a child."

"I'm eighteen." Winnie held her frosty tone. "I have Artos's trust and the things you need to take your side business to the next level. Or not. I have other clubs to visit."

Nick raised his hands in surrender. "Sorry. We got off on the wrong foot. I was surprised. You're not what I think of when I hear charm runner."

Winnie came forward and swung the backpack from her shoulder onto the bar. She'd taken the largest load, and it was heavy, though it would get lighter as she moved through her list. "Artos authorized me to bring you his best. Everything has been adjusted using a new method we use to mask an item's magical nature. Keeps Red Leg scanners from detecting the charms. You know there's nothing like it. And it's only for Artos's top customers."

Nick fidgeted with his rag, looking past Winnie at the door. "Show me what you got?"

She shrugged, opened her pack, then pulled out a small linen pouch. Winnie unwrapped the thin ribbon tying it closed, then unfolded the linen onto the bar and revealed its contents: a diamond stud earring, a small broach, a retractable ballpoint pen, and a hair clip.

Nick snorted and waved a hand at the pile of charms. "I don't have much call for jewelry and such things." He picked up the ballpoint pen. "What's this do?"

"It's a forger. It can duplicate anyone's handwriting, as long as they've used it to sign their name once. So, say you want to get around the health department and sign your own permit? Get the inspector to use this pen to sign his name and you can duplicate his signature whenever you want."

Nick set the pen down. "You suggesting I need to trick my way around the health department? I run a clean kitchen here."

Winnie winced, then picked up the hair clip. "This will cause the wearer to draw attention to herself, make anyone within five feet do whatever she says for five minutes after activation."

"How do you activate it?" Nick asked.

"You put your hair up, then reach back and grab the clip while you shake your hair to let it down. Anyone in the spell's radius will turn to the user, then do whatever he or she wishes for five minutes or until the clip is back in the hair. It's powerful and you should be careful who you sell it to, but —"

"This is crazy. What's to keep someone from robbing my bar and getting away clean?"

"I see your earring, but ..." Winnie picked up the diamond stud. "This will make you immune to charms like the hair clip here."

She was just about to tell him about the broach, but he looked past her to the door again. Winnie turned. Cricket was standing there, holding the door open. His grin was wide as it could probably go.

Cleaver Yorke sauntered into the room, followed by Garraldi. Winnie gathered her items on the bar, save for the clip.

Cleaver turned in place, looking around. Winnie pulled her hair back, placing the clip to hold it in place.

The big boss finished his slow turn and gave Winnie a feral grin. Something sinister sparked in his eyes. "Winnie Durham. I told you I'd have my way."

"So this is how you get it? You follow me to Baltimore? Or are you here for the oysters?"

Cleaver boomed laughter. He pointed at Winnie. "I can have the world's best without ever leaving my room, Miss Durham. I'm here to offer you a final chance to join me." He gestured to Garraldi, who came over and took her backpack. "Like I said, no isn't an answer I accept. One way or the other, you're going to work for me. You know I have the sight, and that I'm telling the truth."

"If I remember correctly, you said we'd work together. Not that I'd work for you. A man like you must respect loyalty and surely understands that it isn't personal. I met Merrilyn first. And he's the boss in Baltimore. Not you."

Cleaver's fists clenched at his side. Cricket and Garraldi were closing in.

She only had a moment.

Winnie reached up, pulled the clip from her hair, and shook her head to send the waves of brown hair spilling back to her shoulders.

Cleaver's men stopped, looking vacantly at Winnie.

A surge of adrenaline. She pointed to Cleaver and spoke to the thugs. "I'm leaving. Don't let him follow me."

Both men turned and walked towards their boss.

"You can play games, Winnie—" Cleaver knocked Cricket to the ground with a firm shove "— but you can't get away from me forever."

The smaller man started to stand, wobbling on his feet. Garraldi reached Cleaver and grabbed him by one arm, but Cleaver lashed out with a fist and sent him stumbling back in a daze easily, dropping to the ground like a toy.

The boss loudly laughed, beating the tar from his men.

Winnie picked up the backpack and ran for the door.

She dashed into the street … and a major dust storm.

She looked around, grit stinging her eyes. She had to find her friends. They were going to get caught up in this, too, if she didn't get them out of here.

Winnie stumbled against the wind, crossing the street to the first club on Cait's list. She was about to open the door when Cait burst out and crashed into Winnie.

Two men exploded out behind her, grabbing Cait by the arms, yanking her toward them as she kicked the larger one with a booted foot. He grunted in pain, but he didn't let go. The second man walloped Cait on the side of her head.

She went limp in their grasp.

The large one saw Winnie. He shouted to his partner, pointing at her as Cleaver came through the Brass Seahorse Saloon doors, snarling loudly enough for Winnie to hear above the storm.

Another two men emerged from the swirling dust, holding a thrashing Tris between them.

Winnie was lost and didn't know what to do.

She couldn't leave her friends in Cleaver's hands. And he'd only hold them until she agreed to his terms.

Cleaver crossed the street and loomed over Winnie. His eyes were narrowed against the grit as he leaned down and shouted over the wind. "You've got balls, girlie-girl, I'll give you that much! But as you can see, I was way ahead of you!"

A bloodied Cricket and Garraldi were pushing through the storm toward them, apparently back in control of their faculties.

Cleaver looked over his shoulder at the approaching men. "Nice trick. You'll have to make one of those for me. Took me a while to unravel it in the middle of the fight. Now, come with me and we'll let your friends go."

Then, something stopped all of them in their tracks.

An angry crowd rounded the corner and came marching toward them. There were hundreds of people, smashing windows along the storefronts and slashing tires with knives. As they got closer, she heard them shouting things like "burn out the chanter scum" and "end the chanters, end the storms."

Cleaver's men let go of her friends, turning to defend themselves as several angry men tried pulling them into a fight.

A bottle flew past Winnie's face, so close the glass brushed her cheek. She fell back from an approaching man who was ready to throw a punch. He never connected. Cleaver intercepted the blow, punched the man, and sent him hard to the ground.

Cleaver looked around, saw his men struggling with the rioters, and shot Winnie a glance as he dodged a punch thrown by his adversary. "Get your friends and go. We'll settle this another day. I won't forget what you did today. There will be payback."

Winnie nodded and shouted for Tris while running toward Cait, still dazed, crumpled against a lamppost. They reached her together.

"I just got a text," Tris said. "The rioting isn't just here. It's even worse in the Enclave. They're starting fires and stopping firefighters from responding. We have to go!"

"Help me get Cait to her feet!" Winnie shouted over the storm. "We'll cut between the buildings to a side street. Hopefully the rioters aren't as bad there. Then we can figure a way to get home. We have to help my mom. If they set fire to our building, she'll never make it out!"

They helped Cait to her feet, supporting her as they wove through the crowd, watching rioters fight with the New Amsterdam crew. A few looked their way, but most people paid no mind as they slipped down an alley and out of sight.

THE THREE FRIENDS MOVED THROUGH ALLEYWAYS, STAYING AWAY from the streets and avoiding the swollen crowds of angry middlings. Winnie kept hoping the rioting was localized to Fells Point, but it seemed to be spreading everywhere as they crossed several major thoroughfares, threading their way between buildings and alleys to clear the riot zone. Garbage burned in the street, wind and storm-tossed embers drifting in the air and endangering buildings.

Cait called for them to stop in an alleyway, asking Tris and Winnie to quit holding her up.

"I'm fine. Let me go. I was just a little dazed back there."

Winnie stepped back from Cait, looked over her shoulder to see if anyone was coming after them, then turned to her friends, panicked. "We need to get back to the Enclave. If it's this bad here, it's worse there. I've got to get to Mom!"

Tris gestured toward the main street. "There's no bus service in the middle of a riot, Winnie. And likely no taxis. We'll have to find another way."

"We can try something I learned in the army," Cait suggested.

"We just need to find a parked car where no one will pay us any mind for a few minutes."

"What are you going to do?" Tris asked. "Hotwire a car?"

Cait nodded. "I learned a spell for quick repairs to broken circuits. My sergeant told us it could be used to steal a car, and that she'd be watching us to make sure we didn't."

Winnie wasn't exactly a fan of the idea, but it seemed like their only option. "I don't know what else we can do."

"Come on." Tris waved them down the alley. "I saw something perfect down this way."

They followed Tris down the twisting alley until they were standing beside a small delivery van for a pizza place, parked by the restaurant's kitchen exit. Tris hefted a broken piece of concrete and turned to Cait.

"You'll have to work quickly once I break the window. I'm sure they'll hear the glass shatter in the kitchen."

Winnie waved her off and walked to the driver's door. "Let me try something first." She leaned over to the door's keyhole and closed her eyes, pulling at the magical flows, teasing them into the lock's mechanism.

She focused on the threads to fashion a key, perfectly designed to turn the tumblers inside. It was one of the most complex things she'd ever done, surely, but she found it disturbingly easy, drawing on the extra power she'd unlocked. After a moment, Winnie was rewarded by a click. The lock unlatched and the door swung open.

Cait smiled at Winnie. "Neat trick. You'll have to show me."

"I'll try and figure out what I did. I was mainly working by feel."

Cait slid into the driver's seat and bent down to see beneath the dash. "You two get in. We'll need to jet once I fire this up."

Winnie got into the passenger seat. Tris climbed in the back and crouched there amid a mountain of unassembled boxes. Cait touched the ignition mechanism, stroking it with her fingers. After a moment, the engine turned, then roared to life. Cait sat up, closed her door, slid the gear lever into drive, and hit the gas.

Winnie looked over her shoulder. A pair of men rushed out of the restaurant, shouting. A couple tried to chase after them, but they didn't get far. Cait turned onto the main street and left the alley behind them.

She turned and sent the van hurling toward the columns of smoke haunting the distance. It looked like the Enclave was burning.

Winnie hoped she wasn't too late.

It took Cait twenty minutes to thread through the debris and looters along their route to the Enclave. They had to back up twice and retrace their route as they reached a burning roadblock. It seemed like the rioters and looters were having a party. Bricks and beer bottles shattered and crashed against the van as they drove through the embattled city. She didn't see police or Red Legs anywhere.

Winnie wanted to rage, thinking they'd given up on her city.

After an eternity, Cait turned down Eastern Avenue and headed into the Enclave. They passed two places where buildings had been set ablaze, fire and smoke joining the unrelenting dust storm in a deadly combination.

They reached another set of makeshift roadblocks — burning tires and rubbish in the street.

Cait stopped the van. "We're only a couple of blocks from your place, Winnie. I don't think I can get any closer. We'll have to chance it on foot."

"I see crowds and smoke," Winnie shouted. "We have to hurry!"

She jumped out of the passenger side and ran towards home.

She'd never forgive herself if something happened to her mother while she was on a job for Artos.

She covered the two blocks with Cait and Tris trailing close behind, the smaller of her companions gasping from trying to keep up. Work kept Tris in a chair, monitoring panels and read-outs. This had to be the first real workout she'd had in a while.

She stopped when a crowd erupted through the dust down the street, waving clubs, a few brandishing Molotov cocktails. The mob swarmed through the street, looking for their next target, swiftly approaching Winnie's apartment. She looked past the mob to a group of people huddled in front of the building — Mom and a few of their neighbors.

And the mob saw them. A shout bit the air as one of the middlings in the front ranks pointed to the cluster of chanters huddled on the concrete. The crowd surged forward with a snarl of rage, like a pack of wolves spying easy prey. Winnie shouted to try and draw their attention but the group paid her no mind with another target already in sight.

Winnie glanced at her friends. She didn't know what the three of them could do against a mob of thirty or more, but she had to do something before it reached her mom.

She turned and ran, shouting, almost unconsciously reaching out for the magic that was always waiting nearby for her. She absorbed torrents, all at once and as much as she could handle, then stretched her mind to draw in more.

Her pores were bursting with magical energy. She boosted her speed with the residual energy still coursing through her.

Surprising. Winnie didn't know she could make magic work on herself in that way. She felt the familiar surge in the pleasure centers of her brain, same as when casting Sable magic, but she didn't care.

Winnie gathered speed and rounded on the crowd until she found herself standing between them and her mother. She was screaming at them to stop, her voice somehow amplified.

The mob stopped about twenty feet away, shouting curses and waving their fists. One threw a flaming Molotov cocktail past Winnie, towards the apartments she was trying to save.

Winnie reached out without thinking, using a magical flow to grab hold of the burning cloth at the end of the bottle. It burst against the building's side, spreading the burning gas in a roaring splash of flame against the brick.

Winnie grabbed ahold of that fire as well, reaching out with her hands and yanking on the blended flows of fire and magic. They swirled around her in a complex pattern that she struggled to control. If she let go now, the resulting explosion would strike anyone within a one-block radius.

From the corner of her eye, Winnie saw Cait and Tris standing off to one side, their mouths gaping. She knew how they felt. Winnie couldn't believe that she'd managed this either. She had to do something with the power surging through and around her. It felt like she'd drawn all of the city's magic to this one spot and now didn't know what to do.

Squinting against grit and smoke from the angry storm, Winnie had an idea.

Instead of letting go, she let the magic and fire spread to the sky, drawing in the air and dust in an ever-widening arc.

Winnie's awareness spread outward as well and she felt other buildings on fire nearby. She invited every flame into her spreading umbrella of magic, fire, and swirling dust until she'd expanded over the entire Enclave and beyond into the neighborhoods nearby who also had rioters looting and fires burning. She drew those flames, too.

Winnie didn't notice that the crowd had stopped shouting, now standing in paralytic wonder. A few had their phones out and were snapping pics and videos of Winnie, moving her arms in complex patterns, trying to maintain control over something she shouldn't even have been able to conjure.

While the crowd watched her work, Winnie struggled to

hold the flood of energy coursing through her and into the sky. She burned inside, as if the magic she was trying to control was scorching her from the inside out.

Soon, it would burn through her, and she would have to let it go.

But Winnie couldn't let that turn into a catastrophic explosion. She had to do something, channel the energy elsewhere, like a lightning strike grounded by a lightning rod.

She searched for somewhere to send the energy, sensing the city below, as if she were flying high above. Winnie looked down and a spot below drew her attention. She smiled to herself, satisfied.

A green glow bled from the steel mill as the dome of fire, magic, and dust yawned out to cover the city. Winnie wished she could zoom in to see the source of that emerald glow, but it didn't matter. The glow beckoned her — it would be the best place to send the energy Winnie now felt at the edge of her fingertips.

With only moments to spare, she spread her arms wide over her head then thrust them down toward the pavement.

The magic, fire, and dust billowing above the city plunged down into a single spot to form a tornado, drawing in the nearby fire and dust, pulling it along with residual magic into the ground under the abandoned steel mill.

The final wisp of magic dove to the ground across town.

Winnie smiled and turned to find her mother's eyes. They met, then her own eyes rolled up into her head.

Winnie collapsed to the pavement, her stare turned upward to the sky.

Before blacking out, she marveled at the sky's deep azure, filled with fluffy clouds and not a single visible speck of swirling orange dust.

23

NILS KANE TURNED FROM THE FLAT-SCREEN MONITOR MOUNTED on his office wall and gave Victor a grim smile. "Well, that was quite spectacular, wouldn't you agree?"

Victor closed his open mouth. The live feed from the Baltimore Enclave showing the riots in action had been the reason for Victor's summons. They had expected to watch the germination of their many planted seeds: doubt, anger, and distrust for chanters among the middling communities. They hadn't expected Winnie Durham to waltz in to single-handedly extinguish the fires and defuse the tension with some sort of wild magic. A bystander had caught the action on her phone before uploading the video to the local news channel. Now it was everywhere.

Victor didn't have an answer. After a moment of watching, Kane waved a hand in the air, dismissing the question. "The Durham girl has resources that I've never seen. That kind of power and control hasn't been present for centuries. She is a dangerous adversary."

"Should I send men to collect her?"

"Oh, God no. That coverage will be played constantly for the next several days. Let people see her and vilify her deeds. They will blame her for everything." Kane gestured toward the TV behind him. "We haven't had blue skies for nearly a month. She makes it happen in minutes."

Victor's right hand pulsed while he watched the live feed and witnessed Winnie's confrontation with the crowd. Something was pulling on him, a gentle tugging over the now constant pins and needles. He had stopped paying attention to the wisps of glowing threads he now constantly saw at the corners of his vision, fearing what it might mean.

"Inspector, what are you thinking about? You haven't been paying attention. I don't appreciate that in a subordinate."

"Sorry, sir," Victor said, trying to hold his anger. "I was considering the hard work we'd done to start the riots. Seems like it was all for nothing."

Kane shook his head. "This is not a total loss. There is still tremendous animosity directed at chanters. We can use Miss Durham's spectacular performance to point out that they could have stopped the storms and prevented Boston's destruction at any time, if they had wanted to."

The Director turned back to the TV. A team of commentators were gathered in a news room, discussing what had happened in Baltimore and showing feeds from other cities, and a cessation of the constant dust storms. Skies weren't yet clear in places like New Amsterdam or Philadelphia, but the dust was no longer eating the streets. The weather was clearly better.

Kane picked up the remote from his desk and turned up the volume.

"Following the change in weather patterns up and down the coast, our team has reached out to a history professor specializing in chanters and their magic. We have Dr. Benton Nash from Princely University here by phone to comment on what we've all just seen. Dr. Nash, can you please explain these extraordinary events?"

The picture cut from the news desk to a repeating sequence of Winnie swallowed by tongues of flame, swirling all around her and funneling up into the sky. A photograph of Dr. Nash, and his name below it, showed up on the screen as he began to speak.

"There is precedent that magic used in one location could have widespread effects on a broader geographic area. I have surmised on this program before that the storms were related to some mistaken use of magic, perhaps by this young woman, or someone like her."

A woman's voice: "You're saying this remarkable young woman may have been the cause of the storms and Boston's destruction?"

The screen switched to a close-up of Winnie. She appeared to be in pain, weaving whatever spell she'd used to fight the fires and dust.

"It is a possibility," the professor said, "but I would like to interview her before jumping to such a conclusion. She is certainly displaying a breed of power we've not seen a chanter wield in our lifetimes."

"What do you mean by that, Dr. Nash?"

"This kind of elemental magic was more common in use two or three centuries ago. Its use has died out; many suppose due to the natural decline of our magical supply. This is the theory among historians such as myself — that magic's been waning for hundreds of years, and that chanters have been limited to minor charms on smaller objects. Even the use of the grander magic to control our cities has required a greater number of chanter technicians to cast new spells for public works, because of the limited amount of magic each worker could wield. This young lady displayed something today that disrupts that theory."

"If you were to guess at why she is only now displaying her powers, what would you say?"

"Well, this is only a supposition on my part, but I would say that either something has changed in the fundamental mechanics of magic, or … This young lady has displayed a power that chanters have said is impossible to wield. Were they lying to hide their true powers, or is there something else happening? I simply don't know without more evidence to go on."

"Thank you, Dr. Nash, for your expert input. We suppose that last question is for our esteemed leaders, like Director Nilrem Kane. I'm sure he'll want a long chat with this young woman about her dangerous powers." The female anchor managed a crooked smile. "We'll be back after this message from our sponsors."

Kane muted the beer commercial and turned to Victor.

"See, our friends in the news are helping manage the Durham situation. If I make a few innocuous statements through official channels, we'll have her become the person of interest, single-handedly responsible for all of our problems, and all in one day." Kane gave a sinister, barking laugh. "It's better than I could have hoped."

"Yes, sir," Victor agreed, though it made him nauseous to blame the girl for everything. He suspected that use of the Harvester had been the inciting magical disturbance, and not anything that Winnie Durham had done.

Victor wondered if Morgan had been watching the news like everyone else surely was. Even if no one else in the Red Legs headquarters recognized Winnie, Morgan would.

"You will return to Baltimore and tell your informants to renew their efforts against the chanters. Miss Durham shall remain at the heart of their ire. Leak her identity and arrest record to the media. Let's put pressure on her and Merrilyn — he'll surely have to provide her protection in the face of what's happened. See if you can manufacture another confrontation where some poor, innocent middlings are directly injured by some sort of magical attack. I'm sure you can come up with something creative."

"Yes, sir," Victor murmured.

He didn't want to attack any chanters, least of all Winnie. He'd not be able to hide his involvement from Morgan, and he now valued her opinion more than he valued even Nils Kane's. She saw greatness inside him. But when Victor was involved in the things Director Kane wanted him to do, he wasn't worthy of her faith.

"That is all, Inspector. I'll want a report on how your efforts are proceeding. You have two days."

Victor straightened. "Yes, sir. Two days."

"Very well. See yourself out." Kane turned the volume back up.

Victor approached the door and was surprised to see a gathering of reporters and cameras waiting for a comment from the Director.

Reporters took one look at Victor's inspector's insignia and rushed him.

"I have no comment on today's events," he mumbled, trying to push his way past the reporters.

He heard the door open, then the Director's voice behind him.

"Yes, yes, I have a statement about today's troubling events in Baltimore. I have just met with my senior officer. Inspector Holmes is heading to the Enclave now. We will get to the bottom of this girl's unprecedented attack on our citizens."

Victor walked faster, desperate to leave before one of the reporters decided to drag him back into the impromptu conference outside the Director's office.

He reached the elevator and pressed the L button for a ride to the lobby.

Victor was startled by a voice from behind. "Hello, Inspector. Mind if I ride with you back to the city?"

The woman was short, and dressed in a red pantsuit. She carried a spiral notepad in one hand and a cellphone in the other.

"I'm sorry, Miss … ?"

"Hallie Carr. I'm a reporter from The Baltimore Observer. Our paper's been following your rise in the department for the last few months. You must be proud of your accomplishments."

"I am. But I can't comment on the current situation. I haven't been there myself, and don't have any new information. Make an appointment with our desk sergeant, and I can arrange a formal interview at the station."

"That's not the story I'm covering. I'm part of The Observer's 'Light on the News' investigational reporting team. We're working on a long-term piece about something else entirely."

The elevator doors opened. Victor entered, followed by the reporter. She smiled at him, continuing her conversation as the doors closed.

"We're investigating the Red Legs' involvement in an industrial accident involving the death of many Baltimore citizens at the Beth Steel Mill." She held out her phone and Victor realized she was recording their conversation. "Would you care to comment about the events that transpired that evening? We have it on reliable authority that you were present during the incident."

Victor looked around the tiny elevator car. He was trapped like a caged animal. The pins and needles in his right hand were now throbbing. He clutched it in his left, kneading it with his fingers. How had this woman stumbled onto that story? They had explained the event as a random industrial accident a month ago.

"Your sources are mistaken, Miss Carr." Victor held an even tone, unwilling to betray his panic.

"I see, well, perhaps we can discuss the reports that recent riots between middlings and chanters were orchestrated by someone high in the DMC?"

Victor nearly gasped aloud. Where was this woman getting her information?

He was still mulling his response when the elevator doors dinged and another crush of reporters tried to board the box to the Director's office.

He pushed his way out of the car, managing to lose the inquisitive woman from The Observer. Victor turned and ran for the stairs, down to the train station's underground access. He had to board the next train out before the reporter could catch up. He refused to spend the entire ride to Baltimore with her sitting beside him and roasting him with questions.

Victor sprinted toward the departing train, showed his pass to the conductor, and boarded just before the doors closed. He turned, looking back with relief as young Miss Carr ran onto the platform, a moment too late.

Thank God something had finally gone right.

Victor found his seat. At least he'd be alone with his thoughts for the ride back to Baltimore and Morgan.

24

WINNIE LOOKED UP, BLINKING AT THE BRIGHT SKY AS A TRIO OF shadowy figures leaned into view. Voices were calling her name and she wasn't sure why she was lying outside while people shouted. Her mind slowly processed the sounds, her mother's frantic voice among the din, alongside Tris and Cait.

"Winnie, honey, are you alright? Wake up, sweetie, it's Mama."

"What the heck was that?" Tris asked, looking down at her.

"That was awesome!" Cait reached down to offer Winnie a hand.

"Don't get her up," Elaine protested. "She must've hit her head. She might be injured."

"Nah. I've seen this before in the army. When you channel too much magic at once, you sort of pass out while your body resets."

"She shouldn't have been doing whatever that was." Elaine waved her twisted hands, mimicking what Winnie must've been doing with the fire and dust. She barely remembered doing it.

"At least sit up," Tris said. "That crowd scattered quickly, but

I bet others are coming. You shouldn't be lying here in the street."

Winnie took Tris's and Cait's hands then moved to a sitting position, still marveling at the bright sunshine washing the world into something new. She squinted up, staring into the pale blue above, beautiful enough to stop her heart.

A neighbor from down the street came over and touched Winnie on her head. "God bless you, Guinevere Durham. Thank you for saving us."

The woman smiled and walked away. Soon others came over to say similar things, none that made any sense. Thanks for protecting us! You're the Enclave's savior! I'm naming my daughter Winnie!

After a few more of these random and almost unsettling comments, Winnie struggled to stand.

"Tell your friends to go home," Elaine said. "We need to discuss how you did what you did. You've been dabbling in things that will hurt you."

Winnie spun on her mother. "I'm not coming inside to have you scold me about saving your life. If I hadn't done what I did, we'd all be dead or severely injured and you know it. Stop telling me what to do!"

"Guinevere Durham, you do not talk to me that way. I don't care how old you are or what you think you did or can do. I am your mother and you will come inside now." Elaine drew herself up as high as her crippled body could go. Anger burned in her eyes.

Winnie didn't care. She was angry, too.

"No, Mom. I'm not going with you. My friends and I have other things we have to do." Winnie turned, looked at Tris and Cait, then walked away.

Tris and Cait followed. They turned the corner in silence, Winnie considering where to go next. There was the neighborhood pub and bistro. She could stop in and gather her thoughts. She was famished, probably from the expenditure, after whatever she did to eliminate the fire and dust.

The Eastern Pub had escaped the worst of the rioting and appeared to be open. Winnie opened the door and entered with her friends behind her.

The restaurant was full of people, all with their attention glued to the TV and a video of Winnie, with fire and dust swirling all around her in ribbons of red, yellow, and muted orange. The image was taller than it was wide, taken on someone's phone.

Winnie began to back out of the bar.

Someone yelled, "It's her! She's the one who stopped the riots!"

Everyone in the restaurant turned and stared once.

Time froze, and so did Winnie.

Then the crowd sucked her in, like dust into a vacuum.

They pulled her towards the bar, clapping their hands and reaching out to pat Winnie on the back as she passed. She looked over her shoulder at Tris and Cait, still standing by the door, both clearly bewildered.

Winnie was freaking out. The crowd was pressing in, pulling her down like undertow, everyone desperate to shake her hand.

A strong arm pulled Winnie to one side, and suddenly she was behind the bar, with the wooden counter between her and the crowd. Winnie was standing next to the restaurant's owner. She recognized the man but didn't know his name.

She smiled and leaned back against the bar, grateful for the space.

"You stay there, little lady," the owner said. "We'll keep the folks from mobbing you."

"Thanks, Mr. ... ?"

"Beecham. Dean Beecham, Miss Durham."

"You know who I am?"

"I do. You and your mother have been coming in here forever, at least for an occasional lunch. Your mom and I go way back. We went to school together, though she's a year or two older than I am. I took this place over from my dad after he passed. Can I get you something to eat or drink? You look half-dead."

"I think I need to eat. I feel like I might faint."

"We can't have that. I'll set you and your friends up at a table in the corner, and get a couple of the regulars to stand by and keep people away while you eat, alright?"

"That would be wonderful. I don't know how to thank you."

"No need. Now let's get you in a chair before you fall right over. I've a shepherd's pie to fill you up."

The man led Winnie to a table and was then joined by Tris and Cait on either side. Beecham was true to his word. Three large men stood between the table and the pub, keeping the eager patrons away. A few minutes later, a platter of assorted appetizers was set on the table, with a steaming casserole of shepherd's pie right beside it. Winnie smiled at the waitress as she set their table. She seemed pleased and perhaps a bit scared.

The waitress left and Winnie turned to her friends. "It's like she's afraid of me, but I don't know why. She's served me before."

Tris pointed to the TV. "What you did was amazing. If I wasn't one of your best friends, I'd probably be afraid of you, too."

"Well, thank whoever for Mr. Beecham. I don't know what I would've done if he hadn't stepped in when he did. That was nice."

Cait snorted, taking a bite of fried jalapeño. "He's not being nice. He has the Enclave's savior in his bar. I wouldn't be surprised if he was charging a fee at the door."

Winnie shook her head.

"Don't believe me? Look." Cait used a chicken wing to point at the door. Winnie saw a man standing with a wad of cash in his hand. He took a bill from a man waiting outside, then stepped out of the way to allow his entry.

"You know what?" Winnie said. "I don't care. I'm tired of everyone needing something from me. At least this time, someone is giving me something back. Besides, if I raise a fuss now, we'll have to go outside. At least here, we have some privacy."

Cait chewed, grinning around her quesadilla. "Just make sure we don't get charged for all this food. And we could use some drinks."

"I'm not drinking, Cait. I think I would pass out if I tried," Winnie said. "Besides, Tris and I aren't old enough."

"Well, I'm of age and plan on imbibing." Cait reached out to nudge one of their impromptu guards. "Hey, can you ask the waitress to bring me a beer? And ice water for my friends."

"Sure thing. Your friend kept my father's home from burning down."

Cait turned back to her friends, grinning. "I could learn to like this. I wonder if we can make it a regular thing?"

Before Winnie could tell Cait she was being absurd, there was a commotion by the door. Someone was shouting.

"But I know her. I'm her friend." Then, louder: "Winnie. It's me. Tell them to let me come back!"

Danny tried to push past the bouncer, but the bigger man was losing patience with the boy.

She leaped to her feet. "Let him in. He's a friend." She tapped one of the closest guards and pointed to Danny. The guy nodded and started toward the door.

There was a brief exchange, then the guard led Danny back to their table.

He looked awful, like a starving zombie. His headaches had probably returned. Something tickled the back of her brain. The euphoric connection to Danny was back, but somehow differ-ent. Now, it felt empty.

Before Winnie could stop herself, she was drawing in energy, allowing the magic to fill her. Someone gasped at the bar. A part of her wondered what she must look like with so much power coursing through her.

But if Winnie kept going, she could fix him again.

Danny embraced her. "Are you alright? I watched that video about twenty times trying to see what happened after you collapsed, but it kept cutting off."

"I'm fine. I just needed to eat. What about you? Are your headaches back? You should have called me."

"I was going to, but I thought you were angry."

"Why would I be angry? I would only be mad at you for not coming back when you needed help."

"I'm here now. You're the one who should be careful. You can't go around manipulating magic like that. It draws attention from the wrong sorts of people. Red Legs, Sable bosses, even hangers-on like the guy who owns this place will all want a piece of you. Do you know what the owner of this bar is doing right now?"

"No, what?"

"He's out in the street doing interviews with local TV stations and posting statements all over social media, saying the 'Enclave's savior' has come to his bar to refuel and rest up after saving everyone's lives. The street is packed. There must be over a thousand people, and the crowd is growing. They all want to meet you and this idiot told them all where you were."

Winnie looked around at all the food and drinks, the several bouncers, and swelling crowd. Most of the people had their phones out and were snapping pictures and videos. For some reason, Winnie hadn't noticed before. Seeing them now made her want to explode.

She looked at Danny. Again, she felt their connection and

the urge to heal him again. But she couldn't do it. Not with everyone watching. They would record it.

Her anger only grew.

Danny noticed something was wrong and tried to come closer, to hold Winnie close. She pushed him away with more force than intended. He stumbled a bit, stepping backward. Winnie turned to Cait and Tris.

"I need to get outta here," she hissed between gritted teeth.

"Come on," Cait said, standing and grabbing Winnie by the arm. "This place must have a back entrance."

Winnie followed Cait down a hallway next to the bar, with Tris close behind. Her connection to Danny broke; he wasn't coming after them.

She should have healed Danny when she'd had the chance.

The open hole was growing wider, leaving Winnie worse than empty, and making her mad at herself for not filling it when she had the urge.

They stumbled out into an empty alley behind the restaurant. Winnie looked around, still in a daze, trying to work out what to do about Danny.

Cait spun her around. "What's up with you all of a sudden? Snap out of it. You need to go home and hole up there until this blows over. Tris and I will come by soon. Stay there until we do, and try not to chew your mom's head off."

Winnie looked at Cait, barely comprehending what she had said. All she could think of was Danny.

"Stop looking back at the restaurant. You're scaring me. Look at me." Cait waited for Winnie's eyes to track back toward hers. "Repeat after me. I'm going home, right now."

"I'm going home, right now."

"Good, now go." Cait gave her a friendly shove.

A shout from the opposite end of the alley was a warning shot: people had noticed the 'savior' standing there.

Cait said, "Go. We'll slow these idiots down."

Winnie nodded, then turned and started walking.

A half-block later she broke into a run, winding through familiar alleys to find her way home.

She had to get away. Hide. Make the world stop collapsing around her.

25

WINNIE ARRIVED AT HER APARTMENT DOOR STILL READY TO explode: angry at the pub owner's manipulations; mad at Danny for not telling her that his headaches had returned; upset with herself for not helping him when his need had been so clear.

She put her key in the lock but the door opened from the inside. Her mother stumbled forward and grasped her in a bear hug.

"Oh, Winnie! I was so worried. I was just about to go looking for you."

"I wouldn't have been that hard to find." Winnie pulled away and entered the apartment.

Elaine shut the door, then glared at Winnie.

Great. Here it comes.

"Hiding your talents makes you look guilty. Like you have a problem."

"I don't have a problem with magic. If anything, I'm too good at it."

"You've been dabbling in the forbidden. I didn't even know it was possible to do what you did today."

"Exactly, Mom. Let it go. I'm eighteen and have been taking

care of you for three years. I've run the shop and paid the bills. I deserve space."

"Keep wielding magic like this and you'll burn yourself out, or worse, kill yourself while trying to manage the impossible."

"You don't know what you're talking about. I've had to do plenty of things that you wouldn't understand. I have it all under control."

"Like your pregnancy?"

Winnie stared at her mother. "How did you know about that?"

"I wasn't as unconscious as you all thought. I couldn't talk, but my ears were fine. I overheard you and Tris."

"Drop it, Mom."

"When were you going to tell me? When you came home with a new baby?"

Oh my God, she doesn't know.

"There isn't any baby, Mom. Not anymore."

Elaine's face withered. She hobbled over to Winnie and sat on the sofa beside her. "Why didn't you tell me … about both things?"

"This is why I told you to drop it."

"You know I can't do that. You used to tell me everything about your life, and now I find out that you're pregnant and already lost your baby. Was it that boy, Daniel?"

"You want all the gory details? Fine. I snuck Danny in one night and we had sex, right here on the couch where we watch TV. I found out I was pregnant after we'd broken up."

Winnie wanted her mother to feel the same anger and loss she suffered thinking about Kane's terror upon her unborn baby. But Winnie's confession would only put Elaine in Kane's crosshairs.

"There was an accident. I fell down a flight of stairs on a job. After I lost the baby, there didn't seem to be a reason for you to know any of it."

Elaine reached out to hold her hand, but Winnie pulled away. Elaine sighed. "So that's how you want it to be between us. You're going to do the things you think are right without worrying about what I think. If you want to act all grown up and keep your problems to yourself, pretending you're alone when you don't have to be, then I can't stop you. But you're going to stop using my illness as an excuse for whatever you've mixed yourself up in. That stops now."

Winnie glared at her mother. She thought this was all about her illness and her medication costs. Winnie admitted that it had started for those reasons. But that had changed. There was so much more at stake. She'd defied the Director of Magical Containment and his Assembly, spit in the face of the New Amsterdam Sable boss, and she was reasonably certain that she'd cracked the magical firmament that had destroyed an entire city. Her mother thought this was all about one lost baby. It was so much more than that now.

"I came home to try and flush some of my anger from what almost happened out there today. That mob was coming to kill people, and destroy the lives of others by burning their homes to the ground. We're in the middle of a race war between chanters and middlings."

"All the more reason for you to not use such powerful magic. It only draws attention to yourself."

"Aren't you even glad that I saved you and those other people on the street?"

"No one else's life is as important as yours, Winnie. That's what I'm trying to tell you."

The women sat in silence as shadows swallowed the flat. Night was coming and Winnie had things to do. She finally stood and grabbed her jacket from a hook by the door.

Elaine looked up. "Where do you think you're going now? You just came home. And I think you've been through enough. Stay home; let the world go on without you awhile."

"You're really saying that if I go, you'll be worried."

"Concern for others is a virtue. You should try it some time."

Winnie whirled around and glared at her mother. She would never understand why she did what she did.

Winnie turned and left the apartment, careful to keep the door from slamming behind her. She wouldn't give her mother the satisfaction of getting under her skin.

She stalked downstairs and out onto the sidewalk. There were a few people nearby, but no one recognized her in the dark. Winnie kept walking, her mind fixed on simplifying a complicated day.

It had all started going wrong on that mission for Artos. If she hadn't gone on that run with Tris and Cait, she might've been here and could have … could have …

What?

There wasn't a thing she could have done differently. It was the steel mill on repeat. Artos had sent her on another impossible mission. It had gone to crap and she'd had to save the day. Even Danny's predicament was his fault, in the end. Artos had entered her life and everything had changed. He was the beating heart of her problems.

Winnie turned on the next street. She was going to the Mender's Hall to give Artos a piece of her mind. The long walk would give her extra time to conjure some truly excellent insults when she told him what she thought of him and how he lorded his position over everyone else from his tower home.

She was pondering the way she would start the conversation when a familiar limo pulled up next to her. The driver's window lowered and she saw Mr. Gunderson smiling.

"Miss Durham, if you would be so kind as to step into the back. Mr. Merrilyn would like a word."

"Fine by me. There are a few things I want to say to him as well."

Winnie walked to the rear door and yanked it open. A familiar voice came from inside.

"You've been a busy young lady. Climb inside. Let's discuss what you've done."

She ducked her head, entered the back, and sat opposite Artos. He was holding a small glass of something dark and smoky.

"Would you like to tell me about it?"

"Would I like to … ?" She leaned across the empty space. "Thanks to you, I've been kidnapped, assaulted, and caught in a riot. I've fought with and pushed away every person I care about. You choose what I tear your head off about."

Mr. Gunderson shut the door, returned to the front of the limo, then climbed inside. He pulled away from the curb and into the night's traffic, unable to hear the raging argument behind him.

26

THE MASSIVE HAND SLAPPED A TABLE IN THE BACK ROOM OF THE Brass Seahorse Saloon. The thundering sound caused everyone in the room to jump.

"Winnie Durham must be working for me. I don't care what it takes or who I have to kick out of the way. I want her in my organization. Now." Cleaver looked around the room at his assembled men. Each one flinched in shame, at least as Cleaver saw it. Only Cricket held his gaze, because he was a captain. He had balls of steel for such a little guy. The others disgusted him.

"Three teenage girls bested you in a fight. Girls! And you outnumbered them."

"We weren't prepared for Durham's magic. Even still, we would've handled it if it weren't for the mob."

Cricket was only making him angrier. New Amsterdam locals knew better than to mess with his crew. Now he had three guys who would likely need some sort of medical attention, and the others had all taken a beating, too, battling their way back to the bar across the street. The mob had passed by after a while and the grateful bar owner at the Brass Seahorse had offered him a place to rest until they were ready to leave. He was probably hedging his bets against the crowd coming back this way.

He didn't think they were. Not after Winnie had somehow stopped the storms. He pounded his fist on the table, thinking back to the first time he saw the video playing on the TV over the bar. The owner had recognized Winnie and called Cleaver over to see her. They had both stood in awe as she pulled the fire into swirling rings around her body, then sent the massive tongue of fire and dust soaring into the sky.

Cleaver stood from where he leaned on the table and walked over to the large window nearby. He looked up and saw the moon and stars as clearly as he'd ever seen them. There wasn't a cloud in the sky. It was as if she had cleared the weather completely.

He glanced over at Cricket, watching him from across the room. "I'm missing something here, Cricket. Something I'm not doing to convince Durham to come work for me instead of Artos. So what is it?"

Cricket shrugged on his way to the TV, which played one of the twenty-four-hour news stations. A panel of experts were covering the magical implications of Winnie's video. It was muted but captioned.

He pointed at the screen. "She was dumb enough to get herself recorded doing this, so she's not a genius all the time."

Cleaver snorted. "Just when she runs into me."

"That's not genius, boss. Some of it's dumb luck. The rest is stubborn teenage girl shit. I dated this woman once with a daughter about Winnie's age, maybe a bit younger. She and that girl were always getting in the biggest fights over the dumbest, most mundane stuff. They'd fight every time the mom told her to do anything. She was fine if it was her idea to help out, but ask her for the exact same sort of help the next night and she'd fight your idea like grudge."

"So I shouldn't be nice?"

Cricket laughed. "Boss, pardon my disagreement, but you've been bossing her around and telling her what she should think. At her age, it's natural to say no to that sort of stuff. And after seeing what she pulled off today —" Cricket shrugged "— maybe the girl's entitled to another level of teen angst."

Cleaver looked back outside at the clear night sky and considered Cricket's words. He had no experience with girls Winnie's age, and had barely understood them when he was that age himself. "Okay, so we approach her by not approaching her."

"Huh?"

"It's like you said about your ex's daughter. Her ideas are filet, others are chuck. We give her filet."

"That might work. If you can get her to come to you on her own, without putting the screws to her or her friends."

Garraldi chimed in. "I guess that means we're not taking over."

"No, Garraldi. We're still taking over Merrilyn's operation. Miss Durham won't stop that from happening, no matter what she does. But we can refrain from interfering in her operations, at least for a while. There are plenty of other things we can do to oust Artos from the local trade."

Cricket gave a low whistle.

Cleaver shot him a look. "If you've something to say, Cricket, say it."

"I'm just wondering about the other bosses, is all. What about Chicago, Philly, or out west? They're watching this, too. And they're all going to want a piece of this action. Everyone will want Durham working for them."

"Let them want," Cleaver said. "It's good for the soul. Like you said before, they're all gonna want a piece, and she doesn't take kindly to that approach. We'll lie back, maybe give her a little cover or protection should anyone want to play rough. We play the long game, wait until she sees us as her best solution."

"Frankly, boss, I'm surprised you have the patience to pull this off. You're usually more direct."

"Well that ain't working for me this time. Durham is apparently destined to save us. I know it as sure as I'm standing here. It only works if she and I are side by side and at just the right moment. That much I know for sure. Knowing what I do, I can be as patient as the next man. Garraldi, bring my car around. Cricket, you're going to stay here. Let yourself be seen, but never chasing after Miss Durham. Be nice. Friendly. Get her to see us as the sane option in the war for her talents."

The New Amsterdam Sable boss waved to his crew and headed out after Garraldi, leaving Cricket and two others behind to start rolling the ball in a different direction.

Winnie would never see it coming.

27

WAVES OF ANGER SPLASHED ON ARTOS LIKE THE ROCKS OF A harbor breakwater.

Winnie unleashed a tirade of anger that he couldn't stop even if he wanted to; she vented the energy that he could see trapped inside her. He could sense it festering, fueling the fires of her anger the second she sat in the back of his limo. It was as he feared, seeing the extent of her growing power. Like nothing he'd seen since leaving Merlin's tower all those years before.

He'd arrived in the modern world to find that man had used his machines to tame and control the world's wild magic. No chanter possessed even a hundredth of the power ancient mages had been able to wield easily. That had been his most shocking discovery. Magic was finite in a way he could never have imagined. And it was fading away, as proved by Europe's destruction.

Winnie had unlocked the wild magic again. She'd somehow opened the floodgates, at least for herself, and she could do things no one in this present could even conceive of. No one told her that she couldn't send the fire and dust asunder, so she had drawn in enough power until she could.

A stunning display of power. It told Artos that she was at a dangerous place in her life. She could let the Sable claim her and destroy all that she'd worked for. Artos had to make sure that didn't happen.

So, he let her anger spill and roll away, waiting for his opening to talk her down from a ledge she didn't even know she was about to step off. She paused after a particularly long tirade about how he controlled everything in the world because he had no one close in his life. He winced at the truth.

"Winnie, I don't disagree with a word that you've said. I'm a wretched old manipulator of a man, just as you say, because of my mission in this time and place. You know what I'm talking about, because you've seen the other side, haven't you, Winnie?"

"I don't know anything about any other side, Artos, and shifting the blame to me isn't going to work."

Winnie stopped talking, waiting with crossed arms for his answer. Fine by him. She'd stopped escalating for a while and that was important. He chose his next words carefully. Trust meant everything.

"Winnie, what you did today with the fire and dust should have been impossible."

"Shows how much you know. I'm not sure it was even hard."

"You opened up something long closed to chanters. That could either be the end to us all, or a gift like you wouldn't believe. It depends on whether the person in control is someone with the proper training and restraint."

"So now I don't have restraint. You've a lot of nerve, Artos."

He was balanced on the tightrope. One wrong move would send him tumbling over the edge. If Winnie went off again, Artos might not be able to contain her anger in time.

"I need to tell you something, but first you must promise to hear me. You don't have to believe what I say, but promise me you'll at least listen. Can you do that?"

Artos studied Winnie's face, searching for any sign that she was actively listening rather than surrendering to her anger again. He remembered a moment he'd had with Merlin — similar to this, but it had happened in a remote castle on the kingdom's eastern marches. Artos didn't have the resources to surround Winnie with stone to keep her magic from hurting anyone else, so he'd had Gunderson drive them to the city's outskirts and the wasteland beyond. All was lost if he failed. The prophecy would never come to pass. The world was depending on him.

"There is a dark side to all things. The sun sets and the darkness comes. Then it fades and the sun returns with the light. Magic is no different."

"I get it, Artos. Sable magic is bad. It's addictive, and abuse can destroy you. My cousin Joey was an addict, remember?"

"That was when magic was limited, and addiction was the worst that Sable could do. But you've unlocked the world's true magic. That means both light and dark — the real Sable, from long ago."

"So, what, is this where you tell me to 'just say no' and make me promise I'll never use the bad, bad magic?"

Artos ignored her mocking tone, refusing to take the bait.

"No, because there will probably come a day when you will need to use the 'bad, bad magic,' but just know that you cannot control it. When you cast magic for the right reasons, such as to help others or save a life, that magic is light. Today's actions were a demonstration of light magic. But being able to do what you did means you can access the dark magic, too. Spells are typically cast on another person for selfish reasons. This egocentricity opens your soul — your very core — to the darkness at the heart of Sable magic. For most people here in the present, that would be a trickle of darkness. Just enough to make you crave more. It always took a strong-willed wizard to resist the urges once the way was open to them."

Artos could sense Winnie's frail shell of feigned indifference finally starting to crack. Soon, he would be able to talk some sense into her, convince her to train with him, accept his help in overcoming the darkness she would eventually allow inside.

The bond between a master and apprentice was enough to ensure obedience ... at least, that had been the way once upon a time. But those bonds no longer existed and children of Winnie's age were known for their obstinance. They considered obstinance a virtue. He must convince her that his way would help her overcome the darkness, and resist the selfish urges waiting to claim her.

"I want to help you, Winnie. Take you into official training. Help you through this time. Come and stay in the Mender's Hall. We can work on the proper meditation and exercises to help you retain control after you access the Sable pool now open to you."

Winnie considered his offer in the limo's silence, her eyes fixed on nothing, head tilted to the side in quiet contemplation. But she had listened. Artos had finally gotten through to her.

Minutes passed before she spoke, and when she did, it was barely a whisper. "I appreciate your concerns, Artos. And that you have your own agenda. I don't know what game you're playing, but you have to stop moving me and my friends like pawns on a board as if we mean nothing to you. Insist on treating people this way and I'll take my own chances."

She leaned over and tapped the glass partition. It rolled down to reveal Gunderson staring back at Winnie in the rearview.

"Please drop me off at the nearest bus stop," she said. "We're finished."

Gunderson found his boss in the rearview. After a brief pause, Artos nodded.

"As you wish, Miss Durham."

Minutes later, the limo pulled up to a well-lit stop with a covered shelter. Artos was thankful for competent underlings who didn't need to be told what to do. He would have to commend Mr. Gunderson on choosing a safe location to drop their precious passenger.

Winnie was key to the prophecy; Artos had never been more certain. She was the one capable of saving the world — if she could survive the magical transformation happening inside her. He couldn't stop it, only help her through the process. All was lost if she surrendered to the darkness.

Artos had hoped that articulating the risks would be enough for Winnie to see the wisdom in accepting his help. But she'd refused so far, and there was little he could do but stand by and watch. It was one of the rare moments when he hated the modern world, along with all of its festered ethics. In his youth, no person Winnie's age would have refused his offer, if only out of deference to his position. Today's youth didn't see things that way; Artos was just another boss she had to resist.

Winnie opened the door, got out, and stood there, staring into the limo at Artos. He was hopeful that she'd change her mind and accept his offer.

"I can't accept your training, but I do thank you for letting me vent. You helped me work out some of my anger, and didn't yell back. I'll be careful and remember what you said."

Winnie shut the door. Artos watched through the tinted windows as she walked to the bus stop with her hands shoved deep in her pockets. She stood alone in a pool of street light as Gunderson pulled away from the curb.

He hoped she stayed in the light. The world depended on it.

VICTOR ARRIVED ON THE TRAIN BACK TO BALTIMORE WELL AFTER dark. He was afraid that young Miss Carr had called ahead to have one of her fellow reporters waiting at the station to continue their awkward questioning about that night at the steel mill. He had spent the entire ride from the capital considering the ways they might have stumbled upon some inkling of what had happened, but all he could think of was a possible leak within his own ranks. It made him wonder if there were others who doubted Kane's direction.

Victor left the train, climbed into his cruiser, and started toward home. He missed Morgan. She'd stood by him throughout the ordeal. And while he hadn't admitted to everything that had happened since that night, he had told her most of it. She didn't know about his strange symptoms or the odd things he sometimes spied from the corner of his eyes. Victor told himself he was protecting her from worry. But that wasn't true. He was afraid of what it meant, and what she might think if his fears were real.

He approached his exit, but kept on driving. At first, Victor wasn't sure why he was avoiding his home. Maybe he was tired of lying, constantly telling Morgan that everything would be alright. That might not be true, especially after what had happened to Boston. He suspected that Kane had sealed the city's doom with his ill-fated plans much more than anything Winnie Durham had done.

Victor eventually pulled off the parkway, driving down random city streets while pondering what to do next. Kane had given him his marching orders. He was to blame everything on Winnie, make sure that people saw and felt threatened by her power. It wouldn't be hard. People were already scared. Most would only need a nudge to see Winnie as the source of their fear. With a public face on the chanter problem, people would see every chanter as dangerous.

Victor realized that he was in the industrial district on the city's eastern edge, near the mill for the first time since that night. Pins and needles returned to his hand with the thought. He was no longer surprised by the odd ribbons of colorful light drifting past the edges of his vision.

Victor turned down the same street where he and Morgan had driven that night, then swung into the lot. The place was abandoned, no guard in sight. He'd been told there was only an open crater amid the ruins of the large central mill.

Victor put the car in park, then leaned forward, reached under his seat, and pulled out his flashlight. He didn't know what he expected to see but he had to get back to ground zero. He had avoided it thus far, despite the pull he felt inside.

He switched on the flashlight and started towards the complex where he'd gone with Morgan all those weeks ago. He tried the handle and found it unlocked. He opened it with a gentle tug, shining his light into the dark interior hallway as hairs on his neck stood on end.

He pierced the gloom for a minute or two before finally managing to take a tentative step into the hallway. Victor wasn't a child. He was a grown man. He knew there were no monsters waiting to attack. True darkness lay inside a man's soul, and that had nothing whatsoever to do with a lack of light.

Victor started down the hallway, weaving through the building's corridors until he found himself at the catwalk leading to the large central room where the Harvester's remains would be located. He reached out with a foot and tested the metal grating. It seemed solid enough, at least for this section. Others had collapsed during the explosion. He'd have to be careful.

He shined his light on the catwalk and saw that it extended around the room's perimeter. He looked up and saw the stars through a massive hole in the ceiling. A significant section of the roof seemed to have been blown open during the explosion, or had collapsed inward since. Exterior walls still stood, supporting most of the suspended catwalk. Victor walked the perimeter, working for a better look at the floor below.

Something illuminated the floor as though someone was shining a bright light from within a pool of water below. A soft, blue-green glow flickered as if refracted by ripples in the water. Part of the crater had probably filled with rainwater and some waterproof, battery-operated light was now submerged. The ribbons of light that Victor had been seeing from the corner of his eyes were more prevalent here. He moved his hands from the railing, shined the flashlight at his palm, and saw nothing. No orange residue from the storms. That dust was everywhere, except here at ground zero.

Victor reached a ladder, tucked the flashlight into his back pocket, and climbed down. He swallowed a moment of panic when the ladder and catwalk both shifted and rattled when he was halfway to the floor. He considered going back up, but if the whole thing collapsed, he'd be better off closer to the floor, with a much shorter fall.

The point was moot. Victor reached the floor without further incident. He looked around, dragging his beam of light along the floor, surprised to see no evidence of the Harvester anywhere. A few of the giant, capsule-shaped holding tanks that had once been connected to the terrible machine still lined the wall. But there was nothing in the room's center except a jagged, gaping hole.

The light emanating from the hole was brighter. Victor killed the flashlight; he no longer needed it to see where he was going. He kept the aluminum barrel tight in his grip anyway, its sturdy weight a comfort in his hands.

Victor stepped hesitantly to the crater's edge and peered down into the chasm below. He didn't know what he expected to see, but certainly not the impossible.

A cavern of sorts had formed below the crater, the floor covered in a deep-green grass amid clusters of small bushes and trees. The amount of growth seemed unthinkable, given the scant weeks since the crater's creation. There was a pool of deep-blue water in the center of the cavern — the source of light he'd seen from above.

The pool's light filled the cavern in blues and greens. Victor fell a step back, shocked to realize that something was moving down there.

Tiny creatures flew from plant to plant, blossom to blossom, landing here and there before moving on. They must be insects of some sort.

His pins and needles were screaming.

Victor started down the rubble-strewn ground until he reached the cavern's edge. The ground turned from hard, uneven rubble to soft, pleasant turf. Victor crouched, running his hands through the thick, luxurious grass. It was cool to the touch, early morning dew dampening his fingers.

He looked towards the crater, longing to know what was causing the light.

A cool breeze shifted as he stood and approached the pool, sending the sweet scent of blooming flowers toward him. This place was practically perfect. It wasn't too hot or cold; the air was clean and clear, with no sign of the dust that was like a blanket over the city. He felt at peace for the first time in weeks, perhaps the first time in his life.

Victor stared into the pool. The light was an invitation, not blinding at all. It was crystal clear and he could see to the bottom of the pool, where schools of small fish were swimming amid the rocks and gravel. He knelt at the water's edge, reaching out with his right hand, the buzzing now stronger than ever.

He touched the water and his tingling stopped.

The cool — not cold but cool — water soothed his fingertips. He leaned forward to immerse his hand, cupping some water and bringing it to his lips.

"Don't drink that, Victor," whispered a soft voice in his ear, high-pitched like a child's. "This pool is not for you. Drinking this water will send you from this life to the next."

Victor turned to see who spoke, but wasn't prepared for the sight of a tiny girl floating in the air a few feet away.

No … she wasn't floating.

Tiny wings whirred in the air behind her, allowing the miniature girl to hover like a humming bird.

Again, Victor fell backwards in alarm, looking frantically around. The tiny insects weren't insects at all. They were all tiny little people, just like this girl.

She waved and smiled. He shouted and crab-walked back. Scrambling to his feet, Victor ran to the crater's edge, tripping and falling many times along the way. A gentle, rolling giggle came from the voice behind him as he ran.

Victor's mind filled with terror at what he'd seen, and what he'd almost done. He felt certain that he would have become one of those creatures in the cavern if he'd followed his instincts and drank from the pool.

He reached the concrete floor and raced towards the ladder.

He needed to leave this room as soon as possible. It had been a mistake to come.

Victor got in his car and raced towards the entrance, back towards his apartment and his bed. He couldn't believe what he'd seen. He wasn't even sure that he hadn't dreamed the whole thing, some sort of waking hallucination.

Had he even left his car? Maybe that was the safer thought. He hadn't seen anything in the crater, or visited it at all.

Victor settled his breathing, convinced himself that he'd imagined the entire incident, and continued to drive towards his exit, forcing himself to think of Morgan and his bed at home.

He was desperate for sleep. And if he got enough, Victor might be able to laugh all of this off in the morning.

WINNIE STARED UP AT THE NIGHT SKY. IT HAD BEEN A MONTH since anyone had seen a clear sky like the one above her now. Again, she wondered how she had the power to do such a thing. Artos said it was a gift. She snorted, considering the irony. This gift had sharp edges and could hurt her if she wasn't careful. They agreed on that much, though she'd never admit it to him.

Winnie was still staring at the sky when she heard a car pull up nearby. Doors opened and slammed shut. She looked toward the noise and saw a pair of men in dark suits approaching her. Winnie stood and looked around, trying to determine whether she should run or wait and see what they wanted.

One of them pointed at her and called her name. "Winnie? Winnie Durham? We'd like a few words, or rather, a friend of ours would."

"My mother told me never to accept rides from strangers."

Winnie backed up as they got closer. The men separated. The taller of the two moved to her right while the short, chubby one kept talking.

"We won't be strangers if you'd let us introduce ourselves."

"You can introduce yourselves from where you are." Winnie

pointed to the taller man now off to her right. She was having trouble keeping them both in view and had to swivel her head to track them.

"Alright, fair enough. Vito, let's stop and talk like civilized people. No need to scare the lady."

Winnie checked to her right. Vito had stopped. She looked back at the chubby guy. "I know his name and you know mine. What's yours?"

"How careless of me. Sorry, Winnie. The name's Ricky Shanks. I'm in town from Philly. Vito and I came down here looking for you. Imagine my surprise when I spot you sitting here, alone, while I'm driving around. Must be fate, am I right?"

Winnie shrugged. "This friend of yours, he wouldn't be Benny Borelli, would he?"

"See, Vito? I told you this girl had to be one smart cookie." Ricky looked back at her, nodding. "I told him. I also told him we'd be able to bring you to meet our boss without any problems. That true?"

Winnie took a step backward. Both men matched her, keeping the distance between them constant. "What if I don't want to go with you? I'm tired of meeting bosses, and of people trying to tell me what to do."

"What other bosses you been meeting with?" Ricky asked. "You haven't made any promises yet, have you?"

Winnie shook her head.

"Then you've nothing to lose." Ricky smiled. "Meet with Benny. I promise, you'll want to hear what he has to say."

Winnie shook her head. This wouldn't end peacefully and she wasn't going to Philly, especially not to meet some guy known as Benny the Blade. But she was also afraid of the possible consequences of her refusal. Cleaver scared her but the man did seem reasonable. The rumors all agreed that Benny was insane.

"I think I'll stay in Baltimore, guys. I like it right here where I am." Fear and anger began to mix, and without thinking about it, Winnie opened herself to the magic around her. She'd never used magic as a weapon, but was willing to now if it meant scaring her attackers.

She took another step back, gaining distance between herself and the goons threatening to nab her, pulling the magic, weaving a complex pattern that she hoped would harden the air molecules between her and the men.

Vito spoke from her right as she moved her arms. "Careful, Ricky. She's pulling in magic. And damn, is it a lot."

They were chanters. Vito had enabled a viewing spell and was observing her flows. He might not be able to see or understand precisely what she was doing, but he'd definitely know she was up to something.

"Gentlemen, I don't want to do anything we'll all regret. Why don't you two get back in your car and head back to Philadelphia? I don't want to work for Benny, or Cleaver, or even Artos Merrilyn. I want to be left alone."

Winnie was about to release the spell, hoping it blocked them from chasing her, but another car pulled up behind the first before she could.

Four men got out and walked her way. Ricky and Vito must have called for help. She was inches from panic when she heard a familiar voice.

"These guys bothering you?" Cricket asked.

Winnie didn't know whether to be relieved or worried even more. "They are," she said, looking Cricket dead in the eye. "They want me to come with them to Philadelphia. I told them I want to stay. That I don't want to go anywhere, with anyone, but home."

"Completely understandable. You've had a long day." Cricket turned toward Benny's men. "I'm sure these gentlemen understand that?"

Two of Cricket's guys had moved over next to Vito. Cricket

and his other companion — Winnie thought it was a guy named Jimmy — had stepped up behind Ricky, who now looked around, considering the odds against him. She could almost see the calculation in his eyes.

Ricky raised his hands, palms outward, and took a step sideways away from both Winnie and Cleaver's men.

"I just wanted to have a chat with the lady. That's all. We didn't know you guys had already made friends. Tell Cleaver that Benny didn't mean to step on his toes, alright?"

Cricket smiled at Ricky and nodded. "I'll pass along the message. Perhaps you should go back and explain how things are rolling here in Baltimore."

"So me and Vito can leave without a problem?"

Cricket nodded and pointed to their car. "If I don't see you again down here, Ricky Shanks, then sure, you can go free. Fair enough?"

"Fair enough. Come on, Vito. Time to split."

Winnie watched the two members of the Philly Mob get back in their car and drive away. After they rounded the corner, she turned to Cricket, still holding the massive amount of magic that had gathered around her.

"So what now, Cricket? I suppose you want me to come for a ride with you. I just swapped one boss for another."

He waved to his guys, laughing. They started back to the car.

"Cleaver had a change of heart. So we're taking a hands-off approach with you for now. He hasn't changed his mind about how important you are, mind you. Or how much he wants you. Cleaver merely believes that we're best served by letting you decide on your own, at least for now."

Winnie couldn't hide her surprise.

Cricket wagged his finger. "And don't think that you can take forever making up your mind. Something big is coming. Cleaver's seen it and I've learned to trust his visions. I believe it if he thinks you're supposed to stand beside him for us to survive. So that means that, at some point in the near future, you'll need to make a decision about who you are and, more importantly, who your friends are."

"I know who my friends are. I'm only confused about my enemies."

"We're not your enemies, Winnie. There's only one bad guy in all of this. He wants us all dead so he can keep the magic all for himself. Nils Kane is the only person you need to worry about. He tried to kill you once, and will definitely try it again."

Cricket turned from Winnie and walked back to his car. The driver started the engine. For the first time, she believed that they'd leave without picking her up.

Cricket stopped at the passenger door and looked back at Winnie. "I don't suppose you'd take my offer for a ride home? Benny and his goons aren't the only bosses that are going to want you to work for them. That video feed is everywhere, and this country's a big place. Be on the lookout for other crews trying to move in on you and your friends."

"I can take care of myself, Cricket. Thanks for the offer. Forgive me for turning it down."

"Suit yourself. Artos is too soft to be operating this close to the capital and Director Kane. The situation calls for a stronger, tougher approach, and Yorke is the man for the job. We'll try and stay out of your way, but we're moving in on the city's trade and you won't be wanting to stand in our way."

"Thanks for the warning. You know I'm going to tell Artos, right?"

"Cleaver doesn't care. This is a promise, not a threat. Artos needs to know. We have the goods on your local boss. It's only a matter of time until we fold things up and move in for good. Then you'll have to make up your mind. We've been told to leave our hands off your business until we have no other choice."

"I guess, then, I say thank you for the help with Benny's

goons and for the warning about your future plans. We'll try and stay out of your way, too, for now."

Cricket smiled, then waved one final time before he got into the front passenger seat. The driver pulled away and drove down the street.

Winnie watched them leave, then looked around at the deserted bus stop. She was alone, feeling more exposed and vulnerable than she had upon her arrival.

She hoped the bus came soon, before anyone else decided to offer her a job she didn't want.

30

Tris's phone buzzed loudly, startling her. The ringtone meant that her boss was sending out an ALL ATTENTION call, alerting his employees that all techs were supposed to report in.

She was tired and preoccupied. The last thing that Tris wanted to do was go into work. She dug in her pocket, pulled out the phone, and looked at the display. Just as she thought — all techs were being asked to report in to the main electrical generation and routing station ASAP.

She was wondering what the problem was when the lights went out.

Damn, she didn't have time for this.

Tris was trying to figure out how Winnie's abilities, and what had happened at the steel mill, were affecting the coastal cities. She'd helped to stave off a catastrophe with the water pumps feeding the municipal water supply. Now, apparently, she was needed to fix the electrical systems, too.

Tris knew everything had to be related. But she also couldn't prove anything. She was operating on instinct, but she'd learned to trust herself before. It was why she was so respected among the other techs. Her ability to troubleshoot and repair broken systems was unparalleled, so far as she knew. Right now, her instincts said that Winnie's newfound ability was involved in this mess, if not downright responsible for it.

She fumbled in the dark when her phone buzzed again, now calling for help at the water and sewer central station.

Which should she reply to? Tris had experience fixing the water pumps, but the electrical station was closer, and with the blackouts, it would be easier to reach than the central station downtown.

Tris used her phone to light a path to the door. She grabbed her coat and ventured into her apartment building's pitch-black hallway. The elevators were out so she went left to the stairwell. A door opened as she passed and a voice called out from inside.

"Tris, honey, are you going to fix the power? I need to watch my shows."

Tris shined her light on Mrs. Swanson's face. Her elderly neighbor had lived alone ever since her husband died. Tris looked in on her from time to time to make sure she was alright.

"That's where I'm going now, Mrs. Swanson. I just got the call. Are you alright? Do you need a flashlight until we get this fixed up?"

"I have one, sweetie. I didn't want to waste the batteries by leaving it on. I've lived here a long time. I can find my way around in the dark."

"Well, be careful and stay inside. You might want to fill your tub and sinks with water. Apparently, the central pumping station is having a problem, too. The pressure might drop and you'll probably need the water before we can get it fixed."

"Good idea. Thanks for telling me. Any idea what's causing all of this?"

"Not yet." Tris shook her head. "But I promise we're working on it. Now, you go back inside and save that water just in case."

Tris waited until the woman closed her door, then turned and started towards the stairs. With the streetlights and traffic signals all out, she wasn't likely to catch a bus. Tris would have to walk the entire way in the dark, and might as well get started.

Tris stepped into the cool, black evening.

Tris disembarked at her stop and immediately turned to look at the city's primary power station across the street. The building's lights were flickering — a terrible sign. The plant should have a steady supply of power for itself, regardless of problems down the line with the distribution network. Flickering lights meant the generators were failing. A complete shutdown might be imminent.

She waited for traffic to clear, then ran across the street and up the power plant steps. The door guard checked her ID and waved her through. Tris headed for the bank of elevators but stopped before she reached them. Boarding a vertical coffin would be an awful idea if the building's power was unreliable, so instead, she took off for the stairs at the other end of the hall.

Loud shouts came from the control room level as Tris stepped onto the landing and started down the hallway outside the main control center. A small group of techs were assembled, getting instructions from a supervisor named Nathan. He sent the group to follow their orders before looking over to see Tris standing nearby. He sighed and waved for her to follow him as he started down the hallway, past the control room.

Tris was surprised he wasn't going in to check things in the control room. She walked faster to catch up.

"Nathan, what's going on? It looks like the generators are failing."

"They are. I just ordered the switch to coal and natural gas auxiliaries, much as I hate to do it. We'll catch hell for the smoke and haze, but we don't have a choice. Come on. I'll show you what I mean."

Tris followed Nathan to the generator floor. She cast a spell to shift her vision to the magical spectrum as they entered, looking toward massive shafts drilled in the chamber floor where the magical flows powering the generators were born. Some magic came from the surrounding air, but the biggest flows rose from deep in the earth. It had always been supposed that there was an endless supply, but you wouldn't know it from the feeble flows rising from the shafts now.

"Nathan, when did this start?"

"We'd been having problems on and off for about a month. When that chanter girl cleared the dust storms and pulled fires from the Enclave, the streams temporarily returned to normal. They even seemed stronger. But that only lasted for a few hours. After that, we started seeing major gaps in the flows. We needed a steady stream of techs to patch and fix the feeder spells. But that isn't working now."

Nathan stopped at the edge of the main shaft and looked over the railing. Tris walked up beside him and turned her magically enhanced vision downward. In the magical spectrum, it should've been like staring into the sun. There should have been a solid orange-white flow ten feet across, blooming from this shaft to enter the massive generator housing above. There should have been a roiling mass of magical energy feeding the generator spell at the bottom. Instead, there was a broken stream of muddy red rising with barely any light at all. It was as though someone had turned off the faucet while the tub was still filling with water. What should have been full of light and energy was now an empty vessel with puddles of light on the floor.

Tris looked at Nathan in alarm. "Where did it all go?"

"No one knows." He shrugged. "I've contacted the university to see if some of the professors in the theoretical metaphysics department will come and take a look. I'm afraid to think what will happen if the city's other sources start failing as well. Baltimore could shut down."

"How long until the backup fossil fuel generators are running at full capacity?"

"They've been offline long enough that we had to rebuild some of the control circuits on the fly. No one was maintaining them, even though they were supposed to be fired up and tested twice a year."

"When's the last time you tested them?"

Nathan shook his head, refusing to meet her eyes. "Ten years ago." He raised a hand. "In our defense, we've never needed them before. Until now, our magical systems just worked. They've been supplying our basic electrical needs without strain for more than half a century. There was even talk of dismantling the auxiliary generators for scrap metal and parts."

"Well, thank God you didn't." Tris was angry, but rage wouldn't fix what was broken. She wondered if what Winnie had done in the Enclave had anything to do with this situation. It could be a coincidence, but probably not.

Tris felt an odd rumbling in her bones. She looked at Nathan, puzzled. She thought it was a piece of machinery, like the auxiliary generators firing up, until she realized the rumbling was getting worse. A crack appeared in the wall of the generator room directly behind Nathan.

Tris turned. "Earthquake! We need a doorway for cover."

Nathan nodded, then they returned to the stairway entrance and rode out the tremor. Tris leaned out into the generator room and looked up at the ceiling, past the glass skylights. If anything failed in an earthquake, surely it would be the glass panels above her.

"Well, that was a new experience," Nathan said. "Since when do we get earthquakes here? I thought that was a West Coast thing."

"Since we've had a catastrophic failure of our natural

ecosystem at a basic level. Something changed the way magic flows in this region. My best guess is it's become a finite resource and will continue to dwindle until we have little, if anything, left for normal chanters to access."

"You said 'normal chanters.' You mean other than that girl who stopped the storms. We should ask her to get down here and fire up the system again," Nathan joked. "You repaired flows into the central pumping station a few days ago. I'll get you help, but I need you to try and do the same thing here. We must stabilize this flow."

Tris looked down into the usually sun-bright pit, assessing the pitiful, pulsing red energy. She shrugged. "I'll try. How many techs can you get me?"

"I have eight on site now and will have another four or five soon. Will that be enough?"

"We'll find out. I'll start with the eight. Have the others come down and we'll start rotating breaks. I managed to fix the pumping station with only three of us, but that was a smaller spell. This will take more hands and time."

"Get started. I'll round up the others."

She nodded, pulled a hair tie from her wrist, and reached up to pull back her long brown hair into a tight ponytail. This would be hard work and she didn't want her unruly hair getting in the way.

Tris approached the railing at the shaft's edge, pulling magic in to form the first patch. She would be here for a while.

31

It was pitch black at the bus stop. Winnie could see the outline of her hand as she raised it, silhouetted by the starlight above. The lights had blinked on and off several times until, in this instance, they'd stayed off.

She could hear car horns and occasionally see a car's headlights coming down the street. She was in a relatively light travel area. Buses only stopped every forty minutes or so. She checked the time on her phone and realized she'd been waiting almost that long. With the power out and traffic lights dead, Winnie wondered if the buses were even running. Maybe it was time to call a cab.

She was considering her flight from bad to worse when the first of the tremors hit. At first, Winnie didn't know what it was. Earthquakes were like tornadoes — threats from another place. It stopped after only a few seconds, leaving Winnie swaying to stay on her feet.

How was her mother faring with the earthquake and blackout?

Winnie looked around, still searching for an approaching bus, a cab, or even a random car she could flag down.

Headlights turned on the street a few blocks away then drifted towards her. The engines of an approaching bus rumbled her way. She blinked into the glare of blinding headlights as it stopped a few feet away.

The door opened and the driver called out. "Last run of the night, young lady. The buses are all called back to the garage until these blackouts are under control."

"Are they happening everywhere?" Winnie asked.

"Supposedly so. I'm sure that between the blackouts and our little earthquake a moment ago, people are starting to feel nostalgic about the dust storms." The driver laughed without humor.

Winnie boarded the bus, paid her fare, and walked past the twenty or so passengers to find a seat at the back. A little girl about halfway down the aisle turned around and stared at Winnie after she sat. Winnie half-smiled, then turned to stare out the window.

A second earthquake struck a few minutes later. The tremor forced the driver to stop, pulling his bus to the curb while waiting for the seismic convulsion to pass. Part of the brick facade on a building a few feet ahead toppled into the street and littered the sidewalk. A few passengers shouted in alarm. Others eyed the trembling buildings outside with terror.

Winnie clung to her seat, riding out the tremor until it passed.

Passengers started to whisper, then the whispers turned to hushed chaos as people wondered out loud whether they would ever get home safely. The driver tried to calm them as he pulled back onto the street, threading his way around the piles of toppled bricks.

Winnie looked forward as they drove, noticing the little girl's eyes still upon her. She was about five or six years old, clutching a well-worn doll in one arm. Winnie gave the girl another smile, but she turned and said something to her mother that Winnie couldn't hear.

The mother turned and glanced at Winnie. Something like recognition passed over her face. Did she know this woman from somewhere?

Another tremor shook the bus.

Passengers shouted, crying out in fear. The driver pulled over again.

The girl's mother shouted at Winnie. "Why don't you stop it?"

"What do you mean?" Winnie asked.

"You're her. My daughter recognized you from the TV. Why don't you stop this, like you stopped the storms?"

Other passengers started to turn, all of them looking back at Winnie. Recognition lit their eyes, one pair at a time. Winnie shifted in her seat, trying to stand despite the tremors, but the bus rattled again and forced her back down into her seat.

Passengers started to point, and demand that she put an end to the earthquakes. But she shook her head.

"You don't understand. I can't stop this," Winnie insisted. "I don't know how. I don't know how I stopped the storms. You have to believe me."

"Why don't you try?" asked a middle-aged man with gray streaking his jet-black hair. "You could save us all."

"I don't know how, I swear." Winnie stood as the tremor finally ended, then walked to the rear exit. She pulled the rope and called to get off. She wanted to go home, but couldn't ride the bus with these people. She had to find another way.

But the door was still closed.

The driver was standing, now joining the passengers calling her to do something — anything — to stop the tremors and restore the city's power.

Someone grabbed Winnie's arm as she tried to push her way through the closed doors.

The world was shouting.

Don't go! Stay with us and stop the earth from moving! You can do it! We saw what you did! The little girl is right. You can save us all!

Winnie shook her head and pushed at the doors. She hurled her body against them, but they would not move.

She looked up, frantic to flee the bus. She saw an emergency release lever and lunged past a few grasping passengers, pulled the lever, then jumped off of the bus as the doors sprung open.

Two men got off, followed by the woman and her daughter. They were all calling for Winnie to come back and save them.

Instead, she took off running up the street. There were people on the sidewalks, exiting their buildings in fear. They heard the passengers calling after Winnie and joined in their cries.

Another tremor shoved Winnie to the ground. Pain shot up one leg as she slid on a knee across the pavement. She scrambled back to her feet, reaching down to rub her knee as she limped away from the crowd now closing in.

Her hand came away from her knee covered in blood and she looked down to see her jeans were torn, road rash marring her kneecap.

She cursed, biting her lip though the pain, pushing on and praying for speed, racing away from pursuit.

A car swerved towards the curb ahead. Winnie thought it would jump the sidewalk and run her down, but it stopped at the edge of the street.

The driver's door opened.

Danny got out of the car and called to Winnie, "Come on. I can get you out of here."

She limped over to the passenger side of Danny's beat-to-hell compact and yanked the door open as he climbed back into the driver's side.

She looked over her shoulder. The crowd was getting closer,

still shouting for her to save them. She slid into the passenger seat and pulled the door closed as Danny gunned the engine and drove away.

He looked even worse than he had the last time Winnie saw him, but she also felt the strength of their connection. It warmed her, set her at ease.

Everything would be fine. Danny had found her. If she stayed with him, it would all work out.

She stopped herself. Danny had found her, but how had he known where she was? Artos and Gunderson dropped her off in an area where she rarely traveled, and yet he had known precisely where she was. It should have bothered her, made her wonder what was happening, but the part of her brain that was so intimately connected to Danny soothed those cautionary thoughts.

She settled for a singular thought. "How did you find me?"

"No, 'thank you?' No, 'you saved my life?' I'm hurt." Danny gave her the smile that always made her melt. Even in his current, haggard condition, it was undeniably charming.

"Sorry, Danny. I'm just surprised to see you. You showed up in the nick of time."

"I had a feeling you might need my help, so I went out looking for you." He took her hand as he drove. "Come on, I'll take you to my new place. It's not far from here. Then we can catch up."

"You have a place? Where — how?"

"My father pulled some strings and got the charges against me dropped. That means that no one is after me, but he also pretty much cut me off and told me we were through. After he left me standing on the doorstep of my childhood home, my mother slipped me enough cash to get a place and told me to come back when it ran out. I can't believe she's defying him like this, but I'm glad that she is."

"So we're both in Hell. Great. Must be destiny."

They shared a long and lingering laugh, a salve to the day's brutality. Winnie was looking forward to being in a place where she didn't have to worry about the pregnant cloud of chaos hovering above her.

Danny's apartment was in the basement of a worn down, four-story building just outside the Enclave's border, a neighborhood of poor middlings who could barely afford their basic needs. It showed in his shabby furniture. He called it furnished, but that was clearly an opinion. There was no place that Winnie wanted to sit. She wasn't exactly accustomed to a palace, but still it was all so disgusting.

But she needed to be close to Danny and that meant staying here. So, she chose the corner of a stained couch cushion and sat. As shocking as this dump was to her, it must have been doubly so for Danny. He'd gone from a silver spoon to a dirty spork in a matter of weeks.

Danny looked around, then put his hand to his head and closed his eyes.

"Are you alright, Danny? Is it your headaches again? Let me help you, like I did the last time. Please, sit."

She pulled him down to the sofa beside her. He didn't resist, leaning forward and tilting his head so Winnie could place her hands like she had before.

Winnie reached up and applied her fingertips, drawing the magic from around her and setting it to work. She felt an immediate, familiar, pleasant surge of satisfaction. She felt happy. The euphoria was electric, sending jolts of pleasure to the ends of her toes and back. Winnie wished she could feel this way forever, rather than only by his side.

Danny's face changed, too, color returning with the fading pain. Winnie could see his transformation as she directed the flows into his head.

His improvement soothed her. She didn't want to just help him, Winnie wanted to cure him; she wanted to delve deep into her reserves, earn another surge of adrenaline, feel the sensation coursing through her with every magical thread coaxed into place.

Winnie finished, sat back, and stared at Danny, trying to gauge how he felt now based on his expression. "How was that?"

"Wow," he said. "It's like I'm a whole new me. I wish you could live here with me."

Winnie cringed, but then considered her mother's reaction to what she'd been doing, and how she had been hounded on the bus. Maybe hiding here with Danny wasn't a terrible idea.

"Maybe I will. My mom and I are on the outs. I might need a place to stay."

Safety was one thing, but her bond with Danny was also narcotic, and she didn't want to let it go.

Danny smiled with twinkling eyes. "Well, then, let me show you the rest of the place. I've even put fresh sheets on the bed."

He winked and Winnie felt slightly ashamed by her own devilish smile. She'd lost a baby because of a moment like this. She couldn't fall for that handsome grin again.

But a full-body euphoria helped Winnie to swallow her doubts. She took Danny's hand and pulled him toward the bedroom.

They were kissing, then fondling, and soon the two of them were swimming into each other.

ARTOS MERRILYN STOOD IN HIS OFFICES ABOVE THE MENDER'S
Hall Building, staring out the windows at his city. The Hall had
a generator, so he'd survived the rolling blackouts better than
most. Many people had come to Artos seeking help over the last
week, and he sent Gunderson on regular missions of mercy for
those who couldn't get to him on their own. It was his place to
protect those in his care as the Enclave boss.

The city lights were on; he could see no darkened patches
where blackouts might still be a problem. The techs at the main
power plant had restored power and reported that it should
remain on for the foreseeable future. Artos wasn't sure the
future was all that foreseeable now. Winnie was the only runner
earning. The others had all stopped reporting — most were
either sitting out the developing drama between he and
Cleaver, or they'd already made their plans to work for his
adversary.

While the city might have recovered from the most recent
changes in power, Artos had not. He keyed his intercom and
called Mr. Gunderson into his office. It was time to put some
contingencies in motion. Opportunities would be harder the

longer he waited. When his assistant failed to enter after an especially long moment, Artos keyed the intercom again.

The door swung open and Artos stood. But it wasn't the dapper Mr. Gunderson who entered his office.

Cleaver Yorke's broad frame filled the doorway. He took his time to occupy the threshold, eyeing Artos before making his way fully into the room. Just past him, two men flanked Gunderson in the outer office. Artos straightened to his full height, though he was unable to match his opponent's stature, and gestured to a chair in front of the desk.

Hard as it was, he found a smile. "I'd like to say this is a surprise, but it isn't. I have been expecting you. Please, have a seat."

Cleaver let out a booming laugh that caught Artos by surprise. But he didn't let it show on his face. The other man kept laughing, shaking his finger at Artos in admonishment.

"Arty, you do have a certain style and panache, don't you? I've always liked that about you. Here I am, standing in your office, ready to kick you to the curb or worse, and you offer me a seat as if it were still yours to offer."

"Power is fleeting, Cleaver. Influence is a currency for trading when something is needed. Your presence doesn't remove the cards from my hand."

"You mean her?"

"If by 'her' you mean Winnie Durham, then you're correct. She still works for me, or at least she did the last time we talked. You and I both know that's the only reason you're dabbling in Baltimore. I can't imagine you want the responsibility of running another city?"

"She intrigues me, Arty. She's one of the few people to get away with telling me no, not once, but twice. She did it to my face both times, as if she had no idea what sort of danger she would be stepping into when she did."

"She doesn't know, Cleaver. She is special, and you should

leave her alone. The girl has work to do — far more important than our petty squabbles."

"Your prophecy? I've heard others talk about a child of prophecy who would save magic for us all. She may or may not be that person, but I have plans for her, regardless. She has power that neither of us have seen in our lifetimes ... even yours, Arty. And that power needs to be working for me. I'm the only boss who can protect her from those who want a piece of her."

"And you don't want a piece of her? Excuse me if I find your altruism suspect, Cleaver. We both know better than that."

Cleaver smiled, all teeth. "Winnie Durham must stand beside me when her most important decision is made, or else all is lost, Artos."

"Your famous sight?" Artos chuckled. "Just because it's never been wrong doesn't mean you're always right. How often do things work out differently from what you imagine? Have you considered the possibility that Winnie is supposed to be your boss and not the other way around?"

Cleaver tossed his head back with a convulsive laugh. "I follow a woman and my crew disowns me."

"Statements that include the words never and always often return to bite the speaker, Cleaver. This world has a few absolutes, but almost none where the affairs of mankind are concerned."

Artos stood and walked around the desk to face Cleaver, the man who was there to remove him from his position as Baltimore's Sable boss. He couldn't stop the takeover. Still, he had to mitigate his losses if he was to remain in a position to assist Winnie. Her being captured on video fighting the Enclave fires had cemented her celebrity. She needed guidance and protection now more than anything. He could only provide that if he was still in the city, near enough to her to help when needed.

"So, Cleaver, what now? I'm prepared to leave gracefully. But if you want Winnie to work for you, you'll have to convince her yourself. I believe that my crew have all defected."

"Arty, you never cease to amaze me. I had some of my boys who said you'd be a tough nut to crack, that you'd never go down without a fight. I disagreed. I knew you were a pragmatist. You'd see the writing on the wall and know to save your hide. See, I was right."

Artos nodded but said nothing. Cleaver was dangerous when crossed. He needed to see Artos as benign. After a moment of consideration and an unbroken stare, Cleaver waved over his shoulder to the two large men behind him.

"Take our friend, here, and his assistant in the outer office down to the underground garage. I believe Arty has a car. Put them in it and follow them until he gets to his place on the edge of the city. Park outside and make sure they don't leave. I'll send you relief in a while."

The two men stepped over to Artos and reached out to grab him by the arms. Artos stared until their hands fell back to their sides, then he nodded to Cleaver and walked out of his office, grateful that everything had played out as expected. Mr. Gunderson joined him in the outer office, then they headed down to the parking garage, accompanied by Cleaver's crew.

Mr. Gunderson leaned close to Artos and whispered, "Where are they taking us, Mr. Merrilyn?"

"To the estate, Mr. Gunderson. That is all. Nothing to worry about. This is a small setback. We'll work through it like always."

"Yes, sir. Thank you, sir."

So much hinged on the next few days. Winnie had come into her power and needed direction if she was to become what the world had been waiting for. Most people thought prophecies were written in stone, that they couldn't be broken, bent, or altered in any way. But that was only partly true. Prophecy predicted an individual's potential to impact change. It used that person's decisions to ensure the prophecy's truth.

The drive to his estate was quiet. He chose to sit up front with Mr. Gunderson, both of them needing the reassurance of each other's company. Another car followed their limo. Artos didn't care about being imprisoned in his home. He had plenty of creature comforts and a full communications center. He'd be able to reach out to Winnie and a few others to make sure he kept his fingers on Baltimore's pulse.

"Mr. Gunderson, I would like for you to try and locate Winnie Durham. She is still the key to everything. We must not lose sight of the prize, despite our setbacks." Artos patted Gunderson on the back. "Find me Winnie and we might just save the world."

Winnie lay back and sighed, her ecstasy draining.

Danny rolled over with a satisfied chuckle. "Is it just me, or are we getting good at this?"

Winnie laughed and poked him in the ribs. He flinched, fending off her attempt to tickle him. She didn't disagree. Their time in Danny's apartment these last few days had drawn them closer than expected. She needed to be close to him, in every possible way. Winnie didn't worry about why her need was so strong, or how Danny's proximity seemed to feed it.

She hadn't left the apartment since her arrival. She was afraid to go out and get recognized by the crowds that spilled from the buildings whenever the tremors returned. She'd rather take her chances with a potential building collapse.

Danny went out every day to get them food. He'd come back and tell her what was happening outside, beyond what she could see from the flat's only window. She'd used the alone time to tidy up and make herself more comfortable. She still worried about her mother but refused to go back and talk things out. Every part of her being drew her to stay beside Danny, exactly where she needed to be.

Her last conversation with Elaine had been a disaster. She'd called her mom to let her know she was safe.

"I promise, I'm fine. I just can't be with you right now. You don't understand what I'm going through."

"You don't understand what you're going through right now, either. Your place is here with me, where I can help you work through this. I'm your mother. No one knows you better than I do."

"No, Mom. You don't. Everything is different. There's so much I've done, so much I've grown into. You can't understand how I've changed."

"I know one thing, Winnie. You're with that boy again. I can tell in the way you talk about need and want. I know how that feels and I know how that fades. He's not as important as family, as our relationship. That boy isn't even a chanter. How can he possibly understand you the way I do?"

"You didn't stop and think about that when you fooled around and got pregnant with me. You thought a middling was just fine for you. Danny is different: he isn't already married and he cares about me. He needs me. And we're good for each other."

"Look, Winnie. I don't really care what you think he means to you. Come home and we can work through this together. He can't give you the support and advice that I can."

"I don't want your advice or your support, Mom. Besides, who's supporting who here? I've been supporting you for years, paying the rent, paying your medical bills. You want me back for security. But I don't have to be home for that. I understand my obligations. You'll be taken care of, if that's what you're so worried about."

"I can't believe you'd throw that back in my face. This isn't how I raised you."

"Well, believe it. I'm going to stay where I am and you won't stop me."

Then she'd killed the connection. Her hand cramped from gripping the phone. That had been two days ago, and Winnie hadn't called or texted her mother since, despite constant messages and voicemails that Winnie didn't bother to read or listen to. Her mother was being selfish and could never care for Winnie as much as Danny did. Right now, he was the only one she could trust to keep her best interests at heart.

Winnie stood and pulled on her clothes. She was hungry and Danny had brought back a small box of delicious-looking pastries from the market. She noticed the orange dust he'd tracked in from outside. The storms had returned, fueling public concerns about the tremors and widespread public works failures.

Tris had been working almost non-stop with her fellow techs to repair the city's failing systems. That didn't stop Tris from expressing her own concerns about Winnie's estrangement from her mother. That phone call hadn't ended well, either. It was like all her friends failed to recognize Danny's importance.

Winnie was surprised by a knock on the door. No one had called on them since Winnie had arrived, and only Danny had gone through the door.

"You in there?" Winnie heard from the hallway outside. "It's Cait."

Somewhere, deep in her mind, Winnie was afraid that Cait would take her away from Danny.

He stepped past her and opened the door. "Hey, Cait. Good to see you. Come on in."

"Hi, Danny. I wondered where Winnie had disappeared to. I should've figured that she'd be here with you." Cait looked around the tiny apartment with a smirk. "You've quite the little love nest, Win. Don't you think it's time to come back? There's a lot that needs doing."

"I … can't … I … don't want to go back out there. You didn't see it, Cait. People know who I am. They begged me to make it stop: the tremors, the dust storms, the power failures. I can't do it. I don't know how I did what I did."

"Hey, Winnie, I get it. I was standing right there, watching you. I couldn't figure out what you did either. You didn't stitch the magic to hold it together like everyone does. You somehow moved it without touching it. Less like a seamstress and more like a conductor."

"Then you know why I can't come out with you. I can't face all those people who think I can do something I can't."

Cait looked around the apartment again. "You can't stay here the rest of your life, Winnie. You'll have to leave at some point. And what about your mom? I've been to see her, Win. She's sick with worry. You know what that does to her arthritis. Flare-ups are always worse when she's stressed."

"We're not talking. She's trying to tell me what I can and can't do when I'm the one who's been running the household for years."

"Suit yourself, Winnie. I wanted to find you and make sure you were alright. I've done that. You don't need our help. Just don't forget that there are people out there who need yours."

Cait nodded to Danny, then left without saying goodbye to Winnie. The glimmer of hurt wasn't enough to overcome her deep need to stay with Danny.

He closed the door behind Cait, then came over and stood looking down at Winnie sitting on the worn old couch. "What's going on? It's not like you to treat your friends like that. She came looking for you because she was worried, and you blew her off like she didn't matter to you at all."

"She doesn't. All that matters to me now is you."

"Believe me, I'm flattered. This is the first week in what feels like forever when I haven't had any headaches at all. The moment I feel the first tickle, you sense it and make it go away. I don't know how you do what you're doing, but I appreciate it."

He sat down beside her and gently took her hands.

"You can't hide here forever, Winnie. You have things you're supposed to do. I know that and so do you. Something is happening out there, and you have a part to play. Hiding here won't make that go away."

"It's not only that, Danny. It's you, too. If I'm out there, I'm not here with you. And I feel … empty when we're apart. Lost. I can't think straight. All I want to do is find a way to get back and be close to you."

She leaned over and tried to kiss him, but Danny pulled away and stood.

"You have to get help. It worries me, how long you've been here. Cait is right. There are things that need doing and you're not the type to run from responsibilities. I don't know what's happening, but I don't think you should be suffering alone."

"I don't need help, Danny, I just need you."

"I'm not sure that's true. Something is … wrong about you staying here. I don't understand magic or how it all works. It would be foolish of me to tell you how you do what you do. But I think you should talk to someone who does."

"Like who?"

"Artos offered to help, didn't he? I remember what you told me about your last meeting. He said there would be problems if you didn't get assistance. This might be what he was talking about. You're not the sort of girl to stay cooped up in an apartment all day, especially not a dump like this. That alone is enough to tell me that something is wrong."

"Artos can't show me anything that I can't figure out on my own, right here with you."

Danny crossed the apartment and stared out the windows at something Winnie couldn't see. He turned and met her eyes. They seemed to shine more than usual. Slowly, she realized they were brimming with tears.

"I think you need to move out. I want you here more than

ever, but I'm afraid this is breaking you. We can meet somewhere else and hang out, but I don't think we should stay together this much anymore, at least not until you figure this out."

"But what about your headaches?"

"I'll have to live with them, just like I did before. Hell, I'm getting a nasty one now."

Winnie went to him, her healing hands extended.

Danny flinched and ducked to one side. "I think you need to finish getting dressed and go. Tell Artos what's been happening. And be honest. He only wants to help you."

Tears welled in Winnie's eyes. Damn it. Everyone was telling her what to do, trying to get her to accept help she didn't even need.

She needed Danny. He was important. If she had to prove him and the others wrong, then fine. After that, she could return to his side.

"If that's what you want, then I'll do it. But I want an apology when it doesn't work."

"You make a genuine attempt and really listen to what Artos tells you to do, then I'll apologize while standing on my head if you want."

Danny held out his arms and Winnie collapsed into the comforting strength of his embrace. They stood there holding each other for a long moment before they finally parted. Winnie went to gather her things.

She'd go to Artos and tell him to teach her. Then she could come home.

WINNIE FELT LIKE SHE WAS STARTING TO DIE THE MOMENT THE door closed behind her. An anchor had taken hold of her soul and was dragging her down to unknown depths. The joy and elation of knowing he was nearby had gone, and in its place, a nagging thought, whispering on repeat that she wasn't supposed to feel this way.

She shoved the ridiculous thought into the back of her mind, inhaled a bottomless breath, and headed downstairs to the street.

Dust storms had returned with a near-constant haze of tangerine. For the first time, Winnie was thankful for the storms; with a scarf wrapped around her face, no one would be able to tell who she was.

People wandered the streets wrapped as tightly as Winnie, physically and emotionally. Tension was thick, as if the crowd believed that they might have to fight for their survival at any moment. It was probably because of the frequent blackouts, water pressure failures, dust storms, and other changes in life's usual reliability. Without the assurance that the sun would rise tomorrow, normality was something to protect at all costs.

Winnie hadn't realized how bad things had gotten in the city. She'd insulated herself by staying in the apartment. Danny made the occasional comment, but she'd discounted the severity. Things were coming apart at the seams and Winnie wondered if she could possibly stabilize the magic like she had in the Enclave. She would ask Artos, work with him to refine her skills until she could figure out how to fix the problem once and for all.

Soon, she stood outside the Mender's Hall, looking up at the tall building before going inside. Artos represented many things in her life: an employer, a mentor, a community leader, and, Winnie reluctantly had to admit, a father figure. Maybe that was why she resisted his offers for aid. Her own father had been around but not a strong presence in her life growing up. She and her mother had always made a point to make it on their own without him. It had dulled her need for a male mentor in her life. Winnie now realized that it might have kept her from learning what she needed from Artos sooner.

She rode the elevator to the top floor but stopped when she didn't recognize the receptionist, curious as to why Mr. Gunderson wasn't puttering around in the outer office like always.

She brushed it off and pointed to the door. "Is he in?"

The receptionist seemed startled. "Uh, yes, but … "

"Never mind, I'm sure he's expecting me. He always seems to know when I'm coming."

Winnie opened the door open and entered despite the woman's objections. She seemed to have interrupted some sort of meeting. She thought about turning around but pushed forward instead. The sooner she got started, the sooner she would be back by Danny's side.

A trio of men stood in front of Artos's desk, and as they turned toward the interruption, Winnie realized that something was wrong.

"Well, isn't this a surprise," Cricket said from behind the desk. "We've been looking for you."

"What are you doing here? Where's Artos?"

"Cleaver told you this would happen. You can't disappear for a week and expect life to keep on waiting. Artos is out. Baltimore belongs to Cleaver now, just like he said."

"Oh, my God. You didn't … ?"

Cricket laughed. "Kill Artos? No, nothing so drastic. Cleaver seems to think the old man will be useful, though we're not sure why. No, Artos is alive and well, holed up in an estate on the edge of the city. I guess you could say he's under house arrest."

Winnie stopped talking, considering her options. She still didn't want to work for Cleaver, but showing up here could be seen as an opportunity to recruit her.

"I didn't know you would move in so completely. So fast. But it doesn't change anything, at least not for me. I'll still never work for Cleaver."

"Gentlemen, can you give Miss Durham and I a few moments alone?" Cricket gestured towards the door. The three men turned and left. Winnie assumed they were businessmen from around the city, here to pay respects to the city's new boss.

The final man left and Cricket closed the door. He smiled at Winnie and offered her a seat opposite him.

She shook her head. "I'll stand, thank you."

"So be it." Cricket sat behind the desk. "Do you mind if I ask where you've been? A lot of folks have been looking."

"I've been with a friend. I had to lay low."

"Well, I'm glad you're alright and that some other gang didn't snap you up for their crew. You need to be careful, Winnie. Word has spread. Your talents will make you very popular in certain circles."

"That's why I need to talk with Artos. He has information I need. Can you tell me where he is?"

Cricket watched Winnie for a moment before he continued.

"I can do better than that. I'll give you a ride. I have a few guys watching his place to make sure he stays put. He's been a good boy, so we've no reason to make an example. I have Garraldi going out soon. He can drop you off, if you want."

"Why help me? You know I'm with Artos."

"Because you need to make up your own mind about who you should be working for. And when you see that Artos no longer wields any power in this town, you'll realize where your allegiance should be."

Winnie didn't want to take a favor from Cricket or any of Cleaver's men. But it would be a lot easier to find Artos if she accepted a ride with Garraldi rather than trying to find him on her own. Every minute not training with Artos was exile from Danny.

"Alright, I'll take the ride."

"Excellent. I'll tell Garraldi to wait for you out front. I assume you would like to go immediately?"

Winnie nodded, unaccustomed to such deference from men in this position. She thought about what had changed since their first meeting. Cricket had always been a polite sort of fellow, but this was different.

"I see you're perplexed." Cricket smiled. "I just want you to see that we're not the bad guys here."

"I'm not sure what I see, Cricket, but thanks for the ride. I guess I'll see you around?"

"You know where to find me."

Winnie left the office confused. Cleaver's guys were offering to help, and despite Cricket's insistence to the contrary, it didn't make sense.

She wondered all the way across town, barely saying a word to Garraldi. After a long drive, he pulled up to a tree-lined avenue with giant homes on walled lots lining both sides of the street. This was where the elite lived. People who were even richer than the Barbers. People with all the influence. She was surprised Artos was even allowed to buy a place.

Garraldi stopped in front of a gated compound. "This is it." He pointed. "Artos is there. You can ring the buzzer and see if he'll let you in."

Winnie climbed out of the car and went to push the buzzer. But there wasn't any need. The gate opened with a hum and a familiar voice sounded over the speaker.

"Good day, Miss Durham. Please come in. Walk up the drive to the side entrance. I'll meet you there."

She pushed TALK to reply. "Thank you, Mr. Gunderson."

Without so much as a backwards glance, Winnie walked through the gates to finally start the training she'd put off for so long.

"Again. Do it again."

Winnie lowered her head, shaking it as she stared at the floor. She'd never exerted herself this much before and was barely moving. She'd also never realized how difficult magic was to hold, or shove into intention.

"Come on, child. Again. Do it once more," Artos repeated. "You've done this already. Show me how you stitched the flows to do what you did in the Enclave last week."

"That was an accident. It just happened."

"You act like the magic controls you rather than the other way around. You must take the reins. To do what you did on that scale requires you to command the flows, force them to do as you wish."

Again, she shook her head. Artos didn't understand. He was trying to stitch the massive flows she couldn't draw into herself, just like she'd manipulated the gossamer threads of magic before creating charms. He tried getting her to do the exercises every chanter child learned from their parents and teachers, the simple enchantments that were part of every chanter's life.

But the more Winnie considered it, the more she grew aware

that, on the two occasions when she'd worked immense flows of magic, she had truly controlled nothing. The flows had been urged, nudged, encouraged to do as she wanted. But she didn't control them, because they had a life of their own.

"Again."

"No. We aren't getting anywhere, Artos. You've had me doing these exercises for days and it isn't working. I keep telling you. I didn't stitch anything together. The flows sort of wove themselves once I'd drawn in enough power."

"I know it seems that way, Winnie, but only intention can guide the magic toward our bidding. You speak as though it is an animal you train for passage, rather than an energy source to be properly wired to perform a task."

"But that's where you're wrong, Artos. The magic isn't just an energy source. I used to think like you, because that's how I was taught. I learned to stitch the threads to do specific things, assembling spells and charms like a recipe. But it's different at this scale. The magic feels alive. I can't entirely describe it. It's like it sort of knows how to do things, and I just need to convince it to do what I want."

Artos started to correct Winnie again but stopped himself. He looked her in the eye, as if trying to gauge her truth. Then he turned, shaking his head. "What you're saying doesn't make sense. It just isn't how it's done."

"What I can do has never been done, or at least not for a very long time. How can you possibly know if I'm doing it right?"

"I don't. But what you're saying turns all we know on its head. If magic isn't a naturally occurring energy source, like a magnetic field or electricity, then what is it?"

"Who cares?" Winnie stalked over to the window, not bothering to hide her frustration. She'd been training for days but had accomplished little.

"You care, girl, or you wouldn't have come out of hiding to find me." Now it was Artos's turn to lose his temper. "You act as though it's impossible when you've proven through your own actions that it can be done. Why won't you embrace that? The possibility exists because of your own abilities. Now, let's try it again."

Winnie didn't want to. She'd already tried and failed a hundred times. "Will you let me show you something? I want to prove that you're approaching this the wrong way. All of your talk about forcing the magic … it just isn't right."

Artos waved his hands in exasperation. "Very well. Do your best, then we'll return to the real work."

Winnie bristled. The old man acted like he had all the answers, but he couldn't help her break through and consciously control the magic. It had always been a reaction, a spur of the moment decision to accomplish her means with magic. Now she had to show Artos what she meant.

"I'm not throwing out what you've been trying to teach me, but it has led me to see the magic differently than before. It might not be as clear as you think."

Winnie opened herself up, drawing magic from the world around her. It came in thick flows rather than the tiny threads she was used to when first using her skills years ago. These flows all seemed to share a sort of group mind that kept them apart from one another in her mind, as if they each had a sort of personality and she had to know it.

Raising her arms, Winnie tried to match the flows' wavering rhythm.

Pure pleasure exploded inside her as she became one with the magic, working alongside it rather than ordering it around. Winnie tried to do something like she'd done the day when saving Elaine from the fire. Still moving like an orchestra conductor, she reached out and pointed to the dust swirling in the wind outside the room. The flows pushed outward without hesitation. Dust thinned and drifted until the sun shined on the grass outside and the sky again turned azure.

Winnie lowered her arms and released the flows, stumbling to the side as a wave of frailty washed over her. She had to catch herself on the back of a chair to stay upright. She grinned at Artos and mopped the sweat from her brow. It felt like she'd just run a marathon, but she'd done it. This was the first time Winnie had consciously reached out and worked her new magical powers without some sort of inciting incident to force it out of her.

Artos pursed his lips, gazing at Winnie for a beat before speaking. "I see what you mean, but I don't think I could do that, and few can even understand my power. What drew you to try this?"

"I was thinking back to when I figured out how to invert the flows so I could hide the charms. It happened when I was sort of stroking the threads of a weave. I think I sort of coaxed them into staying hidden, which is something they wanted to do anyway. The weave would always turn in on itself until it couldn't be easily seen, unless you knew what to look for." She pointed outside. "Same idea today, but bigger. I don't think the magic likes our recent problems, like it somehow knows it isn't natural. I used that feeling to get it to push the dust away for a while."

Winnie realized the magic was fading as dust pushed back in and the swirling orange clouds outside swallowed the blue sky and sunshine.

"It takes a lot of energy and strength, and I don't know how to make it last. Once I let go, the magic stops doing what I direct it to do and returns to simply flowing around and beneath us."

"Don't fret, Winnie. You've made a major step in your development. Until now, you've only been able to do this when upset or angry. Conscious control is an essential next step. We can work on how to create permanent spells later. I must admit, it was nice to see the sun. Thank you for that."

Winnie nodded, and couldn't help but smile. It was nice to

get some recognition for finally doing something right after her days' worth of failures.

"Stand up!" Artos snapped when she tried to sit.

"But, Artos, I'm exhausted. I can barely stay on my feet."

"Exactly. You will never realize your true power until you've reached a point where you can do more than one large spell before collapsing. You must build up your stamina enough to continuously control the flows of several spells in unison, and for an extended period of time."

Artos walked over to Winnie and pulled her to standing.

"Get back up and let's see how many flows you can — how did you say it? Ah, yes — direct at one time."

Winnie stood, throttling her fatigue and opening herself back to the magic. She felt energized, accepting the joy and euphoria into her mind and body. It was easier to ignore her exhaustion while holding the magic.

Winnie was doing it, controlling her new magic for the first time.

Nothing had ever felt better.

Tris checked her watch again and decided that time had literally stopped.

This shift was never going to end and she was looking forward to her first night off since the Enclave riots. Things had calmed a bit since the first day of tremors. There were still system failures to deal with, but either the techs were getting better at patching the spells or things were finally slowing. She hoped for the latter. While Tris liked the idea that her skills were improving along with her co-workers, she preferred a world that was returning to normal.

"Hey, Tris," Jen called from her terminal monitoring the pump station.

Tris straightened in her chair and stretched to gather her senses. These eighteen-hour shifts were brutal for them all. She went to her colleague, leaned over, and looked at Jen's screen. It was filled with numbers, some sort of spreadsheet or database.

"What's that, Jen?"

"You made a comment to me when all of this started. Something about how the sources of magic we were tapping into seemed to be failing. Do you remember?"

"Yeah, I still think there's something either taking the magic away, or our reservoir is drying."

"I've been plugging numbers from the last five years into the database, hoping to see if your instincts were right. Look here." She pointed. "There's a slow decline in the flow into each building over that time frame. Then here, about two months ago, we see a sharp drop in the magic supply as if something drained it all at once. Since then, we've had the dust storms, tremors, and system-wide failures. I don't know what, but something has drastically drained the supply."

Tris studied the numbers, understanding what she was seeing now that she had some context. "I wonder what caused the slight increase earlier this week. Supply surged to a new plateau a few days ago."

Jen nodded. "There are a few days when the supply started to return, only to stay below normal levels after a brief resurgence."

"Print the dates and numbers. And while you're at it, shoot me that database link in an email. I'd like to check it out. I think you may be on to something."

"Sure thing, Tris. I'll do that now. I'm sending it to the break room printer. You can grab the hard copy there." Jen typed a few commands into the workstation and hit enter. "There you go."

"Thanks," Tris called over her shoulder, already heading down the hallway to their tiny break room in the pump house.

The sheets were already printing. Tris grabbed the documents from the tray. She was tapping the stack to straighten it out when she heard someone clearing their throat behind her. She turned expecting to see Kevin, her relief. But two strange men in black overcoats were blocking the door instead.

"Can I help you?"

"Tristan Wellings?" the taller of the two asked.

"That's me … how can I help you?" Tris covertly eyed her surroundings, searching for a means to escape.

"There's no need for worry, Miss Wellings. We're here to escort you to an important meeting. Someone important would like an audience with you."

"I have work to do. I can't just leave the station unattended."

"Our colleagues have brought in someone to cover for you."

As he spoke, Winnie saw Kevin being hustled by in the hallway outside towards the monitoring station and Jen. He was complaining about being pushed, but then, Kevin was always complaining about something, and he definitely didn't seem hurt.

"We'll take you to dinner while we wait for our benefactor."

Tris looked at the two men. She couldn't take them on by herself and they appeared to have help, judging by the other trench-coated men with Kevin.

And yet, these men weren't threatening her. Not exactly. They were offering her a nice meal and a meeting with someone important. She didn't think they would take no for an answer, but beyond that, there had been no threats of violence.

"I'll go with you, but I want to make sure I can go home and get some sleep before too long. I have to work again in eight hours."

"That won't be a problem. I'll make sure you get back to your apartment safely myself. You have my word."

The man stepped aside and gestured for Tris to follow. She gathered the stack of papers then grabbed her jacket and scarf. It was certainly dusty outside. The storms were ever present.

Protected from the elements, Tris followed the men outside.

Tris pushed the bowl of seafood alfredo away and leaned back in her chair. The tall man — he still hadn't identified himself — had asked about her favorite local restaurant. She gave him the name and address for On The Hook. Now, she was alone in the seafood restaurant finishing a bowl of her favorite item on the menu. The pasta had lumps of crab meat, scallops, and shrimp in a creamy sauce.

She was alone because the man had spoken to the owner who, with a wide-eyed nod, had agreed to shut the doors early for a private function, or so he said. That private function consisted of Tris eating whatever she wanted while awaiting her guest.

Now that the main course had been cleared from the table, Tris considered ordering a cannoli from the dessert case by the register. But her craving was interrupted by the bell above the door ringing as someone entered. She looked over to see who it was and her jaw dropped.

"Good evening, Miss Wellings. I trust your dinner was satisfactory."

"Uh, yes ... quite satisfactory, Director Kane."

"Excellent. I wanted you to feel like this was a conversation rather than an interrogation. Our previous meeting was a bit ... awkward, and lacked a formal introduction."

"Well, you were trying to kill me and my friends, so —"

"As I said. Awkward. But that is in the past and there are other things that demand our attention now, isn't that right?"

"I assume you're referring to all the bullshit weather since your monster machine exploded?"

Kane offered Tris his thinnest-lipped smile. "Quite right. I heard you had an interesting theory about the magic supplying much of our infrastructure. I was wondering if you had found anything that might back that up."

Tris surveyed the room. Aside from the tall man in the corner, there was no one else in the restaurant but the two of them. The last thing she had expected was a private dialogue with the Director of the Department of Magical Containment. Tris had many things she wanted to say, but the state of the city's magic supply wasn't among them.

"Director Kane, forgive me if I can't just forget your previous actions."

"I'm not asking for you to forget anything. Or forgive, for that matter. I would like you to answer a few questions and hear a proposition. Is that acceptable?"

Tris pondered the request, then gave a measured nod.

"Very well. Please tell me what you have discovered about the magic that provides for so many of our modern conveniences."

Tris didn't know where to start, but then her gaze found the pile of printed docs. "I've gathered data from the last five years, looking at all the magical supply levels for the cities up and down the coast. Supply levels have been dropping at a steady pace. They hadn't reached critical levels and would have likely stayed high enough to do the job for the foreseeable future."

"Would have? So, you believe that something changed?"

"You could say that. It seems to coincide with a recent explosion in the north-eastern section of the city. The flows have been deficient ever since."

"Well, then it would seem that you and I are both at fault for this current predicament."

Tris didn't see how he could have possibly arrived at that conclusion, but she let it pass. She was quivering inside with rage and terror from sitting so close to a monster.

"Which brings me to the reason I've arranged this little meeting in this —" Kane looked around the restaurant with a smirk "— quaint little venue. I have information that I believe you'll find interesting, based on your other inquiries. They sent a few flags into my systems, set in place to monitor this country's magic use and research. They told me that you are an astute mind who understands the nation's future dangers."

"They're not future dangers, sir. Ask the people of Boston if you doubt it."

"Well, that was an unfortunate series of events. A failure of their techs to properly monitor their city's infrastructure. Had they been more proactive, like you and others around the Eastern Seaboard, Boston would still be standing."

Tris ignored him and said, "You mentioned looking at my queries and research."

"I agree: let's get to the point. Smart young lady." He gave her a serpentine smile. "Who, of course, surrounds herself with intelligent friends."

"You mean Winnie."

Kane chuckled. "Very direct. Yes, like Miss Durham. It is actually her that I'd like to discuss. She is an important young lady for a variety of reasons. I need her help in this crisis. If she keeps trying to fix things, then her meddling will destroy some important plans to save our nation."

The Director fixed Tris with a withering glare.

"You're a smart woman. You've seen what is happening and have extrapolated the ultimate outcome. It is as bad as you fear; maybe worse. Magic is failing us, and has been in decline since before the fall of Europe. That was when we first knew that the world's magic was thinning. Now we have a crisis on this continent, too. If we can't come up with an alternative source of power, we will be doomed to go the way of the Europeans, warring for survival as wandering tribes of hunter-gatherers."

Kane cleared his throat, and Tris could swear that his eyes seemed to be filled with genuine sorrow.

"I was attempting to harvest a supply of magic in a way that would redistribute the wealth to our cities based on need when the existing natural reserve began to run dry. You and your friends disrupted that plan, and in the process caused an acceleration of the declining supply."

Tris kept her back ramrod-straight, standing up to the Director's glaring eyes. They seemed to bore right through her. "I don't see how meeting with me or Winnie can help you. Based on the stats I was looking over today, there might only be a year or two of magic left. Once it's gone, everything will stop and there's nothing we can do."

"I don't believe that to be true, Miss Wellings. The key does lie with Miss Durham. Furthermore, I believe that others see her as the solution as well. The problem is that criminals have only their own limited interests in mind. They want Winnie to support their empires and to hell with the others. I am a public servant. I wish to save our nation, and perhaps even what remains of the civilized world, such as it is."

"I still don't see where I fit into all of this."

"You are the key to Miss Durham." Kane's smile sent chills down her spine. "You will get her to work with me. And in exchange, I will ensure that you and your families receive the same protections as the families of my staff and the Assembly in the coming trials."

Tris stared at the Director in disbelief. Did he know nothing of Winnie? She would never go for anything like this.

"I'll need an answer tonight. You and your friend Winnie, plus your families, protected through the upcoming trials, in exchange for your help bringing her to our side. I'll even throw in a similar package for that Amazonian ex-soldier friend of yours. I believe her name is Caitlyn."

Her friends would never forgive the wrong decision. Tris buried her head in her hands, lost in thought.

"I need the answer, Miss Wellings. What will it be?"

She had to make up her mind, and quickly.

As she decided, Tris prayed that Winnie and Artos had a plan.

Artos could see the improvement in the few days he'd worked with Winnie on her magical control. While he couldn't do the things she did, he could see how she was manipulating the magic and pointed out several places each day where Winnie could improve her technique and refine her control. Her stamina was also improving. He worked her hard and she was near to collapsing when they stopped working each afternoon.

Now, Winnie could practically command the flows to dance, and it was spectacular to observe. It reminded Artos of his childhood mentor working with magic. The young woman was a natural. He wished he knew where she was able to summon up those thick, rich flows of unbridled magic. No matter how he tried, Artos could only draw upon the thinnest ribbons of contemporary magic. Somehow, she had unlocked something ancient, magic like the kind he'd seen in his childhood.

As she worked, he began to formulate his return to power. He must continue to fight against Kane's efforts to subvert the world's magic for himself. Artos could only do that from a position of power, equal in some way to Kane's own position atop the Assembly and DMC. His challenge was Cleaver. With Yorke's takeover of the Baltimore trade, he stood between Artos and the position required to counter Kane. So, Cleaver had to go down, and hard.

Winnie had stopped her latest exercises. Sweat painted the sides of her face. She picked up a towel, mopped her brow, and caught him watching. She offered him a thumbs-up and a smile. He returned the girl's smile and called her over.

"Winnie, there are some things we must discuss. Difficult things."

"Sure, Artos," she said. "I hope I'm doing everything okay. I feel really connected right now. I haven't felt too tired since you showed me that mender trick. Now I feed energy back into my own chakras and finish with more energy than I started with."

"Be careful. That technique can be useful when you're forced to operate beyond your normal limits, but it can be a problem if you use it too much. It's easy to overload your system with too much power and burn out. At least, that's the theory."

"Noted." Winnie hung the towel around her neck. "So, what's up? The training is coming along great, don't you think?"

"It is. You've progressed far, considering the short amount of time you've been actively training. But this isn't about training. We need a way to reclaim my power here in the city so we can continue to fight Director Kane. I fear he's up to something again and I can't figure out what while cooped up here in this house."

"I can do some digging. Danny might have some connections … maybe someone can tell us what's going on."

"No. You must stay away from the boy for now. His presence will only distract you." There was something else going on there that Artos couldn't identify. That boy had a hold on Winnie, even from a distance. He couldn't quite understand it, but when Artos used his mender skills to view Winnie, he saw impenetrable blocks in her central being. It made Artos wonder if

Danny's escape from Kane had truly been the daring getaway he boasted about.

Winnie scrunched her face when he told her not to see Danny. "At least call him on the phone, Artos. I want to tell him about our progress. He'll be so happy for me."

"Very well. You may speak to the young man on the phone, after we're finished here."

Artos could cast a viewing while they spoke, see if there was a connection between them that wasn't supposed to be there.

"In the meantime, let's discuss how we're going to deal with our dual problems: We have Kane doing his level best to turn the entire population against every chanter in the city, and Cleaver Yorke occupying the city enough that we can't properly position ourselves to counter Kane. It's a vicious circle that has us both running to solve problems on both sides at once."

"Maybe we propose a truce with Cleaver. He doesn't like Kane any more than you do."

"Kane isn't the problem to Cleaver that he is to me. He's seen what he wants, and that single-minded focus isn't going to change. Cleaver thinks if he has you, his problems will be gone. He doesn't see how his vision can be seen from two directions, and could represent the opposite of what he thinks he's seeing. We can kill two birds with a single stone, Winnie, so long as you are that stone."

"I'm tired of being the one that everyone relies on for everything. The city already sees me as some sort of savior. I can't go out in public without a mask."

"I know it's tough. But you act as if I've never been in that position myself. I've seen my share of atrocities, believe me. I was there at the end, when Europe crumbled. I was charged with vetting passengers on the last boat out of Liverpool before it all collapsed. Don't ever tell me how tough you have it because people look up to you. At times like this, all people have is hope. A single decision made in haste during a time of calamity can have lasting effects on the world."

"I'm sorry if you think I don't appreciate everything you're doing for me, Artos. I do. Really. I just feel like … "

Artos raised a hand to stop her. "Don't say 'why me,' Winnie. It's beneath you. It's you because you have the privilege to be the one chosen to make a difference. It could be worse. At least you control your destiny in this mess. Everyone else is forced to sit by and wait to see if you'll step up and own your duty."

Winnie looked at the floor, clearly shamed by his correction. Good.

"The plan is simple, Winnie. Kane wants the world to blame chanters. I can't fight his power of persuasion, or stop his many mouthpieces from spreading all of those lies. But we can try and twist what they're saying to our own ends. And we might be able to direct the middling anger and fear at a single chanter rather than at all of them."

"You mean make them all hate Cleaver Yorke and his men."

Artos nodded. "It's the perfect plan. We dull the point of Kane's sharpest blade while using it to excise the cancer in our midst. We simply need to draw attention to Cleaver's presence in the city and match his timeframe in Baltimore to the approximate time all our disasters started."

"What about the other cities where middlings are attacking chanters? Cleaver isn't there. So how do we blame him in those places?"

"If we can make the blame stick in one city, it will spread elsewhere. We only care about unseating Cleaver in Baltimore. And besides, there are other Sable bosses in the other cities. Some of the blame will rub off on them as well."

"Doesn't that mean it will rub off on you? You're a Sable boss, too."

"But I'm not in charge now. I represent a return to normality. If we can clear the skies over Baltimore even part of the day, we'll both be heroes to the people. Kane will have no control over our popularity."

"I can't do this alone. I have to bring Tris and Cait in on our plan. Danny could help with all his middling connections."

Artos winced. But he didn't want to micromanage Winnie. She would develop a plan to move forward with the resources and people she needed. As the prophecy's daughter, she must find her own path as much as possible, without interference from him.

"When will this bloodless coup against Cleaver go down? We've been training hard for the last few days and I'm only now getting the hang of things."

"We should take a break and let your training settle. You can practice on your own while you and your crew plan to unseat Mr. Yorke. I suggest you stay with your mother, so you're within the Enclave and closer to Cleaver than you are here, or with your young man."

"I'm not especially pleased with my mother right now, Artos."

"I'm aware of that, Winnie. But it's been a while since your fight. Go home, dress your wounds. She is your reason for being involved with me in the first place."

Winnie glanced at her phone to check the time. "It's too late to catch a ride on any local bus. Nothing much runs this late in the outskirts. I'll have to wait until morning."

"I'd bet if you went out and asked Cleaver's men for a ride downtown, they'd be happy to do it. They'll imagine they're doing it for Cleaver. They did give you a ride out here to begin with, didn't they?"

"True. Still, I feel like a creep riding back with Cleaver's men while plotting against him."

"We're not in this game to feel good about ourselves. The ends justify the means. Go home to your mother and make amends. Then pull your crew together and set your plans into motion. It's time, my dear, to change the world."

Winnie nodded and went to gather her few belongings from the spare bedroom. Alone, Artos pondered his next steps. He had a few phone calls to make and rumors to start about his adversary from New Amsterdam.

It was time to reclaim his broken throne.

WINNIE UNLOCKED HER APARTMENT DOOR AND STEPPED INTO THE foyer.

After staying with Danny for a week, this didn't feel as much like home. She had mentally burned the bridge to this place while fighting with her mother. Now she was back in her house, unsure of how to make amends.

A familiar creak on a floorboard caused Winnie to turn. She saw her mother standing in the hallway, leaning on her cane. Winnie tried to smile, but tears betrayed her true emotions. Elaine held out a hand and Winnie rushed into her hug.

"Oh, my goodness!" Elaine exclaimed, hugging her daughter tight. "It's alright, dear. I'm here, and everything is going to work out."

They held each other forever, Winnie savoring the familiar touch and other things she had missed, like the scent of her mother's shampoo.

Winnie finally let go and stepped back.

Elaine looked at her, smiling. "You look like you could use something to eat. Mrs. Paulson has been looking in on me and helping to get my groceries while you were gone. I asked her to get me some ground beef, so I could make meatballs if you came home. Would you like to make them together?"

"I'd love that," Winnie said, wiping her eyes, trying to clear the tears. She had been so mad at her mother, and yet here she was, back at home as if nothing had happened between them.

Winnie would cherish their shared afternoon in the kitchen forever. It was a much-needed return to normal, and helped her get comfortable with her mother, without being focused on her whereabouts or the distance that had yawned between them.

Once the meatballs were finished, the pasta was cooked, and their mess was all cleaned, Winnie and her mother settled down to share their meal. Winnie savored the flavors — they were just as she'd remembered. She had prepared this meal many times herself, on those days when Mom's arthritis flared up so bad she couldn't use her hands enough to round out the meatballs. But it was never, ever the same.

Winnie said, "I don't know why everything always tastes so much better when you make it."

"It's a special mom ingredient."

"If you say, 'it's because it's made with love,' I'm going to barf."

Elaine laughed and pointed to Winnie's nearly empty plate. "There's more in the pot. Eat up. I can't imagine that you've been eating well. I worried about that. You always forget to take care of yourself when you get wrapped up in whatever."

Winnie thought about being wrapped up in whatever, like Danny's arms. She tried to change the subject. "I'm glad Mrs. Paulson could help out while I was gone. I'll have to thank her."

"I'd leave that to me, Winnie. She's a bit miffed with you for running off."

"I didn't run off, Mom. I left because you wouldn't let me live my life." Winnie winced, hoping the conversation wasn't about to turn inside out.

Elaine put her fork down and stared at Winnie. Then:

"You've always been a strong-willed girl. In many ways, you remind me of myself when I was your age. And it's because of that connection that I worry about your decisions, and the things you're choosing to get mixed up with."

"It's my life to live, Mom. There are things you don't know about, things going on that I can't explain. Things you wouldn't understand."

"I've not lived my life in a convent, Winnie. I know what happens in the world. I remember the horror stories about Europe's fall. It sounded a lot like what's happening now. People blamed chanters in Europe, too, you know. It's not as new or novel as you think."

"People expect a lot of me, Mom. I have responsibilities to you and to my friends. Artos wants me to—"

"That's your first problem: listening to Artos Merrilyn. I told you not to get mixed up with him. You're needlessly putting yourself in harm's way!"

"That's just it, Mom. There is a need. People are dying. The world is falling apart and there are people who believe that I can somehow fix it all, if I'd only learn to control what I can do. I'm a different person than the girl who used to open the shop to sell household charms to happy customers."

"What about your friends, Winnie? What do they think about all that you're mixed up with? Cait and Tris have always given you solid counsel. I can't believe they think you should be doing all that you're doing."

"Cait and Tris are with me in this. They have been since the beginning. They understand what's happening. You don't see it. But there are people out there like Director Kane who wish to kill us all so that they can have all the power themselves. We have to stand up for ourselves, or else every chanter on the planet will become extinct. That's what I'm trying to stop."

"And you think getting mixed up with mobsters like Artos will make it all better? You know, he's been replaced by some monster from New Amsterdam. I've heard the new boss is even worse than Artos. Are you planning to work with him, too?"

"I've met Cleaver Yorke. He's scary, I'll admit, but he wants me to join him. That's what I'm trying to say. I have to take sides, do things you don't want me to do so I can take care of … my responsibilities." She looked at her mother, trying to make her understand by sheer force of will.

Elaine shook her head. "You mean me. You're using me and my medicine as an excuse to do whatever the hell you want." She reached for her cane and levered herself to a standing position. "I sometimes wonder if you'd have been better off if I'd not survived my last hospitalization. Then you wouldn't have me as an excuse to run off and engage in all of your illegal ventures with your mobster friends. I'm sick of it, Winnie. I want it to stop."

"I can't, Mom, there's too much at stake. The world is falling apart and people like Nils Kane would like nothing more than for me to stand back and let it happen. Whether it's Artos, or Cleaver Yorke, or someone else, we have to stand up and fight back."

"Nils Kane is the Director of Magical Containment. You stay away from him. He's dangerous. If that's what Artos Merrilyn has you involved with, then I forbid you to see him, or the Cleaver guy, or anyone else that has you tied up with Kane. You don't know the things I do about Kane, or what he and his kind are capable of."

Winnie thought back to the night at the steel mill and shook her head. "You have no idea what I know about Kane and what he's capable of. It's the reason I've tried so hard to get in his way. Kane and people like him must be stopped —"

"At all costs? Because that's what it will take. Kane and his compatriots will stop at nothing to get what they want. They will kill you."

Winnie stood. She couldn't do anything to make this better.

Mom wasn't going to change her mind and Winnie wouldn't change hers. She glared at her mother, gathering the plates.

"I can tend to those," Elaine said. "You and I need to finish our argument. You can't stay here if you're planning to use your magic like you have been. It will kill you like it killed Joey. His addiction got him into trouble he couldn't escape."

"I know how Joey died, Mom. I only told you he died from a Sable overdose because I didn't want you knowing the truth. I saw him die. Kane ordered his Red Legs to kill him and they did. Right in front of us. Then he tried to kill me and Tris and Cait. We stopped him and got away, because of my magic. So I can't stop using it — it's the only thing that will keep us alive."

Winnie stalked toward the apartment door. This was all a mistake. She didn't care what Artos thought; her mother would never understand, and she had work to do.

Winnie reached for her jacket and backpack.

"Winnie," Elaine called from behind. "If you go out that door, I can't help you anymore. You can't keep coming home and asking me to take you back when you're doing all the things I forbid you to do. Leave if you must. But understand that I can't take you back."

Winnie spun around and pointed at her mother. She was furious, angry at herself as much as her mother. She tried to think of something to say, anything that might make her understand. In the end, she surrendered, shaking her head. Then she turned, walked out the door, and pulled it shut behind her.

Winnie wouldn't abandon her mother's medical needs, but she couldn't keep coming back and getting pummeled over doing what had to be done.

Her mother's sobs faded behind her. Winnie swiped at her leaking eyes as she approached the elevator. She didn't have time to be sad, or angry, or any other useless emotion. She had a plan to put into action and it had been delayed long enough.

Winnie watched the elevator doors close on this ugly chapter in her life.

Winnie unrolled the air mattress, plugged in the pump to fill it, and looked around at Charmed's back office. It had been her home away from home forever; it was fitting to live here now.

The motor hummed, slowly inflating the mattress. Winnie pulled out her phone and sent messages to Cait and Tris, asking them to come over. The sooner she put her plan into motion, the sooner she could get done all the things she'd been putting off for too long.

The mission as she and Artos had outlined would have a two-fold effect. It would label Cleaver Yorke as the cause of the city's problems, and net Winnie and her crew a significant sum of cash from the New Amsterdam boss's coffers. He'd been taking in all the money from the Baltimore Sable trade since taking over, and Artos had discovered that he was keeping it all in his former Mender's Hall offices. He was supposed to send it north, back to New Amsterdam, in a few days, but if Winnie could orchestrate her strike before then, she and her crew could have it all for themselves … minus a cut to Artos, of course.

That money was the key. Winnie could set up a trust to take care of Elaine's medical needs forever with her share. She'd never have to worry about it again, or see her mother to help. Even after taking care of her mother, she and Danny would have enough left to get started with their lives.

Just thinking about Danny drew attention to a gut-deep need inside her. She wanted to be near him, help with his headaches. Part of her felt guilty because she craved the sweet aftermath from that particular spell, the surge of feeling coursing through her. She never felt quite so alive as she did after delving into his head to make him feel better.

Before Winnie knew it, she was clinging to the energy, moving her fingers in the delicate motions to point the threads and form the temporary patch that blocked his headaches.

Casting about with her mind, Winnie sensed a cat walking in the alley on the other side of the wall. On a whim, she mentally reached through the wall and placed the magical patch in the animal's brain.

Winnie received an instant surge of energy, a bit like a slap — not as strong as what she felt with Danny, but a rush none-theless.

The cat stumbled in the alley, then raced away until it lumbered head-first into a wooden fence. The blow to its head knocked the creature unconscious momentarily, and her rush of power died like a curtain dropped upon a lamp.

Winnie felt guilty, taking her powers out for a spin and using an innocent animal to do it. If she did it again, she'd insert a control spell to keep the animal from hurting itself. It was the right thing to do.

The bell rang and Winnie stood to see who was at the door. It was Cait, entering the shop mid-guffaw.

"What's so funny?"

"I just saw the damnedest thing in the alley next to your

building — a cat, careening around the alley like it was drunk. Then it burst into a sprint and ran head-first into a fence. Must be too much catnip or something."

"Must be." Winnie joined her laughter.

Sure, she felt bad, but the euphoria of the Sable spell, cast on another living creature, was still coursing through her and nothing could dampen the feeling completely. She buried her still-trembling hands into her pants pockets.

"So, what's up?" Cait asked. "You look better than the last time I saw you at Danny's. I can't put my finger on it, but you seem … more energized?"

"I've been practicing with Artos, refining my magic."

"Really? How's that going? I imagine that old man is one hell of a teacher."

"He is. I had some blocks to overcome. He was great at finding a way through them for me." Winnie stole a glance at the door. "You heard from Tris? I sent her a message but she didn't reply."

"She's been off the radar for a couple of days. I've been texting, too. No answers."

"I'll bet she's buried with these tech failures. No worries. You and I can start looking at the plan. She can pick it apart once we're finished."

"A new plan. Awesome. I can't wait to hear it. Just like old times."

Winnie appreciated Cait's enthusiasm, though her memory of the good old days needed some tweaking. Most of their larger jobs had landed them in more trouble than they were worth. This one had the same potential if it wasn't perfectly executed.

"Hold on to that enthusiasm, Cait. We're going to need it. This plan has a big payout, but a huge downside if we fail."

"What else is new? I'm just glad you're back here where you belong. You look better than you have in weeks. We'll figure a way around this job, just like all the others. Lay it out for me."

Winnie took a pad of paper and started scribbling everything they needed to get Cleaver Yorke set up to take the fall for Baltimore's ills. Everything hinged on her position as the city's savior, working with Artos Merrilyn, famed mender and former leader of the Enclave. Cait had questions and pointed to a few places where Winnie would have to push back against Cleaver directly for the final part to work out. They had to start cutting into his business in the south so that he'd be forced to pay attention.

"I can take care of that. I'm much better at a few spells that will keep them from taking advantage of us like they did in Fells Point."

"Good, because I didn't like how that worked out at all."

"How what worked out?" Tris asked from the doorway.

Winnie had been so absorbed in planning with Cait that she hadn't even heard the bell announcing her friend's arrival. She ran to wrap her friend in a hug. Tris looked even more haggard than usual. Strands of her hair had worked loose from her ponytail and her eyes were sunken with fatigue.

Winnie held her at arm's length, shaking her head. "You look like crap."

"Gee, thanks. Remind me to tell you how you look after you've been up for thirty-six hours."

Cait came over and gave Tris a hug. "They're working you guys too hard. How are you supposed to fix anything if you're so tired you can hardly think?"

"It's important work that has to be done. Everyone is afraid that we'll be the next Boston."

"Did they prove it was a magical failure that destroyed the city?" Winnie asked. "I thought it was just more of Kane's anti-magic rhetoric, trying to get the middlings up in arms against the chanters."

"It's the magic everywhere, Winnie. All of it's fading. There's less and less to draw on, and we're having to manually patch all the feeder spells that keep things like electricity and water flowing."

"Perfect. We can use those facts to help us get rid of Yorke."

"What's Yorke got to do with anything?"

Winnie and Cait filled her in on their plan and the overarching strategy to get Artos back in power.

Winnie wondered why Tris looked so concerned. "What's up? You see something we're missing?"

"No, Win," Tris said. "It's the plan itself. We shouldn't be fighting and creating enemies between ourselves and other chanters. Kane is the one who needs our attention."

"But Kane holds all the cards. He controls the media, or a large part of it. He controls the Red Legs and can get the middlings to do things against us that we can't even respond to. It makes more sense to redirect his attention and energy against Cleaver Yorke."

"No, Winnie. This has as much to do with Artos reclaiming his position of power and using your popularity to help him do it." Tris paused, seeming conflicted before pushing on. "I have a reason for my concerns. I met with Director Kane two days ago. I've heard his so-called vision for the new world order and don't think we can afford to ignore him as our primary threat."

Winnie looked at Cait then the two of them stared at Tris in shock. She'd met with Kane?

How could she even agree to that after what he'd done to them and the chanters he'd captured? Winnie was beside herself.

"Tris, how could you? He tried to kill all three of us. He did kill Joey."

"I didn't know it was him. Two men pulled me out of work and said that someone wanted to talk with me. I was treated well, not threatened, then all of a sudden I see Nils Kane standing in front of me, telling me that I should bring you and Cait in for us all to join him."

"Join him!" Cait and Winnie exclaimed in unison.

"Yeah. Join him. Saying it out loud, I realize how ridiculous it sounds, but that's what he said. Kane told me that he could protect our families and that the infrastructure would continue to fail no matter what we did. Only he has the power and control to save the city. I got the impression that he needs you, Winnie, most of all. To do what he wants to do."

"Well, he's not getting me or my powers. You told him no, right?"

"Of course I said no. I was scared to death, but I told him that we'd never join him. I figured I'd be killed on the spot but he smiled and nodded instead. Then he turned and left with all his men, including the ones who had picked me up. I was alone in the restaurant and didn't even know if I was supposed to stay or go. I expected a bullet to the back of my head the whole way home. It's been two days and I've heard nothing else from him."

Cait stared at Tris. "I don't like this. I can't see him making an offer like that and then not getting angry when the answer was no. There's no upside to letting you live after turning him down."

"Maybe not." Winnie shook her head. "He had to know that Tris would tell me about the offer eventually. It's his way of planting the idea without telling me directly."

Tris nodded then turned to Winnie. "Will it work?"

"Of course not. I'll never work for him. Not after all he's done to me and my family. To all those people who died in the Harvester."

"So you and Cait are still committed to this other plan? Artos has his own schemes at play, you know."

"Of course he does. As long as his goals are headed in the same direction as ours, we'll play along. We need Cleaver out of the way no matter what, so yes, we'll continue with our plan.

Are you both in?" Winnie extended a hand and looked at her friends.

Cait and Tris looked to each other then stepped forward to lay their hands on Winnie's. They were finally together again.

Now the plan could move forward and everything would be fine.

Winnie's plan started with trying to move a year's worth of Sable in a day. It wasn't just the largest shipment they'd ever tried to move — it was the largest shipment *anyone* had ever tried to move. But that's how it had to be if they were to lure Cleaver from his New Amsterdam cave.

Trafficking in the forbidden meant the girls were selling their souls. Tris and Cait were nervous. Winnie tried to soothe them.

"We've never been willing to cross this line."

"Dammit, Winnie, there's a good reason for that," Tris said. "Even for Sable magic, this is a terrible idea."

"She's right, Win. You're talking about military-grade stuff," Cait said. She wasn't less concerned than Tris, but she'd used this type of magic in the army and the plan wasn't going to work without her.

"Look, if we're going to step out and do everything we want, we have to accept some serious risks," Winnie explained. "That means doing things we're not comfortable with, even stuff like this."

Tris looked worried. "What if this stuff falls into the wrong hands? Maybe we're handing a grenade to a baby. If this stuff gets on the street … "

"That's the beauty of our plan, Tris. You and Cait will help me make sure that none of this stuff hits the streets. We want to cave in on Yorke and his guys. The authorities will swoop in and confiscate the shipment. It won't fall into the wrong hands, I promise."

Cait shook her head. "You can't make that promise, Win. There are a million ways for this plan to go south. In the service, we said that no plan survives enemy contact. Something always goes wrong."

"That's why we have to plan for every contingency. Cait, you make sure the worst items are secured in such a way that even if they escape us, no one can use them, or at least they'll be easy for the authorities to track down." Winnie turned to Tris. "And you're going to select the perfect location for the sale, then rig the building's systems to help us shepherd the situation once everyone is inside."

Tris shook her head. She didn't think the risks were a fair trade in reward.

"Tell me what you're thinking. We have to be on the same page or this will never work." Winnie waited for her friend to answer.

After a long moment in thought, Tris said, "I don't get why we need military-grade items. A big enough score of regular charms should be enough."

"I know Cleaver Yorke. I've met him. I know how much he wants the lion's share of the magical trade. And I know he wants me to join him. The combination of this type of gear for his organization, and me in the bargain, will coax him out of New Amsterdam and back to Baltimore. He's convinced that we're following Europe. He needs the best in security, defensive, and offensive firepower. We'll have more than that with this score alone. It'll be too rich to resist."

Cait leaned back and stretched in her chair. She looked from Tris to Winnie. "What specific gear were you thinking about, Win?"

"I don't know as much about it as you do, but I'm thinking some perimeter detection gear to protect and shield against magic. Some sort of personal and vehicular protection devices, plus an assortment of weaponized magic."

Cait pursed her lips, tapping her fingers on the table before leaning forward again. "I can get that kind of gear. It's all here in Baltimore's National Guard Armory. I have a source that might be able to help us get in and out without anyone noticing. At least not for a while. It'll be expensive — a career's on the line. But I think they'll do it. The failures are making this guy crazy. You should see his eyes, and he's been biting his fingernails bloody. We can offer enough cash to set him up for life, even if the worst happens. Which I'm pretty sure he's expecting."

Winnie nodded. She'd have to reach out to Artos for the cash reserves. They'd get Cleaver's, too, after he showed up for the buy. They just needed seed money.

"Cait, will your guy accept half now and half after the job is done?"

"I think that will work. It might raise his price, but we can cover that, right?"

"With the money we get from Cleaver for the sale, yeah." Winnie looked up at her girls. "This is the score, ladies. We pull this off and we can all take a long vacation away from our troubles. I'm paying off Mom's medical bills, and then I'm retired."

Tris smiled. A moment of grace on her weary face.

"What will you do with your money, Tris?" Cait asked.

Tris leaned back and stared at the ceiling. Winnie could almost see inside her mind. "There are places in the Caribbean where they don't even use magical tech. It's all wind and solar-powered. I'll retire to an island with no magic to maintain, where no one knows what I can do."

Winnie looked at Cait. "What about you?"

Cait smiled, a feral grin that gave Winnie chills. "I see the way things are going here. But I don't want to run away. I think I'll stick around and start a private security firm to help separate the rich and famous from their wealth in exchange for the comfort of safety. Between what I've learned running charms and from the army, it's the perfect fit."

"Cait's Mercenaries," Winnie said. "Private security for a price."

"Got that right. And steep. Only top clients need apply."

All their dreams might soon be reality. If they could get the pieces to fit in the time that they had. But time and resources were walls around them. They needed more time or more people. Fate gave them neither.

She thought back to the earliest days running, when there had been six of them juggling charms. A bittersweet memory. Joey was dead, and her sister Morgan had turned Red Legged. Now it was the three of them. Four, if she counted Danny.

That tingle in her mind … She looked up and towards the door as Danny tapped on the glass.

Winnie stood to let him in. Her pleasant craving returned. All of her was blushing. She opened the door and immediately saw that his migraines were back, and with a vengeance, judging by his pinched expression and the dark circles around his eyes.

"Sorry, Winnie. I tried to stay away but it's never been this bad. I had to find you." Danny unwrapped the dust scarf from around his neck. Winnie took it along with his jacket then hung both on the rack by the office door. Danny shambled over to the table where they were planning their job.

"Damn, Danny, you look awful," Cait said.

"They did something to him when he was held by the Red

Legs and Kane. He has regular migraines and they won't go away."

"But you can stop them, Winnie. You have to. They're getting worse than before." Danny looked at her, his hopeful expression like a knife through her heart.

"How do you heal headaches?" Tris asked. "You're not a mender."

"I didn't think I could do it, either. But he was in so much pain. I had to try something. I found a spell planted deep in his brain. I don't know what it does, but if I erect a temporary barrier around it, the pain goes away."

"That's dangerous, Winnie." Tris looked at Danny. "You could cause permanent damage tinkering around in someone's brain."

"But I didn't and I can fix it for him. It will only take a few minutes." Winnie took Danny by the hand and sat him down.

She would ordinarily feel self-conscious about doing something like this in front of even close friends like Tris and Cait. The overwhelming urge to cast on Danny was like a taste in her mouth. She didn't care what they thought once she reached out and put her hands on Danny's head. The familiar rush of energy, power, and raw vitality surged through her. She closed her eyes to savor the warmth in her mind, placing the barrier around the spell in Danny's brain.

She drew in a sharp breath as she broke the connection between them. The surge faded and Winnie was left in casting's afterglow. She tried and failed to look normal when she turned around to face her friends. She wanted to keep planning. She took her time walking back to the table. Danny was still sitting on the chair by the air mattress on the floor, head slumped forward, his pain finally subsided.

"I saw what you did," Tris whispered when she came back. "That's forbidden. You used your magic to dive right into his mind. It's the worst of Sable magic."

She knew what Tris meant. Winnie had studied under the same chanter teachers as her friends. Sable magic altered or drew directly on the life force of a living thing. That meant anything from microbes to more complex plants, animals, and sometimes people. Sable was forbidden in any case because of a caster's potential addiction. Spells cast directly on people were considered an atrocity.

Winnie didn't consider what she was doing for Danny a bad use of her magical skills. It was Sable, but she did it to heal him. Besides, she was handling the "addiction" fine. She hadn't seen Danny for days and had avoided using her magic on any other living source other than him since she'd seen him last. She could control herself. No problem.

But there was no hiding the euphoria she was feeling now, and Cait and Tris both noticed. They were watching, faces etched in worry.

"I'm fine. I've got it all under control. He needs my help and I give it to him." She laughed aloud. "It's the perfect relationship."

"Uh, no, it's codependent," Cait said. "I think we're finished for the day. You won't be any good for at least an hour. I've seen what this does to people. You need to think long and hard about what you're doing. You can't be high on Sable when we do this job. You'll doom us."

"She's right, Winnie. You need to stop, or we have to step away from this deal." Tris stood and went to get her jacket and scarf. "Come on, Cait. Let's leave them alone. Winnie needs time to come down and think about what she wants to do."

Part of Winnie called out for them to stay, but the inner whisper never made it to her mouth. The majority of her being didn't care what they thought. Not about her or anything else. Sable's rush was still coursing through her and she didn't care about anything else.

Once they were gone, she went back to where Danny was

dazed in his chair. His headaches had been worse than before so she decided to delve back in, reinforce his barrier a bit.

She closed her eyes and hissed in pleasure.

The connection was made.

Minutes were hours as Winnie faded into infinite pleasure.

Winnie checked her phone for the time, then glanced out the coffee shop's front window again for signs of Tris or Cait. There were plenty of pedestrians, coats bundled about them, faces covered with scarves or surgical masks against the swirling orange dust. None were her friends. Things were tense among them since their discovery that she was using Sable to heal Danny's headaches. She hadn't expected such strong reactions; she had expected her friends to understand that she had it all under control.

Since Winnie had started healing Danny, there had been some sort of deeper connection between them. She could feel his presence whenever he was near, like when they were in the same apartment. But after the intensity of her healing him at the shop a few days before, Winnie could now sense him from a much greater distance. Even now, a mile or more away in his apartment, he was a constant tickle in the back of her mind.

Ordinarily, she might discuss this with her friends. It was a new talent and Winnie valued their input about what it might mean. But right now, she couldn't even consider it. They'd tell her it wasn't real and that it was only the Sable talking. Winnie didn't doubt it was related, but she thought it was a function of her more powerful control. Realizing that the magic was more powerful when directed like the conductor of a symphony rather than forced like stitched fabric had enabled her to do more with Danny's headache. Now, Winnie was sure she could tease out whatever Kane had done to Danny in that prison.

A hand on her shoulder made Winnie jump. She looked up in alarm and saw Cait, and Tris beside her.

"Sorry, Winnie," Cait said. "We said 'hi' several times, but you didn't answer. You just kept staring outside like you were looking for something."

"I was looking for you two."

"We came in the side," Tris explained. "It's closer to the bus stop."

Winnie looked around, still nervous. Her friends sat. The waitress came to take their drink orders.

Winnie waited for her to leave before speaking. "Were you able to talk to the guard at the armory?"

Cait nodded.

Tris leaned forward to explain. "He'll take a cut from our score rather than a single payment up front. I think he's being greedy. Cait says that's just the way he is."

"It's his nature. He was always looking for the big score when we were in the service. It made him a lousy card player. He went all-in on nearly every hand. We figured it out and called him every time. Eventually, he stopped playing. We were taking most of his paycheck. Apparently, he's not learned his lesson."

Winnie chuckled. "Isn't that what we're doing, too? We're all gambling on the backend of this job. Whether it's to get Cleaver out of Baltimore or the chance to take all the money for ourselves, it seems the same to me."

"You're right, Win," Cait said. "Still, him seeing this as a sure thing and a big score for him has me questioning what we're doing, based on his history of bad luck. I'd be more comfortable if he'd taken the flat fee to open up the armory. His bad luck might be our end."

"Yeah, but even a broken clock is right twice a day," Tris offered.

The three of them smiled and agreed. The waitress returned with a refill for Winnie, coffee for Tris, and some sort of frozen concoction with a slice of pineapple sticking out of the top for Cait. She had surprisingly frilly tastes for someone who was essentially their muscle. Winnie had always thought it odd that she was the black coffee drinker in their group rather than Cait.

Tris took a sip and cleared her throat. "So, what's next?"

"I think we're about ready," Winnie said. "We need to set up the sale yesterday. The longer we wait, the longer we'll have to hide the military tech. We have to move immediately once we have our gear together."

"Agreed." Cait nodded. "The Red Legs and military police investigators will start turning over rocks looking for this stuff, soon as it's missed in the regular twice-weekly inventories."

"It'll buy us some time if we schedule our break-in right after one of those inventories. That will give us the most time between when we get the gear and when the loss is discovered." Tris was most nervous about procuring the gear. She knew it would all be returned after the authorities caught up with Cleaver, but she hated having this breed of magic on the street.

"Don't worry, Tris, we'll time it so we don't have the heat on us long." Winnie looked at Cait. "So when do we move?"

"The next inventory is tomorrow morning. That gives us a four-day window before the next one. We could schedule the truck and everything we need by tomorrow night. Our guard said he can swap shifts whenever he wants, and the night shift guard is always asking for people to trade."

"Alright." Winnie leaned forward. "We're in for tomorrow night."

They all nodded, then conversation turned to their plans for life after the score. Each of them was excited for an escape from the countless problems facing young chanters in a society that didn't trust them and offered them little legal opportunity to leave a life of drudgery, punching a clock for middling bosses.

None of them noticed the man nearby, his baseball cap pulled low over his eyes, hunched over a cup of coffee. His posture hid the directional microphone tucked under one arm, aimed at their table.

Victor put the headphones down. He'd heard enough.

His informant had brought the recording directly to him with a promise that no one knew what he'd overheard. Victor had paid him a bonus in exchange for discretion and had waited until he left to plug the recording into his smartphone. Now that he'd listened to the entire conversation twice, Victor was struggling with what to do next.

The plan to connect the city's chanters with the tremors and vengeful weather had moved forward nicely, even with the video of Winnie fighting the storms. They had been able to spin her footage as proof that the chanters were truly in control of all that was happening. People still called her the savior of the city but there was a strong undercurrent of distrust for the average chanter on the street.

He had their plans in the palm of his hand, but wasn't sure if he should turn the recordings over to Director Kane.

Victor absently massaged the palm of his right hand with his left. The pins and needles were constant, ever since his visit to the crater. Knowing what Morgan would want him to do made everything harder. Despite her early and vigorous approval of everything he'd done during her early days in the Academy, Morgan had become increasingly jaded about the Red Legs ever since officially joining the force after graduation. The steel mill had been a turning point. She couldn't justify what Kane was doing under any circumstances. Deep inside, Victor loved her conviction.

How she kept believing in him and his redemption was another matter. Victor didn't understand her pure faith in him and how she believed that he would always do the right thing. Every night, she looked into his eyes in their shared apartment and told Victor that he was a good man. A just man. How was he supposed to stand up to the conflicting pressures of his job and the system he served, against the expectations of the woman he loved?

The tease of a whispered conversation stopped him mid-thought.

Victor pulled himself back into the present and looked around the room, expecting to see no one. He was still alone. The voices in his head no longer surprised him. He could rarely make out more than the occasional word, but that didn't matter. He knew what they were. He'd known ever since his visit to the crater. A fascinating encounter, but still, Victor resisted its meaning.

Victor sighed, stood, and paced around his desk several times, desperate to clear his head. He stopped in front of the large safe in the corner of his office, where they kept the worst of the confiscated charms. Crouching down, he dialed in the combination, then pulled the heavy metal door open.

He peered inside at the shelves, each piled high with enchanted baubles. He closed his eyes and concentrated. When he opened them again, he saw a lattice patchwork of glowing threads, superimposed over the items and pulsing in a spectrum he shouldn't be able to see.

Victor reached out with his right hand and touched one of the glowing patches, picking up a peacock-shaped brooch. Whenever he held something like this, his tingling intensified.

The item itself felt sort of sticky, as if he could pull or peel a coating from its body.

For the first time, he placed the item in his left palm and reached out with the fingers of his right, trying to pull at the stickiness. To his surprise, the edge of the glowing patchwork pulled away, clinging to his fingers.

Victor looked at the edge of the glowing fabric, sensing for the first time what each of the interwoven threads imparted to the brooch, and how it all was meant to work.

He tugged at the threads, and with a wisp of glowing green smoke, the patchwork parted from the brooch.

Once free, the threads unraveled until they'd pulled apart in his fingertips, dissipating into individual wisps of fading smoke.

Victor was left holding a cheap piece of costume jewelry, no longer glowing.

"You did it."

Victor turned toward the voice, but there was no one behind him. He stood, looked around the room, and spoke in a whisper. "Did I do something wrong?"

The voice came from behind him again. "No, silly. You're practicing, that's all."

Victor spun around. "Why can't I see you?"

A giggle, then, "Because I'm not here."

Victor was making himself dizzy, searching for the source of that voice, always somewhere right behind him. "Where are you, then?"

"You know where I am."

Victor sat and pondered the voice. It sounded like a child, though he knew that it wasn't. The voice was right; Victor knew where it came from.

He finally stood, closed the safe, then grabbed his coat and hat before rushing out from the office.

42

THE PARKING LOT WAS DESERTED, AND MIDNIGHT BLACK AS
Victor pulled into a marked space. He smirked at the care with
which he parked his unmarked patrol car in the empty lot. It
was unlikely that he'd find anyone here in this desolate spot in
the city's industrial district. As far as Victor knew, he was the
only person to return after the Harvester's destruction.
Twice now.

He got out of his car and made his way carefully inside the
building's ruins again, to the crater inside. The voice was right.
Victor knew where the whispers were coming from, just as he
knew what the tingling in his right hand meant. His actions
with the brooch proved his theory, and that proof was now a
terror inside him.

Victor Holmes, Baltimore's chief Red Legs Inspector,
favored by Director Kane himself, had long prided himself on
knowing his enemy. Magic would be mankind's downfall. It
could only be wielded by chanters. Yet here he was, drawn to a
magical crater, by magical beings, and by the magic he now held
in his own hand.

He practically trembled with every step.

But fear was never an excuse to do nothing. Victor was a man of convictions, and when those convictions were challenged, he faced his fears and searched for answers. That inner fire that needed the truth drew him back to the crater's edge.

Walking back to the crumbling precipice, Victor looked down at the glowing tableau. Green grass lined the crater's floor, grew beneath a clear and starry sky. It was odd how the pervasive dust storms plaguing the city seemed to disappear while standing here.

Victor could see dots of light flitting about below, swooping and swirling along the crater floor, and around the pool of water in the center. He watched as the tiny lights touched the surface, making ripples on the glassy surface. He was drawn to that pool — the heart of the magic. He could feel its pull, drawing him like a quivering needle on a compass, gentle yet certain.

Victor stepped from the crumbling concrete to the soft turf below and slowly descended toward the pool. His feet touched the grassy floor and a heavy weight was suddenly gone from his body. He felt a peace and belonging he hadn't expected. He would have ordinarily believed that he didn't deserve such peace, but Victor brushed away those thoughts without pause. He might ponder the why later, but for now, he reveled in his existence and belonging.

"You're back," said the voice. "I knew you would be."

Victor turned toward the tiny, child-like voice and saw a winged girl, six inches high and hovering in the air beside him. He craned his neck to follow her perpetual motion, flying dizzying circles around his head, pacing him as he walked.

Victor swallowed. "What is your name? What should I call you?"

The girl giggled. "Everyone here calls me Seelie."

"Pleased to meet you, Seelie," Victor said with a nod. "How did you and your friends come to be here in this place?"

The tiny figure shrugged, hands out at her side as she spiraled by his face. "I don't know. We were different once, I think — more like you. Then something terrible took that away, and for a while we were nowhere, scared and alone. Then the big boom came and we were here, in this wonderful place. I don't remember much about the before place and this is much better, anyway, don't you think?"

Victor nodded, contemplating the many lights bobbing all about. If each of those lights was one of these tiny figures like Seelie, there were more than a hundred in easy sight. He wondered if his suspicions could possibly be right as he stole another step toward the pool.

"How come your other friends don't talk to me, Seelie?"

"They are afraid of you. I think it is the memory of your dress. It scares them, reminds them of their prior lives."

"Why doesn't it scare you?"

"I wasn't like them. I remember being warm, comforted by my mother before the thing took me away. Then I was here. Something about you reminds me of her. Did you know my mother?"

A chill trilled down Victor's spine. He slowly nodded, then finally answered. "I might know your mother, Seelie. That might be why we're connected."

The tiny girl giggled with delight, then spun around before zooming in circles above Victor's head. He couldn't help but smile, despite his earlier dread, and the realization of how all these tiny figures had been born. He couldn't hold onto ill feelings while here. It was as if the location itself was a cure.

"Are you going to see the lady?" Seelie asked.

"Who is the lady?"

"She lives in the water and likes to watch us play. I think she is pleased to see us here."

"Is she here now?" Victor looked toward the pool. Maybe he was here to see the lady that lived at the center of this magical place. Maybe he would finally get answers to his many questions.

"I'm not sure. She's not always there." Seelie giggled and flew out ahead of Victor. "I guess we'll see when we get there."

He followed the tiny winged figure, filled with a surprising hope and undeniable sense of purpose. He was supposed to be here, and time didn't matter so long as he remained a soldier of intention.

Seelie continued to lead him onward, and soon his boots rested on the shore of what Victor now saw as a small lake, bordered by tall, leafy trees, mist floating on its surface and drifting into the wooded boundary on either side.

Seelie hovered inches away. "Wait here. The lady will come if she wishes to speak with you. I'll wait for you up the trail."

Victor turned and watched her flutter back in the other direction. The path back led through a forested track he didn't remember traversing to get here. When he turned back to the lake, a woman in silvery, white robes was already walking across its surface towards him.

It was impossible to describe her. To call her ageless defied eons. She looked at once young and ancient, innocent and knowing, vibrant and frail — a powerful presence that he could barely process and would no doubt remember forever.

The woman walked to the water's edge, her toes inches from the mossy shore. She smiled down at him.

Victor realized that he'd dropped to one knee at her approach, somehow compelled, as if it were the only thing he could do.

"You have come to us at last."

"Where am I?" Victor whispered.

"This is a place that is, was, and always will be. It is everywhere and nowhere." The woman smiled to soothe his confusion. "Let us say it is a convenient place for beings such as you and me to meet."

Victor had met with superiors often enough to know that he wouldn't be getting a better answer. He had many questions about the crater, the fairy-like creatures, and everything else. But his best play was to wait and see what this formidable woman standing atop this mystical lake might have to say.

"Others have had many more questions. You do not?"

"I have questions, but suspect I'm here to satisfy more than my curiosity."

She laughed aloud. The sound filled his heart with a joy he'd never felt or imagined. "You are a pragmatist, Victor Holmes. Much like your ancestor, the one named for the lance he bore in battle. He, too, was pragmatic and noble, though he never lived to fulfill his destiny as the king's ultimate protector."

Victor didn't know anything about any such ancestor. His family, so far as he knew, had an ordinary history, coming to the New World from England a few centuries before. Still, he felt he should say something.

"I am honored to know I had an ancestor with such a noble history."

"Noble, but tragic. His tale was filled with misfortune, because of his hubris and an inability to fulfill his destiny. That fate has come full circle and the chance to accept the quest has returned to your family, as it has to others. But I must warn you: this burden will demand a payment I cannot forestall, as it is with all great quests. The knights of old knew that greatness must always carry a cost. Will you accept the certain burden of payment with only the chance of great reward?"

He searched her ancient eyes for a clue as to what his payment might be, but saw only the soft assurance of a mother urging a child to step forward in faith. Nothing was certain, and in this current climate, that lack of certainty was more fragile than ever.

Victor nodded, meeting her steady stare.

"Speak it, Victor. Accept the quest. I may not assign it otherwise."

"I accept the quest."

She smiled, warm, affectionate, and grim with acceptance of an uncertain future. "Very well, my son, descendant of Lancelot. You will be the once and future queen's protector. You will join her knights in their quest to recover the throne. This new promise may shatter your previous oaths, all second only to this one. Rise and go forth."

Serving a queen as her protector?

"But you've not told me what to do. A quest has a purpose. You've told me to protect some queen and her throne, but there are no monarchs."

The woman receded towards the center of the lake, gliding across its surface rather than walking backward. Her white and silver robes glowed with an almost blinding light. Victor could barely see her form as she whispered her final words.

"Trust, Victor. Continue to do what is right. Follow your heart. The rest will be revealed soon enough."

Light overwhelmed him. Victor squeezed his eyes tight to shut it out. When he opened them again, he was kneeling in the darkness of a starry, cloudless night at the edge of a crater in the center of a collapsed building.

He looked toward the pool and all the flickering lights around its surface and the grassy banks nearby. He saw no sign of the lady or Seelie.

Victor made his way back to his car, unsure of all that had happened, his heart racing with the knowledge that he was now in service to a queen he did not know, nursing countless questions all the way home.

WINNIE CHECKED HER PHONE FOR THE FOURTH TIME. STILL, NO new messages. Tris and Cait were to load all the charmed items, including the military haul from the armory, in a rental van parked across the street from the warehouse, where they'd arranged their meeting with Cleaver. They weren't here yet and Winnie was getting concerned. They had to drive to the warehouse and stage all the gear so that it looked like Cleaver had it in his possession. That way the authorities would swoop in, leaving Winnie as the informant on the outside and in the clear.

Of course, that all depended on the gear being properly positioned before Cleaver and his men showed for the meeting. She'd watched the warehouse for over an hour and saw no sign of Cleaver, his guys, or the rental van.

Winnie had called Cricket to drop a hint about their upcoming haul and ensure there were no mix-ups. As expected, with the gear in their load, he had told her Cleaver was coming from New Amsterdam to handle the trade himself. That part of the plan had worked exactly like they'd wanted.

An engine roared in the distance. Winnie turned toward the sound and saw a white mini-van swiftly approaching, Tris driving and Cait in the passenger seat. Winnie stepped out onto the sidewalk and pointed across the street.

The van stopped in front of the warehouse. Winnie ran over and opened the large sliding garage door. Cait jumped out and helped. Tris pulled inside. Winnie and Cait slid the door closed behind them, a small boom echoing in the empty building's interior.

Tris stopped the van in the room's center, then hopped out to meet Winnie and Cait at the back.

"Any trouble with the rental?" Winnie asked.

"Nope." Tris shook her head. "We put the rental in the name of one of Cleaver's subsidiaries out of New Amsterdam. When the police trace it back, they'll have that going against them as well."

Cait opened the van doors and stood looking at the boxes — drab olive crates stacked to the ceiling. "We need to get all of this out and stacked around the back of the van so it looks like it's being loaded rather than the other way around."

"And we have to hurry," Winnie checked her phone for the time. "Cleaver could be early. We want everything in place, just in case."

It took twenty minutes to unload the van and stack everything around the floor in an arc behind the van. Cait opened a few crates to make it look like the gear had been inspected. Winnie got her first close look at the stolen items: weapons that fired canisters filled with charmed objects, using the magic inside to degrade an enemy's defensive and offensive capabilities; magical defenses that sprayed interference outward from where the pylons were placed. Winnie could feel the powerful Sable magic pulsing inside the crates, like caged animals ready to pounce on the unsuspecting creatures lured by their captors. She could imagine the horrific effects of the weapons, given the magic she could sense.

Winnie was distracted by the powerful magic and didn't hear

Cait calling out until Cait tapped her on the shoulder and pointed to the small, person-sized door set in the wall beside the big sliding door.

"Winnie, someone is knocking at the door, calling out your name. I think you need to answer. I'll keep watch in case there's trouble."

Winnie wondered who that could be. It was early for Cleaver, and Tris still had to call the local Red Legs and alert them to the pending trade. She pulled herself away from the military equipment and went to open the door. Cait assumed her position by the doorway, ready to pounce if she saw any trouble.

Winnie opened the door to the last person she expected to see.

Morgan was standing in the doorway, dressed in a long black overcoat, clearly trying to hide her Red Legs uniform from casual view, though how anyone could miss the scarlet trousers, Winnie couldn't imagine.

"What do you want, Morgan? Haven't you already hurt us enough? Or are you back for another attempt to get us all killed?" Winnie hadn't seen her sister since that terrible night in the steel mill. Now, she found herself with many things she wanted to say and perhaps even do to her sister.

"You have to stop what you're doing," Morgan blurted on her way inside. "You don't know what they've done, or how things are stacked against you."

Cait stepped up behind Morgan and pulled her elbows behind her back. "Just say the word and I'll make sure she never crosses us again. It's the least we can do to avenge all the people she helped kill in the Harvester."

"I didn't help kill anyone, I swear, Cait. I didn't even know what that thing did. My presence was requested by a superior. By the time I knew what they were doing, I couldn't stop it."

Morgan looked from Winnie to Cait to Tris, then back at Winnie. "I promise I'm telling the truth."

"How stupid do you think we are, Morgan? You show up here in a Red Legs uniform. You chose your side in this war a long time ago, apparently well before we knew you were betraying us." Winnie was fuming, inches from Morgan's face. "It took me a long time to figure out that you were the one who bugged us, and that you stood back and let Danny take the rap. Then you let them kill Joey and all those other people … including my … " Winnie bit her lip to keep from crying. "Now you show up here, pretending like you care enough to warn us?"

"You don't understand." Morgan shook her head. "They were supposed to stop your running and make you get a normal job. They told me they were only after Artos, not you or your friends. I've been trying to watch what they were doing so that I could help you ever since."

Cait smacked the back of Morgan's head. "You expect us to believe that you've been helping us? Prove it."

"I haven't been able to do much, but I have been watching and biding my time. Now it's time to come forward. You have to stop what you're doing and get out of here now. Victor and Kane know what you're doing and they're going to send the entire force in to sweep all of you up. I only just snuck away. They're loading up to come here now."

"That's all part of the plan, Morgan. Shows how much you know. We planned on calling the Red Legs in." Winnie laughed, then motioned to Tris, still standing by the van. "Tell her, Tris."

"I haven't called anyone yet. I wanted to make sure we were set and figured we didn't want them to have too much of a heads-up."

Winnie shot Tris a sharp look then turned back to Morgan. This wasn't good. Before she could ask Morgan how she knew where they were, the door swung open and two large men entered the dimly lit warehouse.

They spotted Cait holding the captive Morgan.

One called out. "Boss, there's a Red Legs constable here. Could be trouble."

A voice Winnie could barely hear said something outside the door. The men stepped aside to make room. Their eyes danced across the room, raw nerves evident with every gesture. One of the men had his hand tucked across his chest, resting on something hidden from view. Probably the butt of a gun.

With his thugs out of the way, Cleaver Yorke entered the warehouse, ducking to fit his tall frame through the small access door. He was followed at once by Cricket and Garraldi. Neither looked happy, eyes on their boss for a cue to their next move.

Winnie needed to defuse this situation, or Morgan would disappear for good. She was angry at her half-sister for all that she'd done. She wanted her gone, but not like this.

Winnie stepped toward Cleaver. "You're early. I didn't expect you for another half-hour."

"I make it a point to be early and a little unpredictable. Call it a survival trait." Cleaver pointed at Morgan. "It pays off a lot more often than not. Garraldi, take the Red Leg to the car."

Winnie raised a hand. "That won't be necessary. She's with me, my half-sister, came to warn us that there's a major raid planned on this location, and any minute now."

Cleaver looked at Morgan, then Winnie, before venting a long and wheezing guffaw. He pointed at Winnie, then Cricket, before finally composing himself enough to talk.

"Your sister? She doesn't look much like you, but I do remember Cricket mentioning something about a sister. Something to do with the Harvester and some old-fashioned family betrayal, or do I have that wrong?"

Winnie shook her head, desperate to conjure a plausible explanation. "She was there as part of our plan; we just didn't expect it all to come so close to the wire. If it hadn't been for Morgan, Tris couldn't have rewired the control panel and I could never have overloaded the system and stopped the Director's plans."

Cleaver glanced at Tris, standing by the van. Winnie looked over, too. Tris nodded but said nothing. She was clearly angry, freaking out about their plan going south, just like the last time.

But Winnie wouldn't give up. She had to salvage something. Cleaver had proven more resourceful than she expected.

Cait broke the uncomfortable silence. "Based on Morgan's warning, we need to clear out of here before the Red Legs arrive, or we're all in for more trouble than we bargained for. We don't want a shootout with the authorities."

"No, we don't." Cleaver shook his head and gestured to one of his large men. "Anthony, you and Vincent load the van and ride with the mousy one. We'll conclude this deal at a secondary location I set up for just such a contingency. Winnie, you, your sister, and the tall girl can ride with me."

Winnie could only agree. She motioned for Cait to bring Morgan, then followed Cleaver outside.

There were several black SUVs. Cleaver pointed to one. "Winnie, you join me in this one. Your friend and sister can follow in the other one." He opened the door and held it, waiting for her to comply.

Winnie didn't have much of a choice. She nodded at Cait, who still led Morgan by the arm. Her sister looked petrified. Fine. Morgan owed her for this, and a lot more.

Winnie got in, followed by Cleaver and Cricket, sitting in silence as the driver pulled into the night.

Victor entered the empty warehouse after it was cleared by the tactical team. He saw no sign of Winnie or the stolen gear.

He pounded his fist into his hand. He was torn; he had wanted both the recovery of the military Sable gear and for

Winnie to escape. Now he was stuck with the possibility that the stolen material would find its way onto the black market. That would be bad for everyone. Artos himself had called them in on the bust, citing strong ties to the community and the need to keep a lid on illegal magic hitting the streets. He was sure the old man had more than altruistic thoughts in mind when calling in the raid on Winnie and her compatriots.

The tactical team commander walked over. He was dressed in all-black body armor, night-vision goggles flipped up on his helmet rig to expose his concerned expression. He handed Victor a laminated plastic ID card with a metal clip.

"One of my men found this on the warehouse floor."

Victor turned it over in his hand: Morgan's badge. He growled in his throat, his hand squeezing the plastic until the edges cut into his hand.

"Fan out. Search for any clues as to their whereabouts. They had to leave in a hurry, so let's figure out where they disappeared."

"Yes, sir!" The tactical commander saluted, then ordered his men to sweep the interior and exterior again.

Victor watched them, knowing they'd likely find nothing. Cleaver Yorke was a professional, and unlikely to leave any accidental clues. It was pure luck Morgan had dropped her ID for them to find. He wondered what she had been doing there, though he had some ideas, based on her torn loyalties.

Confronting Morgan was something for another time. For now, his focus was on recovering her and the stolen hardware. He pulled out his phone, dialed, and waited for someone to answer.

This had better work, he thought.

4 4

WINNIE LOOKED AROUND AT THE STACKS OF EMPTY ALUMINUM beer kegs. They were huddled in the back room in a Fells Point club — this was where their collapsed deal would finally conclude. This was where Cleaver had set up his headquarters when he moved in on the Baltimore Sable trade. Now they were back and dealing with the current conundrum.

Cait still had a hand on Morgan who, thankfully, had kept her mouth shut. If she stayed that way, Winnie might be able to talk their way out of this and maybe keep Morgan alive. But that would only work out if nothing else went south. Problem was, Winnie didn't even know what else could go wrong. Their careful plan, scrapped long ago, offered no solutions for dealing with their situation. She looked over at Tris, who fanned herself to ward off the enclosed room's stuffy warmth. Cleaver's men had deposited them in here upon arrival, and now they were waiting for any sign of their intentions.

Winnie turned toward the sound of an opening door and saw Cricket, his stern expression speaking volumes about their troubles.

"Winnie, come with me. Your friends can stay here."

247

"We keep no secrets," Winnie said. "They can come with me."

"Your friends aren't in our crew and Cleaver invited you, not them. Now, come with me."

She looked at Cait, Tris, and Morgan, who was pasty white with fear. "I'll be back as soon as I can. Stay here and keep calm. Everything will be fine."

Cait snorted a nervous chuckle, but said nothing. Morgan and Tris nodded. Winnie turned and followed Cricket out of the room.

He led them towards the front of the club. The thumping bass from the music swelled with their approach. Winnie followed him upstairs to a short hallway, and eventually, a door where one of Cleaver's goons stood guard.

Cricket waved him aside, opened the door, and made way for Winnie to enter. They were in a broad office with a glass wall overlooking the dance floor below. Cleaver stood there, looking down at the patrons below. He ignored her arrival for a while, watching the revelers losing themselves in the music.

Something tugged at Winnie's attention. She turned to see a stack of military crates off to one side in the office. She didn't have to look inside to know they were filled with the world's most dangerous Sable gear. Winnie could feel the magic inside. It made her blood pulse loud enough to hear, despite the booming music.

Cleaver finally spoke. "I'm losing patience with your little schemes and plans. Cricket's convinced me to stand back and let you see the light on your own, but I'm beginning to think he was wrong."

"What good would it do, Cleaver? You have me. You have all my friends. You have my sister." Winnie pointed to the crates. "You have everything you wanted. I think our deal has concluded to our mutual satisfaction. Our joint interests have all been served."

"You think so, eh?" Cleaver gave her a predator's smile. "I

know you tried to double-cross me. You may have your sister on the inside to inform you, but I'm not without my resources. You had no intention of my keeping the gear you stole, or so you assured the guard when he let you into the armory to steal it. Am I right, Winnie? That you told him it would all be back under lock and key within a week?"

"I had to tell him something or he would've never agreed to the plan. I knew once we had paid him off to let us steal the gear, he'd be in our pocket forever, no matter what happened."

Cleaver considered Winnie's words, then slowly nodded. "Be that as it may, it does nothing to resolve our underlying problem. I don't understand your continued loyalty to Merrilyn. He has his own agenda as much as I do, and believe me when I tell you his schemes make mine look like a child's puzzle by comparison. He will never tell you what he has planned. I, on the other hand, have always been up front with my intentions."

"It's not about you, Cleaver. I don't want to work for you or anyone else anymore, Artos included. You've all given me reason to run from your so-called protection. I just want to be left alone."

"There's no room for another Sable boss in Baltimore. Artos will work for me, same as you. It's inevitable." Cleaver tapped his temple. "I've seen it."

"Ah, yes, your so-called sight. But it's not a sure thing, right? You've seen things that didn't come to pass for one reason or another." She waited for Cleaver to nod, then said, "So why this obsession over me? What do you think I'll do that you can't do for yourself?"

The intercom chirped on the desk, then a voice came through the speaker. "We've another uninvited guest. You want I should run him off?"

Winnie felt a sudden, familiar tug pulling her toward the dance floor. She knew what she'd see before she turned toward the glass — a pair of bouncers holding a thrashing Danny between them.

Cleaver looked through the glass, then turned to Winnie with a smile. "Another friend of yours? And how, I wonder, did he manage to find you?" Cleaver walked to the intercom, pressed the button, and asked the bouncer to bring the intruder upstairs. "I think we'll ask him directly."

There was a long, uncomfortable silence while Winnie waited for Danny to get ushered upstairs. Winnie could only think of one reason he would be searching for her like this. Surely his headaches were back.

Winnie felt that familiar itch. She wanted to heal him, even if it meant Cleaver would discover her addiction.

The door opened and Danny was shoved into the office. He stumbled, only staying upright by grabbing at Winnie. She caught his weight while he steadied himself. He looked like crap, his eyes sunken, slitted to invite only the scantest light. The bright room was likely a hammer to his head. Without even trying, Winnie began to draw the magic around her, healing him, lost in the coming rush of euphoria as …

"Stop!"

Winnie looked at Cleaver, standing a few feet away, holding a gun in one hand, his other extended to draw magic like Winnie. He stared in horror.

"What do you think you're doing, girl? You just drew in more Sable than I thought possible for one person to hold. I thought you were preparing to attack, until you directed it all toward our intruder. What are you doing?"

"I'm healing him, Cleaver," she said, without moving her eyes from Danny. "He was a prisoner of Kane's. They experimented on him, left him broken so that now he gets these horrible headaches. I'm the only one who can fix them." Winnie swallowed, and stole a defiant glance at her host. "I have power that you know nothing about."

"That may be, but I can see what you're doing, putting a temporary wall around some spell that's already set in this boy's brain. Whoever put it there is dabbling in the worst Sable I've ever seen. But what you're doing is nearly as bad, and that's not even counting what it must be doing to you."

"Don't worry about me, Cleaver. I can take care of myself," Winnie hissed through clenched teeth and waves of pleasure. She barely heard the intercom chirp with the now-familiar voice.

"Boss, it's Hal again. There's a Red Leg inspector here to see you. Claims he's here to talk. He's alone and isn't wired so far as we can tell."

Cleaver keyed the intercom. "He let you search him?"

"He insisted. He knows the Durham girl is here and wants to see her."

Winnie was still swimming in euphoria and barely registered what was said. What would a Red Leg inspector want with her beyond an arrest?

She was too distracted to think it through and, in her current state, didn't care. She heard Cleaver invite the inspector upstairs. From the corner of her eye, she saw him take a dark blanket from a shelf and drape the crates. It wouldn't hide them from a thorough search, but it would suffice to hinder a casual examination of the room.

She finished her spell work on Danny, then drew her magical tendrils from his mind with what felt like a bottomless sigh. Like always, Winnie was spent from her healing, her pleasure centers still tickled by his proximity.

Danny collapsed to the floor. Winnie leaned against a table for support as the door opened again and Inspector Victor Holmes entered the office.

He looked around until his eyes found Winnie. "Where is she?"

"Where is who?" Winnie asked, most of her mind still fixed

on Danny.

"Morgan. What have you done with her?"

Winnie waved towards the door. "She's fine, with Cait and Tris last I saw her."

Victor turned toward Cleaver. "I think you have one of my constables, Mr. Yorke. I came alone in a show of good faith to retrieve her."

"I suppose you'll swoop back in and take me in for kidnapping once I hand her over," Cleaver said.

"I'll do nothing of the sort. I just want her back and will leave once I have her."

"He's sweet on her, Cleaver. That's why he wants her back so bad," Winnie purred. "He turned her against me, then made her his personal Red Leg officer. Isn't that right, Victor?"

"I'll talk with you another time, Winnie, when you're not high."

Cleaver considered Victor's offer. Winnie could see the wheels spinning behind his dark eyes as a question nagged at the back of her mind.

"How did you find us, Victor? Is Morgan wearing some sort of tracker?"

The inspector turned to glare at Winnie. "No. I figured she was with you. I rounded up lover boy here and sent him to find you. I simply followed."

Winnie tracked Victor's line of thought. Danny did seem to turn up in the oddest places. She looked over at him, dazed in the aftermath of her therapy.

"That's right," Victor said. "Your boy has been turned into a perfect bloodhound by Director Kane. He can find you wherever you are. All Kane has to do is trigger the spell he placed in Barber's brain and the headaches start. You're the only one who can stop them, with predictable consequences for you both. It was always Kane's plan to incapacitate you enough to keep you from interfering with his plans."

"Why tell me all this?" Winnie said. "And why should I believe you?"

Victor laughed. "You can lie to yourself all you want, Winnie. But don't lie to me. You know I only tell the truth. Friend or enemy, I stand by my word. Kane set this whole thing up to keep you out of his way while he solved the problem you started after destroying the Harvester."

Victor crossed to where Danny was slumped in a chair, put a hand on Danny's head, and, with a grasping motion, seemed to pull something imaginary away.

Cleaver gasped. She switched her vision to the magical spectrum just in time to see Victor's fingers peel away both her barrier spell and the deeper enchantment put in place by Kane. Peeling was the only way to describe it. Victor tugged at the edges of each spell until it started to tear from its anchor, then wove the spell's knitted threads into wisps of translucent energy. Winnie knew from her discovery that the magic preferred to follow its own path. Victor was setting it free.

"How did you do that?" Winnie whispered. She could undo a spell she had cast, and sometimes repair broken weaves in other people's work, but he was dismantling the threads like one would unravel the frayed cuff of a sweater.

Victor looked up at Winnie. "I don't know how or why I can do this. I just can, ever since that night at the steel mill. You need to know something else: Neither Morgan nor I knew what Kane was doing there. It was as much a shock to us as it was to you. By the time they had you in custody, neither of us could do anything to help you … not that you needed it, in the end. But you must understand, Morgan had no idea what Kane was up to."

"It doesn't matter. She still betrayed me, and I'm not sure I can ever recover from that, even if she had a change of heart and came to warn us about tonight's raid."

"Morgan had nothing to do with that. We didn't know about

your plans until Artos called and told us that you were planning on selling it all to Cleaver."

Winnie stared at Victor, shocked. She couldn't believe that Artos would turn her over like that. It had been his plan, too. But Victor was right. He didn't lie. It was an irrefutable fact. If he said that Artos had called in the raid on tonight's operation, then she believed in that truth and whatever struggle accompanied yet another reversal in her loyalties.

It was almost too much to bear. She pushed off the table she'd been leaning against.

She had to clear her head and stand on her own two feet. So much had changed in the space of minutes. So much of what she believed to be true was now undeniably false. Her world was upside down.

She looked at Cleaver. "We need to go back down to the others. Victor will want to see Morgan and I have some things to say that everyone should hear."

Cleaver nodded and opened his office door. Winnie followed him down to the storeroom along with the others.

It was finally time to set things right.

WHEN THE DOOR TO THE STOREROOM OPENED, WINNIE SAW TRIS and Cait on one side of the room with Morgan standing opposite them, alone. They wanted nothing to do with her. Their obvious surprise when she entered with Cleaver, Victor, and Danny might've been amusing if the circumstances weren't so dire.

Morgan ran to Victor's side. The way she clung to him, Winnie realized that there was a relationship there that she hadn't suspected before. It forced her to reconsider her opinion of Victor. She'd always seen him as heartless, bound only to his job. But he'd come here alone, risking his beloved job to rescue Morgan. It made so much more sense in light of this new revelation.

Cait and Tris had a world of wonder in their eyes. Surely, they thought that Victor's presence meant they were back in custody, somehow betrayed by Cleaver Yorke. Winnie shook her head, forestalling their questions. She cleared her throat and looked at the New Amsterdam boss.

"I'm through with Artos, Cleaver. He's always had his hidden agenda. And while I knew that, I would have never imagined that he'd turn us in like he did tonight."

"Winnie," Cait said, confused by her revelation. "Artos helped you make tonight's plans. You think he betrayed us?"

Winnie nodded. "I do. We sure as hell didn't call the Red Legs to raid us. If Morgan hadn't warned us, we'd have been picked up with Cleaver and his men. Think about it. Who stands to gain the most if we're all locked up? Who reclaims the throne with no one left to challenge his power?"

Tris stepped forward. "But Winnie, you were on his side in this."

"Maybe my new abilities forced Artos to reconsider how he dealt with me. I could do things he said hadn't been possible for a century or more. I think he saw the way people reacted to what I could do and realized I was the hero of the chanter community. Not him. That makes me a threat to his standing."

She pointed to Victor, who was standing with Morgan.

"He confirmed that Artos called in the raid. He also has some strange power that allows him to dismantle magic spells, says he's had it since the steel mill."

Morgan shot Victor a questioning glance. He half-smiled. The inspector probably hadn't revealed his newfound power to anyone until tonight, after removing Kane's spell from Danny's mind. She filed that away for future reference and turned to Cleaver. She needed everyone to understand what she was about to say.

"Cleaver, you've always said that we were supposed to work together, that you'd seen us standing side-by-side against whatever is coming. Is that still true?"

"Nothing's changed there, Winnie. You and I must stand together against the coming apocalypse."

"Then I accept your offer, at least in part."

Tris and Cait gaped at their friend. Cleaver looked pleased with himself.

Winnie waved them all off. "I said in part because we're partners, Cleaver. I'll not be working for you. I'll work with you, if you'll accept that."

"Partners are bad for business. They always cheat each other in the end. I'll make you a captain."

Winnie shook her head. "I'm not Cricket, and this isn't a negotiation. If anything, I'm offering to let you work with me."

Cleaver laughed, then fell to a hush when he realized that Winnie wasn't kidding. "You're serious."

"Don't worry. I have no interest in your business. I just need your help to fight whatever is coming. I can do more than I've done if I don't have to worry about you and Artos or anything else. I'm in my corner, and looking for allies. You need me more than I need you. I don't know why and I'm not yet sure how, but it's somehow my fate to stop the Director. For some reason that I don't understand, and probably don't even want to know, I might be able to stop the world from crumbling around us."

Cleaver exhaled, deep and heavy. "So, you've no eyes on my business?"

"You run New Amsterdam. I'll keep Baltimore. When the time comes, I'll give you instructions. Follow them to the letter and everything will work out."

"How do you know what to do all of a sudden?" Tris asked. "You've managed to temporarily return things to normal, but the problems always returned."

"Victor gave me the idea when he peeled the magic from inside Danny's head. He picked apart the fibers and returned them to their natural state. They dissolved, back to wherever they came from. I think we've all been working magic the wrong way all these years. It isn't something we control, or stitch into our bidding. The magic is alive, vital, almost aware. It can best be used when you work with it, let it do as it wishes with only the faintest direction. That was how I doused the fires and killed the storms. Magic doesn't seek chaos and destruction. It wants to fix what's broken."

Victor looked puzzled. Then he said, "That makes what I've seen at the crater fit a whole lot better."

"What do you mean?"

Victor described the grassy bowl with the magical pool at its center. Everyone listened as he related his conversations with Seelie and how the crater seemed impervious to the local tremors and storms.

"It's almost as if the magic there has healed the land," he finally finished.

"That's an example of what I think is wrong with the world. We're bending magic to our will. It's meant to shepherd the natural world, but we're abusing its power and forcing it into unnatural things."

"So, let me get this straight: You wanna set the magic free so it can do whatever it wants in the world, even though that violates everything we believe about working magic?" Cleaver laughed, a bit too loud. "And you want me to work for you."

Winnie nodded. "I think this is what happened to Europe. More and more of their public works projects were put under magical control, until they sucked the natural world dry. It's why every major city here in the United Americas is surrounded by wasteland. We've ripped the fabric that holds nature together. We have to return it or suffer Europe's fate."

Cait looked at Winnie. Danny stood nearby, staring at her. Everyone was. She felt self-conscious. She'd just suggested that everything they knew as fact was wrong and that the foundation of their social structure was built on a lie. She was tired of trying to tell them what was right. It was time for them all to decide for themselves.

There was a long silence as the room pondered what she'd said. Winnie waited, feigning patience.

Cleaver broke the silence. "My visions never lie. Sometimes I might interpret things wrong, but that's on me. I can look back and see the mistaken viewpoint rather than the mistaken vision. I've seen us side-by-side, confronting what's to come. I've always assumed it was because you were working for me."

"And now?" Winnie asked.

"Now I need to see it from a different direction. I'm in. New Amsterdam's chanter community stands with you."

Winnie had to throttle her obvious joy. It was a win for her, and for the world, but she wasn't ready to show him.

Victor shocked her next. "I've seen too much of what you can do, and thus, doubt is impossible. Despite all that's working against you, you've come out on top. I'll do all that I can to help."

Morgan beamed by Victor's side. Winnie knew where her sister stood, if only because the man she loved had shifted his loyalties.

"Thank you," Winnie said. "That means a lot. You know this could mean the end of everything holding our society together. Chanters and middlings will eventually have to work together. That's why Kane is working so hard to divide us. He knows that unity will defeat him."

"I know," Victor said. "I also know it won't be easy to beat him. He's stacked all the cards in his favor."

Winnie cocked her head. "Then why side with us?"

"Because I've seen you in action, and I now know what unblemished magic can do when given the chance to flourish on its own."

She nodded at Victor, accepting his allegiance. She only needed to hear from her oldest and dearest friends. Winnie met the eyes of Danny, Cait, and Tris in turn. They each nodded as her eyes met theirs.

Everyone was on board.

Their grand alliance had begun.

EPILOGUE

"Have a seat, ma'am. Please. It'll be a while."

"That's all right. I'd rather stand."

Elaine Durham hobbled back and forth on her cane, looking over the priceless artwork. The ancient paintings were dark, and faded in many cases, but she was sure that someone had assigned extraordinary value to them. The same was likely true for the bronze and marble sculptures standing on pedestals around the antechamber. The woman behind the desk watched Elaine perusing the statues and paintings, eyes like claws on her back.

It was the tail of an endless day. Elaine had done everything she could think of in regards to Winnie. She had to protect her daughter however she could. But this was a true act of desperation, one she'd vowed long ago to never take.

"If you'd like to tell me what this is about, Miss Durham, I'm sure I can take care of this so you don't have to keep waiting."

"As I said, it's a personal matter. I'm happy to wait my turn. It took a full day of red tape just to get this far. I'm not turning back now."

"Director Kane is a very busy man," the secretary said for the fifth time. "I'm still not sure how you managed to get this far. Most people can't just show up and expect an audience with the Director on a whim."

"It was hardly 'a whim.'"

"Be that as it may, it's likely to be a while before you can see him. I've put your name in his digital calendar as you requested. But that's still no guarantee that he'll make time between his other appointments to see you. The Director is expected on the Assembly floor to address members there later this evening."

"We shall see. I expect … " Elaine never finished. The office door opened and she heard men finishing a conversation.

" … I will consider your request, Senator, but make no promises."

"I wouldn't expect any, Director. Only the assurance that my concerns are given their due."

Elaine stepped aside to let the senator by. He nodded as he passed, then Elaine stood facing the man she'd been waiting to speak with. Director Nilrem Kane stood staring at Elaine from the doorway.

"Director." The secretary stood and came around the desk to stand in next to Elaine. "This is Miss —"

"Elaine Durham. Yes, I am aware," the Director said, waving his secretary away. "Miss Durham, if you'll come inside. I have a few scarce moments between appointments. I can speak with you now."

Elaine gave the secretary a satisfied smile, then followed the Director into his office. She looked around and saw the strange sculpture of the stone seat with a sword somehow embedded into the back, as if the blade had been driven into wet cement before drying.

Kane closed the door behind her. Elaine turned to see Kane watching her with a curious grin.

"Ellie, it has been a while since we've seen each other. You told me it was over and that you were seeing someone else. I believed you when you said that I would never lay eyes upon you again."

"I never thought you would. We didn't exactly see eye to eye then, and we're on different sides of the world now." She waved a lazy hand around the office. "You've come far."

"Thank you, Ellie." Nils smiled. It seemed somehow both sad and a little lost. "We parted on the worst of terms and yet you never betrayed my secret to anyone. You could have ruined me at any time."

"Another one of the many differences between us. I always keep my word. I never told anyone you were a chanter. As far as I know, Artos and I are still the only ones to know."

"Others are starting to suspect. I've had to take some decisive actions in the last few years that have exposed me. Of course, from where I'm standing, accusations would be seen as conspiratorial nonsense."

There was an awkward pause. Elaine was unsure of how to proceed.

Nils took the lead, as he always had. "I'm sure you didn't come here to talk nostalgia. Should I hazard a guess?" Kane cocked his head. "If it has to do with Winnie, I assure you, she's gotten off easy considering the several occasions she's crossed me. You should have trained her better to stay within the law's proper boundaries. I understand she's developed quite the criminal enterprise."

"I've kept your secret all these years, Nils. Why couldn't you leave Winnie out of your little plans?"

"Because they're not little plans, Ellie. They are the building blocks of the future, and the world's disposition with magic forever. I do not take them lightly and no one should be exempt from what must be done to protect us all. Including the daughter of an old friend."

Again, fury swelled within her, as angry at herself as she was with Kane. He was still the terrible, self-centered man he always had been. She'd stood by during his rise to power, never saying anything about his true nature. She'd always been proud of her virtue in keeping his secret. Now, after all that had happened, Elaine was deeply ashamed. Everything bubbled to the surface.

"Nils Kane, you are a fool. You have no idea what you almost did, and I'm not sure that you'd care even if you did. You've always been so self-centered that no one else could ever intrude on your life's plans."

"What are you talking about, Ellie? Your daughter decided to get involved with Artos. I even sent a constable to dissuade her, to honor the memory of what we once had. But that didn't matter. She was determined to continue. And in the end, I had to treat her like the others. What did you expect me to do?"

"To recognize your own daughter when you saw how pig-headed she is, just like her father."

Kane stood frozen, his mouth hanging open. His brows furrowed and Elaine flinched, second-guessing her decision to tell him the truth.

"I don't know what you expect to gain from this fiction, Ellie. As I've said, your daughter has placed herself on a direct path in opposition to me and is now standing in the new world's way. There is nothing I can do for her now." Kane moved to the door, pulling it open.

"You know I'm not lying."

"I know nothing of the sort. Now, I must ask you to leave before my next meeting. If you'd like a ride back to the station, I shall arrange for my driver to take you. It is late and you will have trouble finding a cab." Kane turned to his secretary as Elaine hobbled through the door to the antechamber. "Please make sure Miss Durham makes it safely to the station."

"Yes, Director," said the secretary as she rose from behind her desk.

Elaine tried one final plea. "Nils, you must believe me. I'm not lying!"

"Good evening," the Director said. "Please do not call on me again."

The door shut and Elaine was left alone, wondering if now she'd made everything worse.

The End

Continue Winnie's story with *Queen of Avalon*, book 3 in the Broken Throne saga available August 30, 2019.

Queen of Avalon - Broken Throne, Book 3

Winnie's backed into a corner ... and she comes out fighting.

The world's magic continues to fail, but the middlings want their charmed items and Sable more than ever. They can feel the future coming—a future when the magic will be gone forever.

Dust storms continue to pummel the cities up and down the eastern coast of the United Americas. The outer limits are a barren wasteland as magic continues to suck the natural world dry.

It's been a year and a half since Winnie took over as the head

Sable trader for Baltimore and New Amsterdam. With the Philly boss joining her, the East Coast is hers. Winnie finally has a chance to unite the entire nation.

But when news of Director Kane's new Project X comes her way, Winnie must quickly escalate her plans, or else risk the lives of millions.

Get your copy of *Queen of Avalon* today at books2read.com/qofa.

Forced to find passage to the United Americas, Ricky's mother sacrifices herself so that her son can go free, but Ricky's fate lies in the hands of a strange man, and an uncertain future.

A future that the world as we know it will one day depend upon.

ABOUT THE AUTHOR

Jamie Davis is a nurse, retired paramedic, author, and nationally recognized medical educator who began teaching new emergency responders as a training officer for his local EMS program. He loves everything fantasy and sci-fi and especially the places where stories intersect with his love of medicine or gaming.

Jamie lives in a home in the woods in Maryland with his wife, three children, and dog. He is an avid gamer, preferring historical and fantasy miniature gaming, as well as tabletop games. He writes LitRPG, GameLit, urban, and contemporary paranormal fantasy stories, among other things. His Future Race Game rules were written to satisfy a desire to play a version of the pod races from Star Wars episode 1.

He loves hearing from readers and going to cons and events where he meets up with fans. Reach out and say "hi." Visit JamieDavisBooks.com for more books, free offers and more!

facebook.com/jamiedavisbooks

twitter.com/podmedic

bookbub.com/authors/jamie-davis